SUNSET
BREEZER

That's' Life!
Love Rosie
x

-A NOVEL-

ROSIE AUSTEN

TQWM Press

www.tqwmcom

Sunset Breezer
by
Rosie Austen

ISBN 10: 1-84667-029-2
ISBN 13: 978-1-84667-029-9

Book design by:
Pam Marin-Kingsley, www.far-angel.com

TQWM PRESS

Published in 2008
by
TQWM Press

www.TQWM.com

This book is dedicated to the two
most amazing women I know—
my daughters,
Tania and Karen

"We like the plot, Miss Austen, but all this effing
and blinding will have to go."

AKNOWLEDGMENTS

My grateful thanks to all the following:

Mike Bickell who allowed me to sail with him on his yacht in the Caribbean for four years. Without the many experiences he enabled, this book could not have been written; it was a true learning curve.

Ian Frame who chivvied and nudged my inadequacies on the computer with great charm—and to Joy for allowing him the time to do so!

John Maitland-Hudson who designed the lovely cover, achieving this with the sensitivity of an artist and the accuracy of a sailor. For commissions he can be contacted at: **john396@hotmail.com**

Austin Owens and **Dan Perrett** of **Grove Design, Pembridge**, for their guidance and support.

Tania who boosted me endlessly with constructive feedback.

Anthony Pither who was my special friend throughout the writing of this book. He provided unlimited loving encouragement plus invaluable future material by proving the many shades of love.

Peter and **Brian** who gave support in many and various ways.

Other friends who ploughed through the manuscript, giving suggestions and words of wisdom!

Mary Ferris—last, but certainly not least. Amazingly generous last minute help with the final proof.

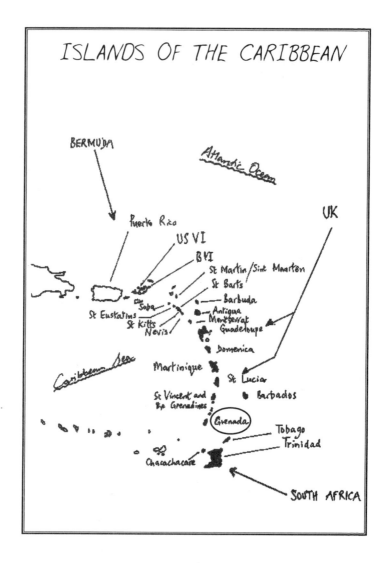

A map Henry drew and put at
the end of his log.

GLOSSARY

ARC	Atlantic Rally Cruise
BATTENS	strips of hard plastic that support outer edge of the mainsail
BILGES	area under the sole (floor) of a boat where water collects
BIMINI	permanent weatherproof fixed cover over the cockpit
BOWS	pointed bit (front) of the boat
BUOY	(1) Mooring: floating device that provides a ring for tying up a boat (2) Navigation: floating navigation marker with specific signs of warning
BURGEE	personal or club flag carried on port halyard
CATAMARAN	boat with two hulls
CLEAT	metal or wood device to attach warps from boat to shore
COCKPIT	the outside well of a boat where crew steer and work
COURTESY FLAG	national flag used when entering waters of another nation
CA	Cruising Association
CHIGGERS	minute bug that bites resulting in tiny itchy spots
DINGHY	inflatable boat usually run with an outboard motor or can be rowed
DLR	Docklands Light Railway
DOLDRUMS	an abnormal state where there is no wind
ENSIGN	national flag
FENDER	hangs off guard rails/prevents damage to boat when docking
GUARD RAILS	flexible steel rails running round the outside of the deck
LIFE LINES	U.S. version of guard rails

HATCH	windows and skylights
HEAD	bathroom/lavatory
HULL	the shell/body of a boat
JUMP-UP	wild Caribbean party with rum, music and dancing
KEEL	stabilising section that protrudes from the bottom of a boat
KNOTS	nautical miles
LEE CLOTH	cloth strip secured by ropes to bunk, used in rough weather
LOG	record of position, other vessels, weather etc
MONOHULL	yacht with one hull
NO-SEE-EMS	colloquial expression to describe biting bugs you can't see!
PAINTER	rope that is attached to a dinghy or tender
PONTOON	land area/walkway where boat is moored
PROP	propellor on outboard motor or boat engine
REEFS	putting a reef in the mainsail makes the sail smaller
SHEETS	ropes that are attached to the sails
SOLE	floor of a boat
SSB	single side band radio
STEAMING LIGHT	vessel under power
STERN	back (usually blunt) end of boat
TENDER	small rigid boat used for ship to shore trips
TILLEY HAT	probably 'the best adventurers' hat in the world'!
TRAVELLER	track to control sideways movement of mainsail
VHF	very high frequency (used between vessels/ coastguard etc)
WARPS	ropes that attach the boat to the shore
WASH	water: usually excessive and created by other vessels
WASHBOARDS	wooden boards slotted between cockpit and below decks, instead of a door
WHO	World Health Organisation

WHO'S WHO

**Lana (Svetlana) Bossi
22**

creator of the Talisman, lives in Rostov,
South Russia

~~~~~~~~~~~~~~~~~~~~~~~~~~

Adam Pitman 46

high flyer in finance

Eva, his wife Eva 43

senior British liaison officer for WHO

apartment:

Limehouse Basin, London

yacht:

Contest 44' Dutch built sloop *Green Flash*

berth:

at Limehouse Basin Marina

their son Paul 17

applied University of London: music
student, lives with Claire, Eva's mumsy
single sister

**their daughter Frances
21**

medical student, lives with other students
on a narrowboat in London

~~~~~~~~~~~~~~~~~~~~~~~~~

Henry Stringer 55

owner of Foxes Club behind the Royal
Opera House, London

Daz (Jo) Lee 24

ex model/singer

yacht:

Fountaine Pajot 46' catamaran *Wild Foxes*

berth:

at St Katharine's Dock, London

Carlos Franco

manager of Foxes; loves and is loved by

Eric Saunders

head of security at Foxes

~~~~~~~~~~~~~~~~~~~~~~~~~

James Bucket 63

retired oil consultant Saudi

his wife Prue 61

met James at Uni: English. Gave up her
career

yacht:

Crealock 37' cutter rig *Sorcerer*

berth:

at Brighton Marina

house:

at Copthorne, Sussex, UK

their daughter **Harrie (Harriet) 35**	senior executive retail industry

~~~~~~~~~~~~~~~~~~~~~~~~~

Sven Pedersen 62	retired engineer highways department
his wife Erika 60	Yoga teacher and a practitioner of all things alternative
yacht:	Island Packet 42' *Packet of Dreams*
berth:	at Stingray Harbour Marina, Deltaville
small apartment:	in Richmond, Virginia, USA

~~~~~~~~~~~~~~~~~~~~~~~~~

Freddy Muller 58	lives on his Van der Stadt 42' ketch *Ducky Do*
berth:	at Royal Capetown Yacht Club, South Africa
Dog	large black and tan mongrel
his nephew George **Muller 26**	newly qualified, rather intense marine biologist
Lily Trampton 50	meets Freddy in Guadeloupe, French West Indies

~~~~~~~~~~~~~~~~~~~~~~~~~

Warner and Margreet	Dutch cruising couple on yacht *Matador*
Trix (Trixie) 20	James' Delight. Native of St Vincent
Treasure	hospital worker in Barbados who became Prue's friend
Sam and Mabel	Montserrat islanders
Roger the Rasta	runs the Hog Island beach bar
Dicky (Richard) Bones	dirty and light-fingered ex-pat. Guards boats, for a price, when owners are away.

PROLOGUE

The Russian girl stroked the silky surface of the Talisman she had fashioned out of white clay and then painted so carefully. Its form was like the small rolling pin her mother used for her intricate pastry work but, unlike the rolling pin, it had a small hole in the top and was finished with a translucent pearly glaze. She smiled as she focused on the tiny exotic hummingbirds that darted round jungle spruce and palm trees, wings flashing brilliant greens and blues as they hovered, caught in a millisecond of time.

'You'll go there soon,' she told them. 'I can't leave but I'll get messages from you about your journey.' As if in affirmation of her situation, the Russian girl lightly touched the arm of her wheelchair, directing her mind to fly, a mixture of fantasy and the internet creating beauty for her. Justifiably proud of her English, she wrote the label. Her friend who worked at the University would laminate it and then attach it, by a bobble chain, to the Talisman. Although he thought her over-imaginative, he would humour her by taking the Talisman to England on his next lecture tour and giving it to a traveller...

I am Lana, from Rostov on Don in
south Russia. I cannot now visit the
world, but my Talisman can. Please
take it with you on your journey,
and send me an email telling me how
you met. I would love a photo too,
showing me where you are. This
Talisman holds my dreams and will
fulfil them with your help.

Thank you.

svetlanab22@hotmail.com

Chapter 1

D az had a slender, lithe body, long legs, and an enchanting oval face. Thick blonde curls topped this sweetness. But above all, Daz had a bottom—a firm, round, wonderful bottom that Henry adored and never tired of touching. Henry owned the prestigious nightclub, Foxes, located behind the Royal Opera House in London. The restricted register and the club's strict adherence to the 'members only' rule, made it possible for VIPs to visit in the knowledge that their privacy and security was sacrosanct. The fees were huge but no one minded that; it was a small price to pay for the quality of service and anonymity. From time to time someone would crack on about super-yachts and the Caymans, but the club was unique and considered value for money.

It was only a year earlier that Daz had appeared, asking to see him. At that time Daz was called Jo, before the stage name of Daz had been adopted. Dressed in a cream silk suit, portfolio held under one elegant arm . . . *What a breathtaking spectacle,* he thought. Big blue eyes looked up at Henry and he was lost—totally, unrestrainedly, lost. The relationship quickly grew from interview to lovers in about twenty-four hours, and of course, Daz was hired to sing—raunchy songs in a soft husky voice—in just one floorshow from 10 to 10.30 nightly. Revered by the members and adored by Henry, Daz remained remarkably untouched by such accolade.

Carlos, the manager of Foxes, was a small, slightly dapper man, always perfectly dressed in a bespoke DJ, silk cummerbund, and matching bow tie. Carlos' 'silkies,' as they were known, numbered hundreds and hung in racks within a cherry-wood facade, displayed on three layers of stainless steel rails. This uniquely designed wardrobe-type structure covered fourteen feet of his dressing room wall.

New club members learned quite soon that Carlos could, and would, provide anything or anyone from his vast repertoire of names. His little black book was secreted within his cummerbund, and a fine chain lay from a fixing on the book to a special stud, which he secured onto all his trouser waistbands. The book was to be buried with him, and the backup files would delete automatically if not used for twenty days.

Eric, an ex British Intelligence Agent, was head of security at the club. He was a tall, fit, humourless man who loved Carlos, cared for him and enjoyed a loyal and gentle response. Affectionately known as the two queens, they shared an enviable lifestyle and status in their industry. Henry knew his business could be entrusted to them, and they were well content with large salaries and a penthouse apartment over the shop.

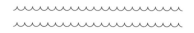

It was soon after their relationship started

that Henry introduced Daz to life on board his 46ft Fountaine Pajot catamaran, *Wild Foxes*. They hosted some weekend parties while the boat was in St Katharine's Dock but mostly the two simply relaxed and enjoyed their mutual delight in each other.

On this Friday late afternoon, Henry's strong athletic legs, the result of three times weekly sessions with a personal trainer, were wrapped round Daz as they sat in the cockpit leaning into each other. His sharply etched features and toned physique reflected a man who lived every element of life to the full. A soft evening breeze moved the canvas canopy as they sipped their first sundowner. Henry enjoyed his drink straight, a fine rum from Martinique, and there were twelve special bottles hidden in the port hull. Daz preferred a light white wine.

The breeze was welcome and occasionally stirred the blades of the wind generator. This was the only sound—a soft whirring—as they chatted and reminisced prior to getting back to the club for the evening performance.

Just before 10pm, the waiting audience in Foxes suddenly hushed in anticipation. They were rewarded with the prompt appearance of Daz, dressed in soft greeny blue body-moulding silk trousers and a matching bolero knotted above a slender bare middle. And bare feet. It was an appearance that raised the rafters every time. Playing the audience skilfully, Daz sang the opening number in an intimately seductive voice. It was the old Marlene Dietrich song, *Falling in Love Again*, and Henry, sitting at his table in front of the stage, was transfixed. He was bursting with pride at this beautiful young creature, *his* love . . . amazing . . . wonderful. Gazing at Daz, he realised how clever the silk outfit was. Its warm colours, reminiscent of the Caribbean sea with the sun on it, rippling gently over sand and coral, constantly changing and shimmering-sensuous, stunning!

The small stage was perfect, very effective in its simplicity, but warm-tone lights added another level of vibrancy to the visual impact.

Daz now launched into *their* song, *Too Much Love Will Kill You*. The raunchy voice, full of innuendo, wooed the audience still further—the club staff and members held equally spellbound.

Henry, the subject of many hot and openly licentious looks from the stage, was enchanted and thought, fleetingly, that it was fortunate they were soon to be sailing away. His focus on Daz was so total he felt his business acumen was not as sharp as it should be. Thank God for Carlos and Eric who would take over while they were away and keep things up to speed.

At 10.30pm precisely, the show ended to tumultuous applause, and one of the two permanent bands took over, providing soft background music for the next two hours.

Daz came offstage, grabbed a cape and went straight over to Henry. They left the club and walked to where Henry's treasured XJS was parked on the forecourt. With relief, they sat in the car for a few minutes prior to driving back to St Katharine's Dock.

'You were amazing tonight, my darling . . . just stunning. The members adore you and so do I.'

Daz, overcome by his words, reached over and rubbed Henry's cheek gently.

'Just how did I get to be so lucky?'

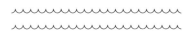

The Limehouse Basin Marina is the link between the lock gates to the river Thames and the entrance to the old Regents Canal—a haven for every type of vessel, nestling together in their berths and mixing a flavour of excitement and constant movement. Surrounding the marina, refurbished warehouses meld with apartment blocks tastefully designed in keeping with the old, while at the same time, giving a strong optimistic feeling for the future.

The yacht, *Green Flash,* was berthed in the marina, almost under the balcony of the apartment. From this vantage point, it was easy for Adam to keep constant watch on the work being done by the chippy he had employed to craft a new teak interior. Adam had re-designed the chart table and quarter-berth space to be extended as an office with instantly activating devices for navigation and, even more important for him, satellite connections to keep up to date with stock market news. Although Adam's business interests would be handled while he was away, it was still vital he receive information about global trends.

The current project for Adam was researching lights and alarm systems for the boat while Eva sought out the latest anti-rat devices and water-making systems. Both were consumed with the planning of every last detail. Weekends were now spent in research and preparation for their big sail to the Caribbean . . . and beyond.

On this particular Saturday, they were together at the Cruising Association, which handily for them, was situated on the Limehouse Basin just a short walk from the apartment. They were deeply immersed in charts and hurricane patterns and happened to notice another couple in the library who repeatedly appeared to be finishing with material they were just about to study. At 4pm the library closed, and heading for the club's bar, they all reached the lift at the same time.

Eva put out her hand towards the young person facing her. 'Eva Pitman, and this is my husband, Adam.'

Daz grasped her hand warmly. 'Daz Lee, and my partner Henry Stringer.'

Introductions completed, Eva then asked, 'Anyone for tea?'

'Make mine Scotch on the rocks,' Henry responded.

It was an interesting evening, cups of tea followed by two rounds of drinks.

'Thirsty work doing research,' commented Adam.

'Must be all the dust that gathers in libraries,' countered Eva, as they all smiled with the ease of a common bond.

The Cruising Association was well equipped for such occasions, and the two couples talked extensively about their dreams. With some excitement, they discovered their ideas of a sail plan to the Caribbean were very similar, although nothing had been firmly planned.

'Let's go to The Bunch of Grapes for a meal,' suggested Henry. 'It's really good to meet you both, and there's still so much we'd like to discuss about the proposed trip. Don't you agree, Sweetheart?' He smiled at Daz, who looked up, and nodded agreement.

They strolled down the streets between the marina and the river—streets now lined with new apartment blocks. They viewed critically some of the less tasteful features that were supposed to blend with the many old conversions but somehow failed and, too often, looked simply gawkish and wrong.

Fifteen minutes later, they arrived at the pub, which was particularly well known for its good food, historical interest, and the earthy good humour of the staff. During the evening the two couples relaxed and got to know each other—no more talk of sailing, or even boats!

A plump and jolly Eastender provided lively banter as she served them, and they all elected to have the speciality menu of the evening, garlic mushrooms served on a bed of wild rice and surrounded by rocket, followed by filets of sole with potatoes au gratin and fresh green vegetables. Two bottles of a fine Chablis showed that these diners knew the perfect wine to complement their meal and could afford to indulge themselves.

Eva felt drawn to Daz, such a sweet person who appeared gentle and almost a little *naïve*, especially for someone who was a professional entertainer. That Daz and Henry were so totally in love was endearing too. No matter that Henry was much older, there was a magic between them—rare but recognised by both Adam and Eva. Henry, generous as always, insisted on paying for their excellent evening, and Adam suggested they meet again on the following Saturday to share their findings, the dinner on that occasion to be hosted by him.

As they walked home, Adam said, 'Pleasant evening, interesting people and that Daz is a stunner, don't you think, darling?'

'Yes, I liked them. Daz is gorgeous to look at and lots of fun too.' Then she suddenly said, 'Let's write a detailed itinerary now. Right now!'

Infected by such enthusiasm, Adam agreed.

It was at 2am—their eyes red and weary from poring over charts, maps and cruising guides—when they finally crawled to their bed.

Next morning, over late coffee and croissants, Eva read aloud the plan they had made the night before, 'Falmouth to the Scillies, and from there to Spain and Portugal, then on to Cadiz. From Cadiz we sail over to Madeira and the Canary islands, and from Tenerife we do the transatlantic crossing to Guadeloupe. What fun! I think it's a brilliant idea to leave from Tenerife with Guadeloupe as our landfall. It's so much more inventive than doing the ARC with hundreds of others all leaving Gran Canaria at the same time.'

'Yes, we've always done things our own way.' Adam paused. 'How would you feel about sailing with Henry and Daz, not together, but in contact with each other?'

Eva stopped, croissant in mid-air. 'Sounds good but, well, let's wait until we know them a bit better.'

'You're right. Always so sensible, as well as being clever, wise, beautiful and oh so sexy.' His hand reached out and softly stroked the back of her neck.

Eva felt herself warming, almost blushing with the tenderness of his compliment and his touch. She was aroused and grabbed Adam's hand. 'Let's go back to bed,' she breathed huskily.

On the following Saturday, prior to eating out locally, Daz and Henry were invited by Adam and Eva to their apartment for drinks.

As they walked from Limehouse Station, Henry commented that he found the revival of all the old dock areas very exciting. Daz was just a toddler twenty years ago and was unable to comment, but agreed that the riverside homes were elegant and attractive. They walked past the harbour-master's quarters, housed in an octagonal brick building at the apex of the lock that connected the Thames to the Limehouse Basin and, as they walked on the towpath by the marina, they immediately spotted *Green Flash*.

'Wow!' breathed Henry in admiration. 'Fantastic yacht, Dutch-built I remember, this one is 44ft, I think. What lovely lines and it's known to be very well designed below decks.'

'Yes, stylish,' agreed Daz. 'But Hen, I thought all sailing boats were referred to as female.'

'Well, historically that's true,' replied Henry. 'But today that often seems a little pretentious—language has moved on and Lloyds has abandoned the use of *she*. The Royal Navy though has stuck out for tradition and will still refer to its ships as *she*. It's quite a history, my sweet. Are you interested?'

'Of course,' Daz answered, 'I need to learn everything about sailing. I feel so incredibly ignorant.'

'Well,' started Henry. 'Many of our everyday expressions in common usage have a nautical root. For instance, being *three sheets to the wind* is not a good sail plan, and of course, in common use it means being drunk and incapable. The idea of a sailing vessel being *she* comes from hundreds of years ago when the crew, often very young men, believed the ship represented their mother. Another tradition is the figurehead on the prow of a sailing vessel, it was thought to bring luck, and she was always a busty female. Her safety was considered paramount to the good fortune of the ship, and sailors went to great lengths to keep her safe.'

Daz nodded. 'That's really interesting. It never occurred to me how all those expressions came about.' Then turning to Henry, 'Would you fancy me if I was a busty female?'

'My darling Daz,' Henry replied, 'I always fancy every single bit of you—just the way you are!'

They walked to the refurbished warehouse building that housed the Pitman's apartment.

'Lovely place,' said Henry warmly as Adam opened the door. 'Beautifully restored and that Contest of yours is a joy to see on the water.'

'Yes, we're very pleased with both,' responded Adam as he shook Henry's hand and gave Daz a kiss on the cheek.

Eva came up behind him saying, 'Welcome! What can I get you to drink? Scotch on the rocks for Henry and dry white wine for Daz, I remember. Is Semillon Chardonnay all right for you?'

Daz nodded thanks, following her over to the handsome drinks cabinet.

Drinks dispensed, they all sat on the balcony in the late afternoon sun and relaxed with the sheer pleasure of the company and the view of the marina below, full of boats: yachts, power boats, converted riverboats, and narrow boats.

'I've always been drawn to narrow boats,' offered Daz. 'But when I seriously looked at one for sale at Little Venice, I decided it would be too time-consuming. It would be mucky too—wellies and that sort of thing. Also, a narrow boat is so small, it would have to be kept incredibly tidy, and there is nowhere to keep clothes, no real facilities of modern living, not at all like the catamaran where there is room to spread. Anyway, it would drive me potty, walking up and down in straight lines all the time.'

'Yes, I can understand that,' agreed Eva. 'Our daughter, Frances, is renting a narrow boat with a couple of fellow students. They share the costs, or rather we do!' She smiled. 'They love the canal-side life, but being students, stylish living is not an issue—and the interior of the boat is like a tip.' Seeing their guests' interest, she continued, 'When you see how they live you seriously wonder how medical students can be so lax about basic hygiene, but they say that a bit of dust never hurt anyone as long as the loo is kept clean! When Frances fancies a bit of civilisation, she comes home for the weekend. However, there is a certain charm to living on water, I must admit.'

Naturally this turned the conversation round to the proposed sailing trip ahead of them all. Adam stood up and walked over to a desk where he extracted several large paper sheets from a drawer. 'We drafted out a rough sail plan last weekend and, on further reflection during the week, saw no reason to change it.' He handed it to Henry. 'What do you think?'

Henry and Daz studied the plan with the accompanying maps and charts that Eva had scanned and printed out.

'Looks terrific to me,' said Daz. 'In fact, it looks very like our own route.'

The sheets of paper were spread out on the balcony table while the two couples discussed in more detail where they particularly wanted to visit. Henry said he and Daz preferred to spend a little time in Lisbon on the way south, and Adam said they would like to do the river trip up to Seville, staying there for a few days. Both couples planned to go to Cadiz prior to sailing to Madeira and the Canary Islands.

'Let's meet in Cadiz,' suggested Eva. 'That would be about four months from when we leave London. We can keep in touch by email or SSB radio.'

They all agreed with this broad plan and, after another round of drinks, strolled round to Bootles, an excellent pub close to where they had eaten the weekend before.

The hosts, Kevin and Andy, greeted them. Recognising Adam and Eva as frequent diners, they showed the two couples to a special table overlooking the river.

'Adam, Eva. Good to see you as always,' welcomed Kevin.

Daz giggled, and speaking with the boldness of two glasses of wine, said,

'Adam and Eva . . . amazing! Did you realise when you first met? Did Eva simply offer you an apple immediately?'

They all laughed and Adam responded. 'Actually, she offered me a symbolic apple—her phone number—and it wasn't long before the serpent was rising nicely, I can tell you.'

Bawdy laughter erupted. The evening was off to a good start.

Two hours later, very mellow and with feelings of great optimism, they went their separate ways. Henry and Daz took a taxi back to St Katharine's Dock, and the others elected to walk rather than be dropped off *en route*.

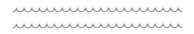

'What a gorgeous bum Daz has,' mused Adam as they strolled back to their apartment.

In the tradition of women, Eva asked, 'So what's wrong with my bum?'

'Nothing, my darling, your bum is most wonderful, but I also think that Daz's bum is noteworthy.'

They both laughed at the absurdity of the conversation.

Mundane activities, like loading the dishwasher, is also useful for stretching the hamstrings, thought Eva.

Adam had no such thoughts as his eye caught a movement that lured him away from his *Financial Times*. Eva's long shapely legs—slightly apart—and a frankly large bottom, moved temptingly as she pushed glasses and plates into place. She wondered if the last mug would be safe…

'Don't move,' came the gruff command. Adam slid in closer and gently rubbed himself against her.

Feeling his hardness, Eva wriggled just a little. He stroked her thighs and lifted her skirt, immediately feeling the easy access afforded by French knickers. Eva raised her hips, dropping her body down a little, and in just a few seconds, he slipped inside her, moving slowly until her body responded.

'Mmmm,' she breathed softly.

Then all conscious thought vanished as he wrapped himself closer until his fingers could play with her. He felt her gasp as he filled her with deep thrusts, and her muscles gripped him, increasing his excitement. She tightened her hold on the worktop as she bucked against him. Adam climaxed with her. He could not have done anything else, feeling and hearing this amazing sexy woman who never ceased to turn him on and was always ready to receive him. They stayed joined until the last movement left them, then sank onto the old sofa nearby—the old sofa that somehow never got thrown out—the sofa that had hosted so much fun, sex and love.

Soon Adam's soft snores became the only sound.

Eva relaxed in his arms and drifted. *Wow,* she thought. *That was, well, just something else…*

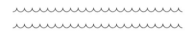

Another seven weeks of detailed research, planning and maintenance work had to be done on the boats before *Green Flash* and *Wild Foxes* were ready to leave for the Caribbean.

A few friends of both couples had gathered in St Katharine's Dock for a final lunch at Dickens Inn and an affectionate send-off. Adam and Eva had locked up their apartment and sailed to the dock to join this pre-arranged party. It was being kept fairly low-key as the major participants needed to keep clear-headed in order to negotiate the river—and anyway, they'd all agreed long ago that drinking while under sail was totally out.

Daz was spending a few quiet moments at the waters edge, simply reflecting on life and the twists of the last few months. At this moment excitement was finally overridden by feelings of terror. But they were carefully hidden. Above all an actor, the hours of dedicated practice took over now, on cue. However, the Russian man standing nearby, had been watching the body language and must have seen a succession of facial expressions and hand-clenching that fleetingly exposed vulnerability.

'Stage fright!' Daz asserted out loud. 'That's all it is.'

'Forgive me interrupting.' The Russian bowed imperceptibly.

Daz looked round in surprise, noting a slender well-dressed young man whose fair hair and high cheekbones gave a hint of his ethnicity. He carried a small bag, as was the custom of European men—and the immediate identification of not being English!

'Please listen. I have a friend in Russia, a young woman aged twenty-two, who was hurt in an accident. She is now paraplegic and confined to a wheelchair.' The man hesitated.

Is he going to ask me for money, wondered Daz, but aloud spoke encouragingly. 'Go on.'

'Lana was a brilliant artist whose work had attracted the attention of a renowned specialist in restoring rare works of art. She had just finished her third year at Art College in Moscow. She longed to travel and had accepted a years work experience in America when she was knocked over by a car. After many months of suffering on every level and learning how to be disabled—suddenly—how can I put it? Yes! Her spirit soared, and she was moved to design and make a Talisman. Please look.'

On taking the Talisman, Daz felt a slight but definite sharp electric-type shock followed by a sense of uncertainty. A slender finger gently traced the artwork, and another feeling was engendered—this time a sense of calm, of acceptance and peace. 'How bizarre! How weird! I felt shock and uncertainty and then calm, but the feelings came from the Talisman, not from me!'

The Russian man nodded, as if such an event was not extraordinary—so much so that Daz wondered if he had understood what had just happened!

Daz was completely hooked into the mystery by now. 'But how absolutely lovely. What an exquisite piece of work. Let me read the label.'

I am Lana, from Rostov on Don in south Russia. I cannot now visit the world, but my Talisman can. Please take it with you on your journey, and send me an email telling me how you met. I would love a photo too, showing me where you are. This Talisman holds my dreams and will fulfil them with your help.

Thank you,

svetlanab22@hotmail.com

Feeling deeply moved and inspired by the words, Daz continued, 'Of course I'll take it with me. I'll write to Lana and tell her who I give it to. Do you want to take a photo now? Hey, but wait a minute. Let's just walk to the lock gate. A photo from there would give a background of Tower Bridge.'

Together they walked to the dock entrance. The Russian produced his camera and took a photo of Daz, delightedly swept along by this new adventure— smiling and holding out the Talisman—pictured as a precious piece of treasure lying in two pale and sensitive-looking hands.

'Thank you. I too shall write to Lana. She will be thrilled. Thank you again for taking it.'

The Russian man inclined his head courteously as Daz, stroking the Talisman, acknowledged, 'It's a beautiful idea. Thank you for trusting me.'

They shook hands and parted. Daz, endlessly curious and loving the enigma of the situation, walked back to the pub filled with feelings of secrecy and optimism. The Talisman, back in its protective leather pouch, nestled deep in the jacket pocket, just below Daz's left breast.

When the time for departure arrived, two car loads of friends drove over Tower Bridge to the south side of the river, down Jamaica Road and eventually to South Dock where they could access the river and wait for the appearance of the sailors.

Henry, always the showman, had suggested they execute a stately sail down the Thames in tandem. It took quite a time for the two yachts to clear the lock from St Kats into the main waterway, but eventually the elegant Contest and the impressive Fountaine Pajot, sounding their fog horns, motored slowly and majestically downriver towards the Essex estuary.

They had all enjoyed dressing the boats. Henry had shown Daz how to thread the little flags in correct order and then hoist them above the catamaran.

'It's a time-honoured gesture of maritime celebration to dress boats overall,' he explained.

A great noise erupted as they rounded the bend in the river.

Are there no staff left at the Club? Henry muttered to himself as he recognised many of those waving and shouting on the riverside—but secretly he was very chuffed that so much affection was being shown to Daz and himself in this wonderful farewell. It was clear Carlos had arranged for some of the staff, along with close friends, to meet up at this point on the south bank.

On the north side of the river, quite a few Cruising Association members, plus Frances and Paul, the offspring of Adam and Eva, sent up fireworks and shouted words of encouragement.

'Send us a postcard!'

'Don't fall in!'

'Watch out for pirates!'

'Don't hit a whale!'

'Good luck!'

'Good luck!'

'Goodbye!'

'Bye!'

'Byee!'

Soon they had left the more residential part of the river and could no longer hear the shouts of good wishes. But there was one more surprise in store for them. A close friend of Eva and Adam, who was also a gifted trumpeter, had stationed himself by the river wall next to Chichester's *Gypsy Moth* at Greenwich. As the two yachts drew level, he started playing, and the emotive sounds of the *Maori Farewell* echoed hauntingly across the river.

> *Now is the hour when*
> *when we must say goodbye*
> *Soon you'll be sailing,*
> *far across the sea . . .*

'Strewth!' said Adam softly, swallowing hard, his strong craggy face softened with emotion.

Gradually the sound faded, and the two boats were left on their own, sparkling in their finery, but apart from the hum of the engines, now silent. Both couples were quiet, reflective of this moment and what lay ahead—suddenly aware of the enormity of the dream they were now transforming into reality as they started the adventure of a lifetime.

Chapter 2

The two yachts separated at Dover. Henry and Daz crossed the channel to France and then travelled south, whereas Adam and Eva wanted to cruise down the English coast to Falmouth, visit the Scilly Isles, and then do the crossing to Spain. But they kept in touch every four days or so and both couples, although content with their own environment, found this of great interest and, strangely, a comfort too.

Adam and Eva found the sail from Falmouth to the Scillies unpleasant. It was cold and wet, and the swell made life uncomfortable—added to which, they both felt a bit queasy after such a long break from offshore sailing. Eventually reaching the coast of northern Spain, things improved, and they were able to thaw out and relax.

Adam reclined in the cockpit, surrounded by green deck cushions that matched all the canvas and sail trim. 'This is what it's all about,' he declared. 'Sails set nicely, bowling along at a healthy eight knots, and you at the helm.'

Eva smiled, happy with what she was doing. She felt a sense of reward for the years of hard slog. Caring for their two children, and for the last fifteen years, juggling her employed work and family life had been tough. Now, although still technically working for the World Health Organisation, she had taken two years out for this adventure. If an international crisis were to blow up, she had declared her willingness to fly wherever needed, as had Adam. The adventure had its limitations...

Slowly sailing south, they stopped in anchorages. They wandered around on shore, simply enjoying being away from their work and the chilly English summer. The water-maker was doing a reasonable job, the wind generator and solar panels kept the electrics going and, as they were able to sail most of the time, not much fuel was being used. They only needed to top up once before arriving at Vitamora. Here they planned to buy fresh food, charge the batteries, and fill up the water tanks.

As Adam checked into the marina, he was shocked that some of the staff were brisk and frosty, more interested in chatting to each other than helping the visitors. *But didn't that only happen in English supermarkets?* And he was not impressed at having to pay sixty euros deposit against a key to the marina showers and facilities.

The pontoons were arranged in fingers so the land end of each one went directly onto a large concrete semicircle. This housed shops, bars and restaurants. But the noise coming from karaoke bars and drunken visitors was dreadful, and they decided to leave the next day.

Their decision was reinforced by a meal out. The fish was only just tolerable, and that was never an acceptable result. And tinned peas! Eva struggled with the Spanish for 'tinned peas,' but the waiter eventually understood.

'*Si, Señora*, no problem. Is normal.' He smiled, bowed, and departed.

'So much for marina facilities at Vitamora,' she said. 'And this looked like the best of the restaurants. Tinned peas in Spain, just imagine!'

'Probably just hit a bad day. Market traders on strike or something,' Adam countered cheerfully.

Back on the boat, they amused themselves by composing an unflattering mnemonic on the word Vitamora! Early next day, they were ready to leave at 0800. This was the opening time published by the marina office so they were further irritated at having to wait, along with four other yachts, for the office staff to arrive forty minutes late. However, once under sail, the unpleasant interlude was forgotten as they headed south, down the Spanish coast towards Seville.

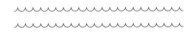

Henry was cautiously pleased with everything about *Wild Foxes*. Having been a sailor all his life, boats were second nature to him. But it didn't do to tempt fate by being too happy! He thought of the novel by Han Suyin. She told her lover how the rice workers in the paddy fields would cry out, 'Bad rice, bad rice,' in case the gods thought things were going too well for them.

'Bad rice,' he shouted into the wind, feeling rather silly when Daz came into the cockpit.

'Did you say something, Hen? It sounded like *bad rice*.'

'No, my sweet. I was thinking out loud and said *hand vice*, wondering about a piece of equipment we need,' he bluffed desperately.

Daz, looked a bit suspicious, shrugged, and disappeared below!

But Daz is shaping up well too, thought Henry. *Though to talk about shape and Daz in the same breath is superfluous, synonymous whatever. I am a sailor, an engineer, a club owner—not a damned poet.* Daz's character, Henry was pleased to see, greeted each new situation as a positive challenge, learning quickly and becoming truly useful crew.

The journey south was without major incident. Daz especially enjoyed the new way of life, while acknowledging that most things in Henry's company were good. 'And thank goodness I'm not seasick. I had no idea how it would be for me. What a relief!'

Neither of them had visited Portugal so they were enthused by how different everything was. They put into the harbour at Viana do Castelo.

That evening, Daz, having devoured the *Cruising* and *Lonely Planet* guides, said, 'Hen, my love, have you read about the history here?'

'No, only the pilot books. What's interesting?'

Daz's eyes gleamed. 'Well, this was a small fishing village until four hundred years ago, at which time cod was first brought back from the fishing banks of Newfoundland. They salted and dried the fish to preserve it, and bacalau became famous. The sleepy fishing village was no more!'

'Now, that *is* interesting. Shall we try some on shore?'

Daz needed no further encouragement and was ready inside ten minutes, looking svelte and lovely in mint green harem pants and a snug top.

'Gorgeous!' said Henry.

'It's all so easy with a tan, it makes me look so much better.'

'Impossible to look better. Just different,' responded Henry warmly.

The little local restaurant and the bacalau were memorable. Henry had already discovered the patron spoke some English, so he asked how to prepare and serve it.

'*Senhor*, you catch him, put him in salt, and hang him for half a year. No problem.'

Henry laughed. 'Okay, well can I buy it ready to cook?'

'Ah,' said the patron, whose eyes were firmly on Daz throughout the exchange. 'Now you soak him for one day and one night. You make new water two times and you cook him softly with herbs and make the gravy to serve him.'

At this point they were both finding it difficult to hide their amusement so Henry quickly responded. 'Thank you for that and for the meal. It was a wonderful evening.'

With much hand shaking, hand kissing for Daz, and goodbyes being repeated, they finally left the restaurant. Shops were still open so on the way back to the boat they bought a pack of bacalau.

Henry thought it would be a good idea to keep some as backup. 'Only problem is,' he observed, 'the smell is just awful.'

'Put it deep in the hull where you keep the fuel,' suggested Daz.

The fish was duly stowed, and forgotten!

Next day, again inspired by the guidebooks, they treated themselves to a luxury night on shore at an elegant mansion, now a state-run Pousada, near to the Basilica de Santa Luzia. The basilica dominated the skyline on a hill north of the city, and they enjoyed exploring the ancient monument, before the midday sun became too vicious and drove them back into the cool interior of the Pousada.

Here they relaxed with drinks in a dining room annexe that formed a balcony overlooking the stunning view of forests and mountains, with the sea in the far distance, and homes dotting the foreground.

'Just another slice of heaven,' murmured Daz.

Much later, after looking at postcards in the hotel foyer, the concierge guided Daz to a tapestry in one of the salons. It depicted a scene from the Roman invasion in 135AD, and with huge excitement, Daz rushed over to Henry and persuaded him to view it immediately.

'Well worth being interrupted,' he said, smiling, as he stood before the incredible work of art.

Daz was breathless with excitement but still managed to give a fair account of the scene. 'The subject is the soldiers at the banks of the River Lima, which was called the River of Forgetfulness. They didn't want to cross so the Commander dispelled the myth by crossing the river on his own. Then he called his men by name, one by one, to prove he hadn't forgotten anything!'

'Amazing,' said Henry. 'You know, you have a good memory for facts and a lively way of telling a story. When you get too old to ensnare the masses with your body and voice, you'll make a successful courier! Follow me!' he sang out, leading the way out of the salon with his hand held high, as if holding a tour guide's umbrella.

Daz, finding it difficult to walk from laughing too much, managed to reach reception soon after him.

They decided to get postcards to send home, and Henry paused reflectively.

'You know, Carlos and Eric would love that tapestry. We must send them a card. Do you think, my love, that they would like to join us for a week in the Caribbean? And would you mind?'

'Yes, just say the word. I think they would love it. And no, I wouldn't mind at all.'

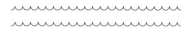

After their disastrous experience at Vitamora, Adam and Eva decided to head for Mazagon and then think about their trip upriver to Seville. The marina staff at Mazagon were friendly and helpful. They warned them the river had areas of uncertain depth, the current was very strong, and robberies had been reported recently from yachts moored near town. On that evidence, there really wasn't much of a decision to make, and arrangements were made to leave *Green*

Flash at the marina where security was excellent.

The trip to Seville was easy. They took a taxi to the bus station and then a luxury coach to the city. On arrival at the bus terminus, they checked into the nearest modern hotel.

Their first day in Seville was memorable because of the heat. They were flattened by the forty-three degree temperature that was so much more apparent after leaving the cool hotel.

'No wonder everyone leaves the city in August,' said Eva. 'This is killing.'

They both wore hats and carried bottled water but still found the heat, rising up from the streets and coming down onto their heads, too much.

'Let's escape into this air-conditioned shopping complex and read the leaflets about the city,' suggested Adam.

They entered the cool stone building with relief. Once inside, they sat on stone seats, sipping water. After a while, they ventured out and headed for the Alcazer Palace, which was also wonderfully cool and, with its mixture of exotic and elegant architecture, visually rewarding. The Cathedral was similarly beautiful, and they did their tourist walk, stopping many times for juice, ice cream, and to rest.

I'll be fat as a house at this rate, Eva thought. But out loud she said, 'I wonder if this heat, and sweating so much, balances the input of juice and ice cream.'

Adam's unhelpful rejoinder was, 'I like cuddly women!'

Next day, they did the City Tour in an open double-decker bus and were amused to see from some of the features that it was originally part of the London bus service! They could leave and join the bus as they wished and so were able to enjoy a lot of time studying the extraordinary bridge over the River Alquivir. This appeared to be supported by huge diagonal metal bars on one side only.

'Stylish in the extreme—a miracle of modern engineering and architecture.' Adam was completely bowled over by the structure. After he had taken many photos from different angles, they sat by the river under the shade of a tree to rest and take time away from the heat before going back to their hotel.

That evening, they enjoyed a drink and tapas at an outside bar, shaded by huge palms and masses of thick foliage.

'A bit like grazing in the jungle,' said Eva.

An elderly couple at the next table smiled at the comment.

A few minutes later, the slender and well-dressed man came to their table. He inclined his head courteously. '*Señora, Señor*, my wife and I would be honoured if you would care to join us for a drink.'

Adam and Eva accepted with pleasure and learned their host had been the Spanish ambassador in London some thirty-five years earlier. On recognising Eva's BBC English, as it used to be known, the Spanish couple felt drawn to converse, to reminisce, and to talk about the London they remembered.

Inevitably, they all dined together much later in a local restaurant, Roberto saying graciously, 'As my guests in our beautiful Seville.'

The food was excellent. It complemented the sparkling conversation. Talking about Andalusia in particular, Adam and Eva, who were united in their denouncement of bullfighting, asked their hosts about its popularity.

'Not so popular, my friends,' said Roberto. 'It is a myth that all Spaniards are cruel and bloodthirsty. Some are, of course. There is a tradition in some regions, but the more educated amongst us, well...' His voiced tailed off expressively.

Elena finished the answer. 'Passionate, yes! Barbarians, no!'

Roberto and Elena were only in Seville at this time of year for Roberto to fulfil a medical appointment and would return to their *hacienda* in the country the next day. But so great was the *sympatico* between them all that Adam and Eva were invited to join a weekend gathering in four weeks' time. Adam explained that, sadly, their schedule would not permit, and it was with real regret they parted—but not before exchanging contact details. The Spanish couple drove them to their hotel and, vowing to keep in touch, wished them good fortune and good weather.

'And may Neptune always be on your side,' added Elena with a warm smile.

With that, they waved briefly and were gone.

On reaching their room Eva said to Adam, 'Elena is so graceful and so beautiful. She must be eighty plus. She is my role model for old age.'

'You've chosen well there,' responded Adam. 'What a terrific evening!'

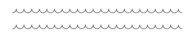

After leaving Viana, Henry and Daz continued cruising south, with only two brief overnight stops. Five days later, they sailed up the River Tagus towards Lisbon, and upon seeing the huge monument of Henry the Navigator, Daz insisted Henry's photo be taken in the same pose on deck!

They loved Lisbon and spent a day on local buses, simply going round the city and in and out of the outlying areas. They took many photos of the intricate ceramic tiles on the outside of all the old buildings, some of them even telling a story, but they were sad at the level of dilapidation.

'Many really lovely buildings are simply falling down. I can't understand why the government doesn't put money into preserving them,' said Henry. 'Or what about EU funds? They've put a lot of euros into Ireland, among other countries, but I happen to think this bit of history is worth preserving too.'

'Yes, I agree,' said Daz. 'But look at the economics of that. In Ireland, roads and harbours get upgraded and that in turn helps the people. But here in Lisbon, a few old buildings being restored, rather than roads and schools, would not be popular I think.'

Henry was impressed! 'You're right but it's sad, very sad, to see such magnificent old buildings crumbling. I wish some fund could be set up to restore the city. It must have been glorious a hundred years ago.'

They fell silent for a while, and the subject was abandoned as they continued walking, both deep in thought.

In the evening they went to the Via Graca restaurant where the subtle interior design complemented the spectacular views over the rooftops of Lisbon. The city lights were just coming on, and the sun, huge and red as it set, caught the red roof tiles in a luminous glow. It was, as Henry put it, 'truly awesome.' They were moved by the spectacle. Later, not wanting to end the magic of the evening, they decided to walk the mile or so downhill from the restaurant to the harbour, quietly absorbing the sounds and smells of the part of a city that probably had not changed much in two centuries.

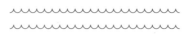

Leaving Lisbon, they day-sailed down the coast until they reached the old port of Cadiz. The marina in Puerto America was not well positioned. Commercial shipping created a big swell, and that made life on board very uncomfortable. The facilities were very basic, so once again, they were glad to be self-sufficient.

They planned to have one big shopping expedition in El Corte Inglés, a renowned Spanish hypermarket and department store. But in the meantime, they wanted to learn about this Castillian city, to explore its narrow alleyways with high buildings each side and, above all, to enjoy its culture.

The ancient city of Cadiz had the usual grim history of battles, executions and slave trading. Daz was completely overwhelmed with the knowledge and evidence of the original settlement established by the Phoenicians around 1000BC and found it difficult to absorb the enormity of it all. The city was at once romantic and exotic. The buildings blended a little of each culture—Carthaginians, Romans, Visigoths, Moors and Christians, the latter epitomised by Drake, Raleigh and Essex.

Henry commented that the mixture of blonde children with blue eyes and dark skin among the peasants could be the result of the English privateers.

'Or,' he added sagely, 'perhaps it's just modern prostitution and rape, rather than pillage and rape . . .'

They allowed themselves plenty of time to ramble through the streets and the fort. As they stood on part of the original wall overlooking the approach from the sea, Henry said that he quite expected to see a fleet of invading vessels rounding the peninsula, or even the sleek lines of *Green Flash*! They didn't have to wait long. Two days after their own arrival, they spotted the yacht as it motored slowly into the marina.

That evening, Daz and Henry provided a wonderful dinner of roast beef and Yorkshire pudding.

'Good Hereford beef,' said Henry. 'I bought it in the UK and froze it myself. Nothing to beat it, and so welcome after the fare of the last few weeks. Not that I didn't enjoy the local food,' he added quickly, not wishing to sound like the worst type of British tourist who just wanted egg and chips!

Suddenly Daz remembered the bacalau and said with perfect timing, 'Next time, *mi amigos*, it will be deeeelicious salt cod with the gravy to serve him.'

Adam and Eva were taken aback by this but thought it very amusing when the whole story was recounted later.

Henry put an arm round Daz. 'My little wag,' he said tenderly.

Chapter 3

Eva was on night watch. She scanned the horizon for any other vessels and noted a merchant ship and its position. Then she went below to take readings from the instruments and entered all the information in the log. That done, she was faced with another two hours of nothing. Nothing? Eva actually enjoyed night watches.

Totally alone ... but never really alone ... A glorious full moon was with them, and she enjoyed watching the shimmer of moonlight as it touched the sea.

Phosphorescence too was dancing on the water, and a satellite displayed its usual crazy jive in the sky, skidding every which way as it chased a signal. *Is it magic or mischief I'm reminded of?* As if to add weight to these thoughts, she suddenly saw a distorted reflection of herself in a piece of sheet metal Adam had been working on. Instead of her own pretty face framed by artfully streaked brown hair, she saw a gargoyle gazing back at her. Her usual dainty features—gently sloping hazel eyes and cleft chin—looked more like an ugly female Puck, and as she grinned at the reflection, her generous mouth twisted back in a lascivious leer. *Not my best shot,* she acknowledged wryly to herself! Just as suddenly the image vanished as cloud drifted over the moon. Now the night was velvety black, wonderful, and terrifying. No less mind-blowing was the depth gauge that registered '0' when it couldn't cope with the enormity of measurement. There were miles of depth under the keel—depth beyond counting— subterranean events and creatures down there from time beyond time. *It's a bit like trying to understand the concept of eternity.*

In common with such thoughts she felt a little confusion creeping in. The image of her daughter came to her mind. Frances hated sailing, and somehow Eva could hear her saying, 'Mad, quite mad,' which was not unusual in her assessment of her parents' mental wellbeing. Eva smiled and relaxed. She set the tiny plastic egg timer to fifteen minutes and clipped it onto her lapel. This way she could doze before her next check was due.

At 0200 Eva woke Adam so he could take over the next watch. He came up into the cockpit, and after updating him with details of her watch, they sat together for ten minutes in companionable silence until Eva yawned and said she was ready to go to bed.

'I'll wake you when we are two miles off Porto Santo.'

'Aye aye, Skipper,' she said softly, blowing him a kiss as she went below.

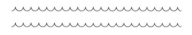

The lights of Madeira Grande could be seen in the far distance but the street lights on Porto Santo were very clear, as the island was now only fifteen miles away. Reluctantly, Adam decided to turn on the engine as the wind was giving them no progress at all. He wanted to get inside the harbour as soon as possible, thereby avoiding the foul weather that was forecast to blow in over the next few hours. As he scanned the horizon, he saw distant steaming lights being switched on and wondered if they were on *Wild Foxes.* Perhaps they too were changing their heading and motoring in to seek a safe haven. He was right, and the two boats arrived inside the harbour within an hour of each other, the catamaran having made up speed with her two powerful engines.

After a day of resting and doing boat jobs, Henry and Daz invited Adam and Eva to join them for drinks and supper on *Wild Foxes.* Forward plans were discussed, and they decided to meet up at Funchal Marina on Madeira Grande. Just three days after arriving, the two couples weighed anchor and left for the forty-mile sail.

Funchal was lively. The four friends decided to eat on shore the evening of their arrival and, as they strolled from their boats, they were able to enjoy the famous graffiti painted by visiting sailors on the inside harbour wall. Some of the contributions were works of art, with vessels and crew faithfully characterised or caricatured. Henry, a fair artist himself, said he would do a drawing of *Wild Foxes.*

Adam, not to be outdone, countered, 'Okay, perhaps we could do a likeness of *Green Flash*, too.'

'We could have dolphins bow-leaping,' suggested Eva.

'Wonderful idea,' responded Daz. 'Could we do that too?'

'No, my sweet,' Henry answered. 'We'll have to make do with flying fish.'

Daz looked disappointed and, showing an innocence of sailing, asked, 'Why?'

'Because dolphins prefer bow-leaping mono-hulls,' explained Eva. 'I guess it's more fun for them. In fact, I've only ever seen dolphins racing alongside cats, not leaping over them.'

'Now I feel foolish. I should have realised.' Daz looked a little crestfallen.

'Don't worry, we were all beginners at one time,' Eva was quick to say, giving Daz's shoulder a warm squeeze.

Fired with the enthusiasm of a new idea, a mini hardware store was found within a chandlery, and many small tins of paint were purchased. They elected to share the paint, although an element of competition was now evident. Eva and Daz said the winner would have a prize, and much whispering ensued!

A couple of days later, after an early morning walk to get bread, Adam came back to Eva. 'I just met a couple of cruisers who did an amazing sledge run.'

Eva looked up at him in surprise. 'Surely they don't get snow here?'

'No, not snow, but cobblestones!' Eva looked even more amazed as Adam continued. 'Apparently, before motorised trucks, the farmers used sledges to transport vegetables and fruit from the hill farms down to the town markets at sea level. These days, the same run is done by adventurous tourists just for the hell of it.'

'Wow!' said Eva. 'Let's do it!'

After breakfast, they walked round to the berth where *Wild Foxes* was tied up. Henry and Daz were sitting close together in their enormous cockpit, both reading. They appeared to be delighted at the interruption and to be informed of this latest adventure. It was decided to do the run the next day before it got too hot. In the meantime, they would gather more information about the history of the event and its location.

On the following day, as they walked out of the marina, Adam nudged Eva and pointed to the harbour wall.

'Oh,' she breathed with admiration. 'How brilliant! Hey, Daz, Henry—just look at this.'

There it was! An incredible geometric painting of *Green Flash*, about two foot square. Eva at the helm, and Adam looking through a telescope would not have been instantly recognised by everyone, but the group stood round, praising and commenting on the unique style of a man with engineering, rather than artistic, skill.

'Now that is sneaky but terrific,' said Daz, warmly. 'When did you do it?'

'Well, I woke early, couldn't sleep, so I decided to start the fresco. It didn't take as long as anticipated.' Adam, true to form, was self-effacing.

'Hard act to follow,' said Henry. 'But I'm used to following hard acts,' he added as an afterthought, leering at Daz who blushed and said nothing.

They took the bus to the hillside town of Monte and walked to the place where the run began.

'Oh look, Daz,' said Eva. 'Just look at those gorgeous hunks.' She indicated the young men who would guide the sledges down the hill.

They were indeed a sight! Splendidly clad in skin-tight stretchy white trousers with little jackets and coloured shirts that matched the paint on their particular sledge, their taut young biceps and gluteals displayed to maximum effect. Eva and Daz conferred with a bit of lusty lip-smacking while Adam and Henry, the latter scowling, waited impatiently.

Just as suddenly, all enthusiasm evaporated as Eva noticed the gradient of the hill for the first time! 'Oh no,' she squeaked. 'Can't do that—no, no, no!'

Then Henry said to everyone in general, 'I'm with Eva. I'd throw up with fright, and if that didn't get me, vertigo would.'

Adam looked at Daz, and Daz looked at Adam.

'Yes?'

'Yes!'

They both agreed and, walking as sedately as their excitement allowed, they selected a sledge. Or, to be exact, Daz selected the sledge being driven by the two sexiest-looking young men.

'See you at the bottom,' called Daz. 'We'll be at the nearest bar to the end of the run.'

'Take care,' shouted Henry, clearly suffering a lot of misgiving.

He and Eva watched their beloved mates settle themselves into the wooden sledge that looked far too flimsy for the job. Once strapped in, the sledge started its precipitous run. Eva took video shots and was pleased to record Daz's screams and Adam's shouts of horror!

'Come on,' Henry said. 'Let's race them by cab.'

Of course, by the time they had joined Daz and Adam, the two adventurers were already halfway through their first drink and buoyant with success.

'What kept you?' A flushed Daz, with sparkling eyes, smiled up at Henry, grabbed his hand and kissed it. 'That was such fun ... but I missed you!'

Everyone laughed, and while more pre-lunch drinks were ordered, Eva re-played the camcorder. Adam, always very articulate, talked them through the thrills, and near spills, of their terrifying sledge run over cobbles, round sharp bends, and steeply downhill. Both he and Daz had been impressed with the incredible expertise of their guides, who stood each side of the sledge and used their outside leg as if on a scooter, guiding and steering it.

'There was also a rope to aid the steering, though it was difficult to see how. One of the most frightening experiences of my life,' he said. 'But I'm glad to have done it!'

'Absolutely terrifying!' Daz agreed whole-heartedly. 'But those boys in tight trousers were sensational, and Adam gave them a huge tip. Well worth it, I thought!'

Daz grinned wickedly at Henry, who tried to smile, but failed.

They all acknowledged that nothing useful could be done now, or for the rest of the day, so Henry ordered another round of drinks. It was clear that things would soon deteriorate into siestas all round.

'Ah well,' said Eva. 'It's not good for us to rush around in the afternoon heat!'

Before leaving for the Canary Islands, it was decided that a day should be spent looking at the famous lace-making industry in Madeira. Fortunately, Spanish was understood by the Portuguese-speaking islanders so Eva, with her good communication skills, was elected spokesperson for the group. They walked around the town, then took a local bus to a village in the mountains where the out-workers lived.

Every woman making lace by hand—often little old ladies or mothers with a bevy of small children—had the same answer, 'No, *Senhora*, buy your lace from a shop.'

Eva enquired from a bookshop owner why this was. She found out that all trade was centrally monitored by a quality inspectorate with what they called *factories* controlling the design and supply of raw materials to the out-workers. The owners of these *factories* sublet the skilled craftwork to women in the villages and then sold the finished product in their showrooms.

As she relayed this information to the others, Eva became more outraged. She had particularly wanted to buy a lace tablecloth for her sister but direct from the worker, thereby getting some money into a poor household. 'It seems these women work their fingers to the bone and jeopardise their eyesight so the *factory* owners can grow fat. Fancy having such control that they don't dare sell direct to us.'

'We don't understand how the system works,' soothed Adam. 'Perhaps it's a good option for them— no responsibilities, free education for the children, and they don't have to worry about medical care, I expect.'

'That's *naïve*,' butted in Eva. 'I bet they are being exploited. It's like a modern slave trade. After all, Madeira isn't the only country in the world to use such tactics. But usually it's hidden under words like *co-operatives,* incidentally putting genuine co-operatives under suspicion. The workers' skills here are still being abused. These prices are huge by any standard, and I reckon I could get a lovely fair trade cloth in the UK, guaranteeing that the workers are well cared for and getting a good reward. But it wouldn't be from Madeira, that's for sure!'

Eva strode off, and Daz followed her, linking an arm in hers in silent support. Nothing was said for a full five minutes. Then Eva spoke, 'Sorry Daz, I get very lit up sometimes. These situations are not uncommon, and no one seems to care or be prepared to do anything about it. But in order to be fair, I'll check it out properly.'

Daz nodded. 'You are amazing, so articulate and clever. Let's go and have a drink. We can join the guys later,' and turning, gave a thumbs up signal to Adam and Henry, who until that point were undecided what to do.

Eva's anger soon dissipated, but she resolved to find out more about the system. She had been deeply moved by the sight of so many women working hard and, judging by the quality of their homes, for very little. *There'll be plenty more of that in the Caribbean and South America. Better get a grip right now. These outbursts serve no purpose. But I must find out who may be interested enough to write about it and has enough clout to get it published. Maybe me,* she mused . . .

~~~~~~~~~~~~~~~~~~~~~~~~~
~~~~~~~~~~~~~~~~~~~~~~~~~

Funchal was about two hundred and sixty miles from Graciosa, the first of the Canary Islands, but Adam and Eva decided they would sail straight to Tenerife where some old friends had a villa. They had no desire to visit Lanzarote or Gran Canaria again as they had good memories from holidays taken when their children were small. In those days, the islands were fresh and unspoilt by tourism.

They walked round to *Wild Foxes* to tell them their decision. Henry and Daz were deep in boat work, cleaning and polishing below decks. A boy of about fourteen was busy hosing, scrubbing and polishing the cockpit, decks, and equipment. They waited on the pontoon until Henry and Daz appeared, hair tousled, stripping off their rubber gloves as they walked. They all decided to meet up in Tenerife in three weeks but keep in touch in the meantime. Henry and Daz said they wanted to spend a couple of days on Graciosa.

When José heard the word Graciosa, he called out, quite unashamed at having eavesdropped.

'Graciosa is my home. It is a beautiful island and very friendly people.'

Eva answered him in Spanish, complimenting him on his English and asking if he wanted a job doing deck cleaning for them on the following day.

'*Si, Señora,*' he said respectfully. But his black eyes said something else entirely as he looked at her with undisguised admiration, bordering on lust.

'Jesus!' exploded Adam. 'We're not having any of that around when I'm not on the boat.'

The group grinned, and Eva smiled sweetly. She then arranged a time for José to start. '*Mañana, en la mañana,*' she told him.

They had learned, as most travellers did, that *mañana* had to be fixed very specifically or the arrangement became too casual!

Walking back to the boat, Eva suddenly spotted a new painting on the wall. 'Look Adam,' she pointed. 'It's *Wild Foxes*! What beautiful work. You can even see the burgee flying, its two foxes grinning at each other.'

The painting was impressive and showed the catamaran in some detail. Daz was there at the helm, a peaked skipper-style hat atop the curls, and Henry stood slightly behind, a hand raised in greeting.

'He painted it yesterday,' Adam said, 'when you and Daz went off for a drink together after your little tizzy.'

'Good! At least something positive came out of it.' Eva was unrepentant.

They walked back to their boat, and Eva collected her new camera, a professional model she could use for her work if necessary. She took photos of the wall with its many inventive and skilful paintings, and then swung round to take a shot of *Wild Foxes*. José, now precariously balanced, as he carefully cleaned two of the solar panels, made an interesting study. Eva decided to take a photo of him, with Daz sitting in the cockpit, mug in hand. But as she focused, she was surprised to see José looking at Daz with something approaching a sneer. Certainly dislike was obvious.

How odd, Eva thought. *Daz looks sensational, as always. One of the few people who can wear Bermuda shorts successfully. Wonder what's going on there...* She walked back to *Green Flash* and told Adam what she had witnessed.

Adam thought for a moment, then said, 'You know, Daz is a successful performer, used to having men falling over themselves, making fools of themselves. Perhaps forgetting José is only a young teenager, he was slapped down too hard. The teens are funny sometimes where lust, hate, love, and social skills are all mixed up. Do you remember Frances and that guitar player who seldom washed? He composed songs to her, ogling her with total adoration. When she gave him the heave-ho, he turned quite nasty.'

'You're right,' said Eva. 'Thank you for reminding me. Let's have a beer.'

Henry and Daz were really enjoying the catamaran and all the superior facilities. They used a holding tank for toilet waste and discharged it well offshore, as directed by the cruising guide for each country. Their water-maker was efficient and supplied plentiful amounts of water, and the generator boosted sufficient power to enable a modest amount of air conditioning when they really needed it. But the thing they enjoyed most was the *camaraderie*. That they loved each other was never in question, but the day-to-day living in a relatively small space was hitherto untested. They had both wondered if their relationship would thrive while sailing.

As Daz had said, 'Much as I love you, shall I need to get away from time to time, and will you also have the same need?'

Happily, Henry liked to rise early and enjoy a peaceful time with no conversation before 0900. This was no problem as Daz slept until Henry brought cups of tea into the cabin. Then they would sit on the massive double bunk and chat. Daz, being a sunny and uncomplicated character, was a joy to be with, and the only drawback was the night watch—long deep sleeps being a real need—and night watches were an agony. After much thought, Henry devised a system where he catnapped during the evening, took the watch 0200 to 0800, and then slept. Daz, being a serious noctural anyway, had no problem in keeping awake until 0200 so it all worked out. But they both disliked those nights because they were unable to indulge their most treasured moments—sitting close to each other, reading and talking, or lying in each other's arms in bed. Overall, they were both aware of the need to give space during this enforced togetherness. They made an agreement that if one of them wanted time on their own, they would go and sit forward of the main saloon or on the platform aft of the boat, uninterrupted.

As Funchal grew smaller in the distance, Daz took out the cruising guide for the Canary Islands. They also studied some of the ideas given in the *Lonely Planet* guide to help them plan land-based trips.

'Although we don't need to economise, doing a trip geared to the younger, less well-off traveller can be more fun sometimes,' commented Henry, sounding just a little pompous.

The anchorage at Graciosa looked inviting— clear water, good for swimming, not too many boats, and most important, good holding for the anchor. Henry had arranged a huge bimini that covered the whole cockpit area so they were able to strip down and not get burnt in the direct sun. Daz, sounding youthful and happy revelling in this surfeit of sun and sea, called out, 'Playa Francesa, here we come.'

Chapter 4

Although it was mid June, Brighton Marina was unusually quiet on this Thursday afternoon. James parked the Merc in their reserved space, narrowly missing a bollard as he backed in. Prue, as was expected of her, rushed off to collect a trolley. She was a small spare woman of sixty-one with a slightly nervous demeanour. Her no-nonsense attitude to life was in sharp contrast to pandering to her husband's excesses, both in and out of bed.

She started to fill the trolley and, predictably, James said, 'No, put the spare sail on the bottom and stack the beer round it.'

She said nothing, except to herself, and here she was very eloquent, *Why am I doing this? I can't stand him*. Prue smiled, realising that her verbal restraint gave her control of the situation, although he didn't know that . . . yet. *One day* . . . she said to herself, continuing to smile.

'Don't just stand there smiling inanely,' James called out, his face a little red, his double chin wobbling.

He needs a serious facelift. Prue smiled even more at this mental picture of James, bandaged, in pain, and unable to speak.

Eventually, after three trips from car to boat, everything was on *Sorcerer*, a handsome 37ft cutter rig Crealock, awaiting their pleasure. James' pleasure was to spend the summer sailing to the Canary Islands. There, at great expense, they were booked to join the famous Atlantic Rally Cruise, known as the ARC.

Maybe a parody on Noah's Ark, Prue wondered.

In order to meet up with the other rally yachts, they needed to get to Gran Canaria in early November for the crossing to St Lucia in the West Indies.

Prue's pleasure, James considered, would surely be in accompanying him! He eased his bulk onto the saloon bunk with a loud whooshing sound, which described the sudden expulsion of air, as buttocks, belly, and neck concertinaed.

'Pass me the Scotch and a glass, will you love?'

Prue took the bottle and glasses from the well-stocked locker and, with a sudden feeling of rebellion, poured herself a tot, *en route* to James. His expression of disbelief amused her again. 'For dinner, a tin of this and that alright this evening, dear?' she asked.

'My God, Prue. After heaving all those bags and sails around, I feel more like a large steak.'

'Its okay, dear, just teasing. In fact I have a pre-cooked chicken casserole in the cool bag.'

'Are you feeling alright, Prue? You don't sound your usual self. I hope you're not getting a bug that will delay our departure.'

The worm is starting to turn. Prue smiled at him again, broadly this time.

'Oh God—women,' James breathed into his second Scotch.

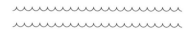

Around 0600 the following morning, Prue eased herself gently from the double bunk. James' drink-soured breath disgusted her, and realising he would need pleasuring sexually if she remained in bed, this early option seemed more appealing!

After dressing in a warm tracksuit, she took her mug of tea into the cockpit and sat there peacefully. She sipped the tea and relaxed as the sun slowly climbed into full glory. In common with many English summers, the sky was cloudless and blue, but by 1100 it would probably be overcast. Then her thoughts returned to the current situation, and her shoulders tightened as tension moved them into a hunched-up position near her ears. When James was working, she could just about hack it. His work as an oil consultant had caused him to be away a lot, mostly in Saudi, and the occasional week or two back home could be endured in the knowledge he would be away again soon.

Prue came from a working-class background. But her academic achievement at university, then as a published writer—*The Life of a Victorian Novelist*—set her apart from the rest of her family. After becoming pregnant at twenty-three and a quick marriage, she decided to concentrate on her family and let go her previous ambitions. Researching literature and philosophy through Victorian and Edwardian England, she realised the subjects she loved would need more dedication than she could give while looking after the children. Anyway, James did not support her writing, preferring to chip away with his criticisms until her confidence started to ebb, little by little. Strong family values, from both her background and her generation, had caused her to believe her marriage must be honoured at all costs, but now she wondered if the price was too high.

Prue loved the home she had created in Copthorne, a pretty Sussex village. The quiet peace of the pastel walls and soft furnishings soothed her, and now she had to adjust to life on a boat with no such backdrop, but rather the harsh reality of the elements.

Most of her beloved books were left behind. James had told her to bring no more than six of them, but the entire Patrick O'Brien and Wilbur Smith collections, plus the necessary books on navigation, cruising guides, and pilotage, took up all the available space. Prue felt the resentment edging in again. She displayed her chosen six: a handsome dictionary, a thesaurus, one book of modern poetry, the complete works of Byron and Wordsworth, and a large volume of Dickens. Eight more books were hidden under her underwear, and she decided that Charlotte Bronte would have approved! It was not that she disliked sailing or life on board. It was the reality of living with James in an interior space of approximately 20' x 12' and being unable to get away, have a walk . . . be alone!

Prue sighed and stretched. She gathered her towel and wash bag and, climbing off the boat, headed for the marina facilities.

~~~~~~~~~~~~~~~~~~~~~~~~~~~~~~
~~~~~~~~~~~~~~~~~~~~~~~~~~~~~~

James gave a huge snort and woke with a start. His belly felt tight and distended, his mouth dry, his eyes a bit puffy. He farted loudly and immediately felt better. *Hell*, he thought. *That's a terrible stench, even for me to tolerate, but satisfying.* He lay in bed and thought about his life. A successful career, retirement six months ago, his current cruising plans, and his marriage. He missed his consultancy work with all its perks, but most of all, he missed the respect and flattery from his Arab colleagues. His money was safely invested in the UK. He didn't approve of people who invested offshore, but that was largely because he hadn't thought of it until it was too late to change his arrangements and he had no wish to draw the attention of the Inland Revenue to himself. But even so, they enjoyed a very comfortable lifestyle.

James thought about Prue. He'd been married for forty years and felt satisfied that all was well. She had been a dedicated and caring mother, a good homemaker, and clearly adored him. Although never a highly sexual woman, even when young, she was always willing to accede to his fantasies and needs. When abroad, he had enjoyed affaires with European women living in the same area, so his huge sex drive was indulged and satisfied. He occasionally wondered, though he didn't dwell on it, why they always left him after a few weeks. He had been generous, occasionally buying a little gift, usually chosen for its glitz and low price, and he let them share the cost of meals out.

After all, he knew that modern women liked to be treated as equals . . . James sighed. *Women are certainly very strange creatures.*

A day later, *Sorcerer* sailed out of Brighton Marina and headed for Falmouth. More provisioning of fresh consumables, words that James liked, necessitated a two-night stay before leaving for La Coruña on the northwest coast of Spain.

Once in the West Indies, James wanted to sail round St Lucia, spending about a month there. Then, because he had memories of a brief affaire with a Bajan woman many years ago, he decided they would visit Barbados. It was not an island that many cruisers felt drawn to, due to the lack of facilities for visitors on yachts. But maybe that was another reason for James to go there. He enjoyed ignoring popular opinion, as he believed himself to be a bit of an adventurer—one who would *boldly go where no man had gone before*—well, almost!

Privately, Prue thought he was just plain bloody-minded. Having learned over the years not to challenge James and his ideas, she persuaded herself that Barbados would be a wonderful experience. *Libraries*, she thought. *There will be libraries everywhere, won't there?* A tiny panic started within her. She pulled herself together and decided there would always be an opportunity to find a theme or a cause, and write about it, maybe even get published. *Dream on*, said a little voice inside her.

Chapter 5

Henry and Daz agreed that Playa Francesa was outstandingly attractive . . . and different. They dropped anchor, had a swim, and then a cup of tea in true British style. The finest quality foil-wrapped teabags had been bought in England and were now travelling with them in weatherproof tubs. As they sat together in the cockpit, they enjoyed the view of a long, wide beach—just an occasional walker came by and a couple of old men with fishing rods. A far outcrop of rocks seemed to be the place to fish, and Henry said he reckoned the two old guys had probably been doing this together since they were children. After two days at sea, enough time to get into the swing of changed sleep patterns, they were glad to get an early night and do their exploring on the following day.

The sand dunes beckoned, and Daz, for once up early, agitated to go ashore as soon as possible. His early morning peace disturbed, Henry hid his irritation and complied. The main village at La Sociedad had only about one hundred dwellings and a few restaurants. There were also a couple of small supermarkets that were not at all super and, understandably, overpriced. The views over the strait were fabulous, and they decided to have a picnic of local bread, cheese and red wine. When they bought the wine, the shop assistant gestured whether they wanted it opened or not and gave them two plastic mugs. Obviously many sailors coming off boats were seduced by the view and bought food and wine for an alfresco lunch.

After a siesta in the dunes, where they behaved impeccably, they strolled back to the dinghy, hand in hand. When they reached the boat all restraint dropped—along with their clothes—and they indulged their love for each other until passion was spent and slept in each other's arms.

Next morning, Henry suddenly called to Daz. 'Look through the binoculars, my sweet. Your eyes are better than mine. I think *Green Flash* is sailing towards us.'

Daz confirmed that it was, and they called their friends on the VHF, telling them of the one rocky place to avoid when anchoring and adding how glad they were to see them again, and so soon. They invited them on board for sundowners and a meal that evening, which meant that Adam and Eva would first be able to catch up on sleep after their long sail. It wasn't long before *Green Flash* was safely anchored, and two brown bodies were seen diving off the boat— gloriously naked like a couple of kids.

That evening, a man and woman in a dinghy came alongside and hailed them.

Henry, recognising the pair from the only other British yacht in the anchorage, invited them for a drink. 'You're from *Sorcerer*, I think. Welcome on board.'

James put out his hand. 'Very good of you to invite us. I'm James, and this is my wife, Prue.'

Introductions were made all round, and they talked of various adventures, shore trips, narrow misses at sea, and future plans. They were invited to stay for supper. As Daz said, the catamaran had marvellous freezer facilities, and it was easy to thaw another bag of bolognaise in the microwave. Prue insisted on going back to *Sorcerer* to collect a dessert she had made earlier and returned with a large treacle tart and a bottle of wine.

'What a feast!' said Eva. 'Spag bol, salad, treacle tart and cheese.' With a flourish, she produced a large plastic box of ripe camembert and crackers.

'Camembert!' they chorused.

'How on earth did you keep it since Cadiz—and then get it to such perfection?'

'Aha,' said Eva, 'my secret.' She tapped her nose triumphantly. 'But seriously, I simply found a very cold spot in the bilges, perfect for cheese. Bananas can be stored there too but they must be in airtight containers.'

The three couples talked with the common obsession of cruisers about food, its storage, preservation, and the vagaries of cookers on board. Then the conversation moved to the usefulness of miniature hammocks to save space, and the huge problems of stowage in general on a live-aboard boat.

Prue, slightly bored, went off to find the visitors' bathroom. *Far too grand to be called a head,* she told herself. Then she decided to go out onto the foredecks of the catamaran and have a look round.

Soon she was joined by Daz.

'What a beautiful vessel,' Prue acknowledged.

'Thank you. We're very happy with it. Henry is especially delighted with the boat—it's his first twin hull. He used to hate the idea and said that cat owners weren't proper sailors, as real boats had only one hull! Then we spent a weekend on a friend's cat, and Henry had to admit being smitten. The rest is history, as they say. Prue, changing the subject somewhat, there's something I'd like to tell you about.'

'Of course,' Prue responded immediately. 'Is there some way in which I can help?'

'No, it's nothing like that.'

Daz delved deep into a trouser pocket, pulled out the leather pouch, and held it out to her. Prue, looking mystified, took it and, undoing the fine leather ties at the top, pulled out a smooth object, which in the dark she could not identify,

'Just a min, let me use this.' Daz rummaged again and pulled out an infra red torch, beaming the light on the Talisman.

Prue exclaimed with pleasure. 'Oh, how utterly lovely. What artwork! Look at those tiny birds. They are in flight, or are they? And it's warm. How can clay be warm, almost as if it has an energy of its own.'

'Exactly! Please read the label, Prue.'

Prue read the words and looked at Daz, waiting…

'I'd like you to take this Talisman to another person in another place. Is that okay with you?'

'I'd be honoured,' Prue replied, softly. She stroked the Talisman gently and affirmed to herself that she felt more a *sense* of warmth, rather than *actual* warmth . . . and peace. *Perhaps it's just a giant worry stone*, she told herself! But out loud, smilingly, said, 'Thank you, dear, for thinking of me. But you know I think it will be hard to give it away.'

'The right time will come for you. I felt the same but now I'm happy to let it go.'

Once more diving into pockets, 'Such capacious pockets,' Prue murmured, as Daz extracted a tiny camera.

'Prue, I need a photo to send to Russia with my email.'

'Of course.' Prue loathed having her photo taken, but complied.

And somewhere amongst the millions of pixels, a sweet study was stored, showing Prue holding the Talisman in softly clasped hands, almost in the pose of a mother holding a precious newborn. Even her smile was maternal and nurturing.

'Lovely!' Daz nodded at the image. 'And thank you.'

Prue smiled again at her new acquisition. *No, not an objet d'art, more a new friend*, she decided as she stowed it in her bum bag. 'Let's get back to reality,' she suggested to Daz, and they carefully climbed back to the group in the cockpit who were deep in conversation and hadn't seemed to notice they were missing! It was just before midnight when Prue said, 'Home, James, I think. It's near the witching hour.'

James looked astonished. Prue didn't usually assert herself in this way. 'And just as I was getting into my stride,' he grumbled.

'No, just as you were getting to be a bore,' Prue corrected, displaying observations born of a long marriage!

The group laughed in a companionable way, and even James joined in. All the visitors departed soon afterwards, Prue and James waving to their hosts from the dinghy platform.

'What a truly lovely evening.' For once Prue felt tranquil inside, as James drunkenly bounced and swerved the dinghy across the bay to their boat.

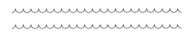

'Mmm,' said Daz, a little later. 'Prue's nice. In fact, she's rather special. Not so sure about the leery-eyed James though. Bit too familiar—well not exactly familiar, but sort of sleazy.'

'My thoughts entirely,' said Henry. 'The sort of chap I'd never trust, but okay on a superficial social level. Made his money in Saudi he told me.'

Daz paused, then said, 'They're doing the ARC, exactly what we said we didn't want to do. Bet there'll be lots of partying though.' Daz looked wistful.

Henry was suddenly more than ever aware of the age gap between them and realised that this abstinence might be hard on such a party animal. 'My darling, when we reach the Caribbean, we can go dancing with the locals, learn the tin pan, and party many nights away.'

Daz smiled up at Henry and then kissed him softly. 'I love you, my wonderful man.'

Chapter 6

*S*orcerer sailed into Gran Canaria within a day of the target, which James found very pleasing. A Seat had been booked well in advance so they were able to be tourists while preparing for the transatlantic passage. They found the island chokingly touristic, but having a car made all the difference. The scenery, away from the main roads, was lovely with its variegated colours of rock and vegetation. They stopped for lunch at Puerto de Mogan, which proved to be as attractive as described in the guide book. They bought fish in the port, for later, and had lunch in one of the many attractive waterfront restaurants. Bougainvillea and exotic flora adorned the many buildings, both old and new, which seemed to blend in well, each with the other.

'Charming and peaceful, don't you think? Quite a change from the ghastly noise and bustle of the city.'

For once James seemed to be in total agreement, and their day continued companionably enough.

Over the next week they worked hard to prepare *Sorcerer* for the crossing, with fresh and frozen food carefully stowed in the small freezer unit. As a backup, they had also purchased tinned food of various types.

Starving was not a possibility! Time sped by, and suddenly it was the day before departure. Everyone was in a state of high excitement. Rather than join any parties, James and Prue decided to have an early night and went below for a final tidy-up.

James suddenly looked at Prue and said, 'I'm sorry Miss Blossom, I've been a very naughty boy.'

Oh please. Not now. But out loud, Prue responded in the way she had been groomed, 'So, you've been a very naughty boy! What have you done?'

James looked down at his feet in a shamed pose and said in a little voice, 'I didn't put my shoes away.'

'You didn't put your shoes away,' roared Prue. 'Well, you know what happens to naughty boys who don't put their shoes away!'

James opened his eyes wide and with trembling lip said, 'Oh no, not that. Shall I bend over now?'

Prue followed the usual routine. 'Yes, you horrible little boy. Pull down your pants and bend over the bunk.' She reached up for the cane, hidden behind the bookshelf.

'Oh, please don't hurt me,' he whimpered.

Prue swished the cane through the air in preparation. In a stern, loud voice she replied, 'You must take your punishment and, if it hurts, you will be a good boy in the future.'

James screamed out, his mouth buried in the pillow, as the cane hit his naked bottom.

Swish! Swish! Thwack!

His screams became a prolonged loud whimper until Prue said, 'Right, that's enough. Get up, you nasty little boy, and don't do it again.'

James stood up, his massive erection nodding at her. 'Can I do something nice for *you* now, Miss?'

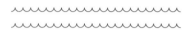

Over the next few days around two hundred and thirty yachts sailed out from the Las Palmas Marina, all heading for the island of St Lucia in the Caribbean. Their £500 fee for joining the ARC was to cover various issues: a comprehensive safety check of each vessel undertaking the transatlantic crossing, a radio web available each afternoon with weather forecasts, and a berth available in Gran Canaria and St Lucia. But for many transatlantic sailors, the provision of a platform for partying and frolics before and after the rally with like-minded people was the most satisfying thing. After four days at sea, they picked up the trade winds and bowled along at a good pace.

'Head south and turn right when the butter melts,' said Prue, irreverently.

James had the grace to smile and agree.

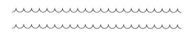

Twelve days out, the wind dropped, often completely. Progress now was about thirty miles in twenty-four hours. They were in the doldrums. This was a time to read, write, and watch the fish that provided a spectacular display. Whole squadrons of flying fish were very active, their bodies providing a cascade of lights in the sun. Often tuna and dorado leapt right out of the water. They were easy to catch but James and Prue didn't have to put in any effort for their meal that night as several flying fish landed on the boat. Prue was able to cook them, a very welcome change from the tinned food they were now reduced to eating. After four days in the doldrums, they were further entertained by the incredible frigate bird, swooping and diving so fast it could also catch a flying fish while on the wing. White-tailed tropic birds and shearwaters added to the spectacle, and Prue commented that it was amazing to realise that each species—fish, bird, and human—was relying on the flying fish for their supper!

Just under four weeks after their departure from Gran Canaria on 14th November, James and Prue sailed into Rodney Bay, St Lucia to the sound of tin pan playing, *This is my Island in the Sun*. This tune greeted every yacht as it arrived and was therefore one that all participants felt they never wanted to hear again. The celebrations were well under way as many larger boats had arrived much earlier, but everyone was on a high after their individual achievement in crossing the Atlantic, whether taking two, three or four weeks. The cruisers were either new arrivals and on an adrenaline buzz, or had been there awhile and were on an alcoholic buzz! There was a plethora of mad partying: dancing, singing, swimming and tall-story-telling whilst consuming vast quantities of rum, and indulging in all the excesses available after their privations at sea. After securing *Sorcerer* on the reserved berth, James leapt off the boat and disappeared for three days . . .

That's it, peace on board at last. With a smile, Prue went for a brisk walk, turning down offers to join various boat parties on the way, her personal excesses being to stand under a hot shower for five minutes and then enjoy a large and extremely expensive Scotch at the bar. Then she walked back to the boat and, with earplugs firmly in place, stretched out on the bunk and slept.

When James returned to the boat, he looked wrecked, complete with two days' stubble, red eyes and filthy clothes.

Prue dragged out his spare sleeping bag and put it on the foredeck. 'In there,' she said, pointing.

He was too far gone to even notice being told what to do. When he surfaced some sixteen hours later, he would find a bag of fresh clothes, toiletries and a towel beside him on the deck. The washboards were in place and locked so he would have no choice but to go to the marina showers. Prue would be nowhere in sight.

At around 1700, Prue arrived back at *Sorcerer*, having spent a rewarding day sightseeing. She had travelled on local buses, joining in with the chatter of the locals and was entertained by the equally lewd comments of the women passengers as they berated the driver for his obscene shouts to young women on the pavement! When she had seen a market or area that took her fancy, she simply got off the bus and browsed. *Bliss*, she thought. *No orders. No criticisms.*

James was sitting in the cockpit—clean, spruced up and looking suitably contrite. It didn't last long though. That evening, he told her he would like to sail to Barbados. 'Which you will love,' he added.

Before that, he said they should visit Marigot Bay and Soufrière.

Prue, knowing there was no choice, busied herself reading all she could about these two anchorages on St Lucia.

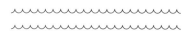

Two truly spectacular mountains, the Pitons, looking like elongated twin pyramids with emerald green slopes going down to the old town, provided a magnificent backdrop to the little port. The town itself had lots of character and much charm, in spite of wrecked boats on the foreshore. They had been damaged by a hurricane a year earlier and were as yet unrepaired.

James decided to join the two other yachts already anchored off the small beach by the Hummingbird Hotel. A boy appeared, paddling himself on a homemade raft, but James waved him away.

Prue was moved to counter his decision. 'James, look at the boy, he is only about ten-years-old, and so skinny.'

'Don't want to encourage them,' said James, completely missing the point. 'Prepare a sturdy warp to the stern cleat please.'

Prue obeyed. After securing a bow anchor, James got into the dinghy and took the stern line onshore where he wound it round a palm tree in line with the other yachts similarly moored.

While he was busy, Prue went below

and put a packet of biscuits, some cheese and a box of chocolates into a carrier bag. She signalled the boy, who came alongside, looking nervous. 'What's your name?' asked Prue.

'Jim,' he replied. 'You won't tell the school, will you?'

'No.' She smiled. 'Here are a few goodies for you, Jim, they all come from England.' She handed over the carrier bag.

'Thank you,' said the boy, then added, 'My Dad went to England to get a good job five years ago, but we only heard from him once after he arrived.'

'How old are you, Jim?'

'I'm twelve. I should be at school I know, but Mum needs my help so I try to earn money. Michael, my older brother, had a fishing boat, but that was wrecked in the hurricane.'

Dear God, here we are floating round the Caribbean in luxury, on a yacht worth over £150,000, and a child of twelve has to work for survival rather than be educated. Prue felt ashamed. 'Hang on,' she said. 'Just wait a sec.' She went below and found five US dollars which she gave to Jim. His huge dark eyes were enormous as he thanked her. *Okay, she said to herself. I know I can't feed the world, but I can try…*

James came back and suggested they go for a drink and lunch at the hotel.

'You go,' said Prue, thinking about Jim. 'I just want some scrambled eggs.'

James left and she settled with her book. Around two hours later, Jim was back.

'For you, Missus,' he said, handing over the

carrier bag with a freshly caught tuna inside.

Prue was moved. She took the bag, thanking Jim and wishing him well.

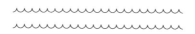

Next day, following a walk into town for fresh vegetables and fruit, they sailed round to Marigot Bay, but it was overcrowded. The too-famous and beautiful anchorage immediately lost much of its appeal, but as it was now evening, they needed to stay overnight.

This time, James was forced to employ a lad to help attach their line to a buoy.

This lad, though, was well fed and quite confident about his role. 'Five dollars first please,' he said. He held the line in his hand and asked for the money—*before* securing it.

Prue was delighted! *Great! At last someone steals a march on James. Hurrah!*

Chapter 7

The date set to start their transatlantic crossing from Tenerife was 10th November, so Adam and Eva decided they had time to visit Fuerte Ventura. They found the island was well named as the strong wind enabled them to sail with two reefs in the mainsail, and even then they were making eight knots. Both were glad to reach the anchorage at Isla de Lobos, and when Eva translated this as *Island of Wolves*, they hoped it was not!

The plan was to spend at least two days and nights at this peaceful place in blissful nothing. A slight tear in the mainsail on one of the batten pockets needed repair, but apart from that, they were able to swim, read, and fish. They enjoyed being naked and thought that by now their bodies had a good enough base tan to be in the sun safely, especially as they had the bimini as a permanent fixture over the cockpit. Forty-eight hours on and, wonderfully, they were still on their own in the anchorage. Adam had been successful, and the fish meals had been simple and delicious, perfect for their current lifestyle. There was enough left to freeze for a future meal and no waste as he even filled a freezer pot with the grotty scraps to use as bait.

'Be sure to label that carefully!' called Eva.

With Friday approaching, they decided to leave, as undoubtedly the anchorage would quickly fill up with weekenders. They sailed round to another spot, just outside the bay of Gran Tarajal, and enjoyed a trip on shore to buy fresh milk and local bread. The area was undeveloped for tourism but Tajita, where they next visited, was even quieter. They couldn't even find a post box. From their view on the boat, the landscape was sandy and barren with mountains as a backdrop, totally uncompromising in its austerity. Eva said that she half expected to see a Bedouin tent each time she looked at the shore.

~~~~~~~~~~~~~~~~~~~~~~~~~
~~~~~~~~~~~~~~~~~~~~~~~~~

On their fourth morning anchored off the island, the wind strength had increased and sand was being blown onto the yacht. They emailed Angie and Stuart, who had a holiday apartment at Los Cristianos and, after receiving a warm reply, set sail for Tenerife. Adam contacted Radazul Marina to book a berth for the next few weeks and, upon learning how busy the marina was, asked them to book a large berth for *Wild Foxes* too, ETA to be confirmed. He then faxed the information to Henry and Daz.

Adam and Eva also planned to spend five days with their friends. Friends who had met Eva, and each other, at university. They had all kept in touch ever since.

The apartment was small but comfortable and cool with the air-con constantly buzzing in the background.

Eva had anticipated enjoying the luxury of shore life for a few days. But later, in the privacy of their bedroom, to her own surprise and after only two days, she told Adam of her feelings. 'Darling, I feel restless and a little stifled. I want to get back to *Green Flash* and be rocked to sleep by the ocean.'

'I know how you feel, my love. Perhaps we can suggest a couple of days out sailing, as a change for Lou and Stewart. In the meantime, let me rock you to sleep in a more traditional way!'

Making love for Adam and Eva was usually an adventure, still full of mystery and passion, but tonight it was gentle and familiar, loving, soothing.

Angie and Stuart were excited to have the opportunity of sailing so they all set off for Radazul Marina and *Green Flash*. On arrival, Adam and Eva were delighted to see *Wild Foxes* sitting snugly in her berth, but their friends were nowhere to be seen.

'This grade of catamaran doesn't have ordinary washboards like ours,' commented Eva as she stuck their note, *BREEZERS AT 1800 GREEN FLASH*, on the saloon door.

That evening Henry and Daz appeared, and after warm greetings, introductions, and a couple of rounds of drinks, they all headed for Casa Tito, a highly recommended marina restaurant. An evening of the very best mixture followed.

As Henry said, 'What could be better than good food, very drinkable wine, and interesting company!'

'Love!' said Eva emphatically.

Everyone turned to her.

'Yes, love. That is more important.' She raised her glass. 'The toast is *love!*'

Everyone joined in. A man at the next table called out, 'I'll go along with that—I love fishing.'

'I love chess,' countered Angie. And so it went on, and on, and on!

It was 12.30am when the waiter approached the partying group. Some of them were dancing, but most were just talking noisily, having put all the tables together to make this easier.

'Please, *Señors, Señoras*, we have to be back here at six in the morning to serve breakfast.'

Good naturedly, the group agreed to leave and apologised for keeping the staff away from their beds. A big tip helped put the smile back on tired faces. The whole group, twelve in all, were then invited for a nightcap on *Wild Foxes*.

An hour or so later, just four couples remained as the evening wound up. An invitation for drinks on *Matador*, a Spanish registered yacht owned by a jovial Dutch couple, Warner and Margreet Frank, was extended for the following evening.

'Much to talk about,' said Warner as they shook hands and kisses were exchanged.

Then, with Adam, Eva and their guests, they lurched and laughed their way off the catamaran and back onto their respective boats.

~~~~~~~~~~~~~~~~~~~~~~~~~~~~~
~~~~~~~~~~~~~~~~~~~~~~~~~~~~~

The next three weeks were busy with preparations for the transatlantic passage, though the cruisers allowed plenty of time for socialising too. Much conferring on backup safety issues, plus cleaning and testing of equipment, took place. Food was bought, and great galley activity produced pre-cooked meals, just in case!

Suddenly it was 10th November and at 0400—right on target—the three yachts, *Wild Foxes, Green Flash* and *Matador*, motored quietly out of the marina. As soon as they were clear of the harbour, each yacht turned into the wind and raised its sails.

'*Vaya con Dios*,' breathed an early fisherman on the harbour wall, crossing himself.

The catamaran immediately took the lead with the two sloops not far behind. But this was not a race, and they were all aware of that. Although they may only see each other from time to time, they would each do what best suited their needs and the ability of each vessel.

With cries of 'Fair Winds' and 'God speed,' they settled into the pattern that would dominate their transatlantic passage over the next two or three weeks, each person feeling a huge sense of anticipation and of excitement that even Eva had difficulty describing in her journal.

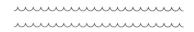

After eighteen days at sea, Daz and Henry were pleased to make landfall at Guadeloupe. The crossing had been easy enough, but they were tired from keeping watch round the clock. With hindsight they agreed that one or two crew would have been helpful. They slept a lot to catch up and enjoyed eating and drinking off the boat. Although the water-maker was efficient during the crossing, they had been careful just in case there was a malfunction. So laundry had piled up, and one whole day soon after arrival was dedicated to the washing mountain, as it became known. Against all the marina rules, they were pegging out sheets and towels on a line they had put up, running from the portside guardrail round the mast and over to the opposite guardrail. It was quite a sight, according to Eva and Adam, as they rounded the point and into the marina.

'But no smalls,' said Adam. 'I was disappointed not to see little wisps of this and that flying from the halyard.'

Green Flash was escorted in by two marina attendants in a skiff with outboard motor. All the cruisers entering Pointe à Pitre were impressed how marina staff always appeared in time to assist tired transatlantic sailors to secure their boat and then guide them to the check-in procedures.

Eva and Adam joined Daz and Henry for a quick beer on the way to the Customs and Immigration office and recounted how their cruising chute got snagged and torn in the mid Atlantic. This of course made the boat handling more tedious. Instead of being able to relax with the chute doing most of the work, they had to use a more conventional sail plan that needed frequent adjustment. Now all they wanted to do was sleep.

It was another three days before Margreet and Warner motored in. They had suffered a broken traveller that rendered the mainsail useless. All Warner's best efforts failed, and they were totally exhausted when they finally took their berth.

Everyone realised how devastating this must have been and how it would have slowed them down.

Daz, puzzled and keen to learn, questioned Henry. 'Hen, what is the traveller?'

Henry responded by pointing out, physically, where the main sheet threaded through a shackle and onto the traveller. This in turn controlled the movement of the sail from side to side before it threaded through a cleat and into the cockpit.

'But why is it called a sheet?' Daz asked.

'Daft word I know. I haven't a clue why a bit of rope attached to a sail should be called a sheet.'

'I reckon it's an elitist thing, just to make the ignorant feel more so,' supplied Daz.

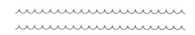

After a week in Guadeloupe, Daz and Henry had seen all they wanted and were keen to move on.

The three couples gathered for a lunchtime pow-wow at Le Petit Chou-fleur, a local restaurant well used to providing a congenial background for cruisers. Adam and Eva now rested, were ambivalent about moving immediately. Margreet and Warner had no choice. They were stuck in a queue awaiting urgent repairs. Thus it was agreed they meet in the marina of Fort de France in Martinique for Christmas.

Margreet commented that it was good to see how well France looked after its colonies in the West Indies—maintaining excellent roads and communications, providing French items to the supermarkets, and offering cheap flights to anywhere French.

In response, Eva was moved to say that Britain had a very poor record in that area. 'We seem to have a history of invading, re-structuring to our needs, and then abandoning. So many Caribbean islands were left floundering with no direction or economic expertise.'

In the pause that followed, Henry, changing the subject, said, 'We'll see you in Martinique then. We plan to leave tomorrow for a few days on Dominica.'

'Okay everyone, how about supper tonight on *Green Flash*?' invited Eva.

'Great'.

'Wonderful'.

'Good idea, thanks.'

They all accepted immediately.

'Bit of a send-off for Daz and Henry,' Eva added.

As they all started walking back to their boats, Daz linked arms with Eva and said quietly, 'Can I help prepare the meal. There's something I'd like to talk about with you.'

'Yes, of course. How about after siesta. Around 1600?'

Daz nodded. 'Thanks, Eva.'

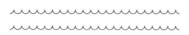

Eva quietly sipped a Scotch, not a usual drink for her, but she was a little un-nerved, her composure slightly rattled as she came to terms with Daz's confidence. Sworn to secrecy, Eva would never betray this but she needed a strong drink, just tonight, to help absorb the shock. *Why shock?* she asked herself. *Everyone must do what they have to do.* She had said to Daz, 'That took courage. Thank you for telling me. It makes no difference how I feel. You are still the Daz we know, sweet and funny. You are glamorous and talented . . . and my good friend.'

They had a big, warm hug, and Daz murmured, 'Thank you, Eva. I just wanted you to know, you of all people.'

Eva had smiled warmly and gently patted her young friend's face. 'No worries. See you later.'

The evening went well, but the finale was memorable. They had just finished brandy and coffee when Daz stood up, walked over to the music centre, and put on a pre-selected CD of backing music.

'I'd like to sing for you.'

Without any more preamble, the fascinated audience was treated to one of the most sensual and evocative performances they would ever witness. Hips that mesmerised swayed gently in time to the introductory music and big blue eyes homed in on Henry's, looking deep into him. The rich and sexy voice that had made Daz famous flowed through the boat and echoed out across the marina, stopping people in their tracks.

> *You ask how much I love you, must I explain*
> *I need you, oh my darling, as roses need rain*

Everyone who heard felt something like a little kick in the solar plexus, hairs on arms stood up, and breaths came a little quicker.

> *You ask how long I'll love you, I'll tell you true*
> *Until the twelfth of never, I'll still be loving you*

Moonlight danced on water and streamed through the saloon portholes, creating a diffused spotlight. The whole effect was surreal . . . a piece of time out of time.

Henry stood up and, moving over, took Daz's hand. This song was just for him.

> *I'll love you 'til the poets run out of rhyme*
> *Until the twelfth of never and that's a long long time*

He then enveloped Daz in his arms, and they held each other close. A minute or so later, unable to speak and arms round each other's waists, they walked quietly off the boat.

The group, still sitting, appeared to wake from a powerful dream. They were moved beyond words, and soft goodnights were exchanged.

'Are you all right, sweetheart?' Adam asked Eva, putting his arm round her. 'You seemed a little pre-occupied this evening. And Daz too seemed different, somehow more relaxed. Anything to do with your earlier *tête à tête?*'

'Yes,' said Eva. 'And yes to everything you've asked. You know, Adam, you are the best, and thank you for not probing me on this one.'

Chapter 8

arbados had proved a difficult place to visit by yacht. There were no marinas and the anchorage was crowded and busy. Prue successfully lowered the anchor after much instructional shouting from James. He would not trust her to helm so each time she had to struggle to do her heavy designated task. They decided to go on shore but found the beach landing hazardous. Rolling waves hit the shore with force, and the outboard motor only helped their direction up to a point. The prop had to be lifted just before the dinghy was swept into shallow water, then onto the beach.

James told Prue to jump clear while holding the painter so the boat would not drift out again. Terrified, she did so and was submerged briefly as a roller overtook her. Scrambling out, rope still in her shaking hand, she sat down heavily on the sand, her normally sweet round face contorted by fright, her brown hair plastered on her head like a hood.

James took one look and laughed. 'What a sight you look, Prue.'

'Pig!' Prue responded violently.

James, unaccustomed to her outburst, said, 'Hey sorry, Prue, I didn't mean ...' his voice tailed off. 'You did well. I couldn't have done that beach landing on my own.'

Prue shivered.

'Come on,' said James. 'Let's get a drink.'

'Panacea for all things,' Prue managed to mutter.

Next day, disaster! They had planned a day in Bridgetown with some shopping and meals on shore. With clean clothes secure in dry bags, they motored in. James urged Prue to wait for his call before she jumped off the dinghy. James shouted and Prue jumped.

But a second roller, unseen by him, was waiting to catch her. This time she was picked up, and the rope torn out of her hand as she came down with the wave, hitting her leg on the engine, and gashing it on the rotor blades of the prop. Her leg snapped, and she was hurled unconscious onto the shoreline. A local man who witnessed the incident came racing to help. Because of the event, James was forced to land the dinghy on his own while Prue's rescuer pulled her clear of the water, turned her onto her side, and covered her with his sweater. As he sprinted off for help, he shouted back to James that he would get an ambulance.

Prue awoke in agony as James tried to stem the flow of blood by holding a pressure pad, made from a handkerchief, tightly against her injured leg. When the paramedics arrived—fortunately the ambulance from the Bridgetown Clinic was in the area—James thankfully handed her over to them. He then tied up the dinghy, locked the motor, and went to the hospital with his wife.

Five hours later, heavily sedated following extensive surgery, Prue looked very small and white-faced in her hospital bed surrounded by drips and drains and all the mysterious paraphernalia of hospitals.

Dr Ernest Browne, the hospital surgical director, introduced himself and Dr Amos Bartlett, a renowned orthopaedic surgeon from the US who visited Barbados once a week, to James.

'It will be three months,' Dr Bartlett told James. 'There's damage to the left anterior tibial artery, some severe lacerations and a complicated fracture to the tibia and fibula. More surgery may be needed later.'

James sighed audibly, seeing the months ahead as wasted here in Barbados, instead of sailing. The doctors must have interpreted his sigh as anxiety for his wife.

Dr Browne put a consoling hand on James' shoulder. 'My friend, we'll do everything possible to keep your wife comfortable and pain-free. You may visit her any time you wish, but let her rest now until tomorrow.'

'We are well insured,' said James. 'Spare no expense, please.' With that he left and checked into a local guest house before getting paralytically drunk.

Next day, he visited Prue. She was pale and drawn, but a drip controlled the pain from her leg wounds and the multiple bruising all over her body.

She smiled weakly, saying, 'Go and do what you need to do, James. I'll be fine.' With the effort of speaking, she drifted off to sleep almost immediately.

James went back to the boat, collected clothes, personal things, credit cards and money. He checked the anchor and, putting everything into a bin bag, stripped to his swimming trunks and motored along the shoreline until he found a more hospitable-looking landing site where there were boats already tied up on the beach. The landing area, he guiltily observed, was much easier than the one made two days earlier, but he decided to keep that information to himself. He secured a heavy chain round the outboard motor and then to the dinghy itself. A nearby tree trunk provided a sturdy place to wrap the chain and then padlock it. Walking down the beach, he found a man who said he looked after boats for a small fee. James told him the story of Prue's hospitalisation and paid him ten dollars to care for the dinghy.

Then he hailed a cab and went to check into the island's famous and exclusive golf club. He was awarded temporary membership when he produced his member's card for Surrey's premier golf club, The Royal Chiddington. Observing the facilities at the club house, the style of the members, and his personal situation, he allowed himself a small smile. *Done quite well here. Not so bad. Not bad at all …*

As Prue settled to her second night in hospital, James went to a club in Bridgetown, where he spent the next few hours trying to lure a young black beauty, with the sort of large bottom he loved, into his bed. However, this did not happen. He was mugged, robbed and dumped on the street. At dawn he was found by the police, and as a Caucasian, the ambulance from the private clinic in Bridgetown was called. It was fortunate for James that the crew who attended Prue were on an early shift. They recognised him, and whisked him away to the same hospital. He was conscious but unable to speak due to a badly swollen mouth and possible broken jaw.

The police said they would interview him after making further investigations in town. Normally, muggings for theft were not so violent. This attack was particularly savage, clearly carried out with intent to inflict serious harm. But why? Ten hours later, James had been cleaned up, x-rayed, and his substantial injuries treated.

'Only a broken nose,' was the report from the amazed radiologist.

Next day, the police returned, and the officer in charge spoke to James. 'Sir, you was tryin' to lay the woman of a local,' he said pausing, 'shall we say, businessman. He din like this and some of his friends try to get helpful. We can't trace these men of course, but we've issued a warnin to the club boss. That was not a good place for a white guy to be in. I suggest, sir, you remember that blood is hot here. Passions run high. You was lucky. Please take care in future.'

For once in his life, James could not reply but he indicated that he wanted to communicate in writing. Paper and pen were put in his hand. 'Get the black bastards,' he wrote.

'Thank you, sir,' the policeman responded with dignity. Taking the piece of paper from James, he inclined his head courteously, and left.

~~~~~~~~~~~~~~~~~~~~~~~~~~~~~
~~~~~~~~~~~~~~~~~~~~~~~~~~~~~

Two weeks later, after James had been advised by a local lawyer to let the matter drop, he sat next to Prue in her wheelchair out on the verandah. 'Look, Prue, they've closed ranks on me. No point now in me staying here. Why don't I take the boat off to St Vincent and then Grenada. What do you think?'

Prue was glad to hear his plan. The idea of being able to read, uninterrupted, for a few weeks, sounded blissful. 'That's fine by me. You go on and let me know via the hospital where you are. And look after those bruises,' she added.

A link was organised through Dr Browne's Secretary, Treasure, and a treasure she proved to be, helping Prue in many ways beyond her hospital duties.

But Prue was suffering, suffering in silence. Her nights were punctuated with long painful stretches, having been woken by nightmares as she re-lived the horror of the accident. It was the evening following a particularly bad night that she remembered the Talisman. She asked her nurse to look for her body-belt and was very relieved that its waterproof exterior had protected everything inside. The leather pouch with its contents was intact! She took out the Talisman and smiled with pleasure at its glowing face. Holding it, she relaxed and slept.

The nurse, observing the softened lines on her patient's face, did not disturb her with a meal and simply left her some fruit. Prue slept a deep dream-free sleep and woke the next day feeling refreshed and almost buoyant, the Talisman still clutched in her hand.

A few days later, James spoke to Prue of his plans. 'I must get back to the boat soon. It needs to be moved from the anchorage. All things considered, I think it would be best if I left Barbados in a week or so and sail to some hurricane hole, probably Grenada as I mentioned before. But first I need to get the boat ready for the passage and get in some consumables.'

Sounds like a rum run! How about drinkables instead of consumables. Prue managed a small smile as she nodded to James, replying, 'Yes, of course.'

'I'll arrange for you to fly to join me when you are strong enough.'

Ah, reprieve. Prue nodded. 'See you in a day or two then.'

As she lay in her bed that night, Prue felt calm and untroubled. Her thoughts turned to Daz's words at the time of passing on the Talisman: 'From the moment the Talisman came into my care, my life changed, or maybe it was me that changed. You'll see…' *How strange. I was carrying the Talisman in a body-belt at the time of my accident, yet I still had the accident so it doesn't protect.* Suddenly it hit her—*IT DIRECTS! I've been unhappy in my marriage for a long time but I let it drift on. I wouldn't listen to that little voice inside telling me to leave, and there was no need for all those wasted years. This Talisman has a profound effect on me. At last I'm questioning the validity of my life!* Then a new thought. *Changes need to be made. I must make those changes, and soon.*

Up to this moment, mild-mannered and non-assertive, Prue felt as if she'd had a dynamic revelation! The accident had brought about positive changes. But for now, with her mind at peace and a new feeling of optimism, she drifted into another deep and healing sleep.

James found it difficult to do everything for himself. He had been indulged as a boy and as a husband. In his business life, his subordinates and secretaries served him in all capacities. Five days after the talk with Prue, where he had outlined his plans, James weighed anchor and left Barbados. He set the wind vane, poured a beer, and reflected on his fate. *Not so bad*, he told himself, *at least once my nose is mended*. To Prue's horrific injuries and enforced stay in Barbados, he gave only a brief backward thought.

Wallilabou Bay, St Vincent was the place for checking in, and James was irritated by the boat boys coming alongside and offering help for a fee. He shouted to them to go away, he needed no help. He was to regret this later when he was offered no fresh bread, fish, fruit and vegetables and had to make the tedious journey on shore each time he needed anything. Help with provisions would have been useful while he was doing essential repairs on the boat.

Three mornings later, it appeared that the two bow anchors had dragged overnight and, on closer inspection, James was alarmed that the boat was adrift in eighty-seven metres of water, the two anchors hanging vertically off the bow. *Must have dug in on a steep slope,* he thought, *and the wind direction changing one hundred eighty degrees caused the anchors to loosen and get free.* At this point he decided to leave and sail round the coast to Cumberland Bay, a very pretty protected anchorage. Here he accepted the help of a boat boy as the depth gauge now appeared to be faulty.

Moses, who clearly was no boy, knew the best anchoring plan in the bay. After securing forward and aft anchors, he asked, 'You like some nice black pussy, sir?'

'Could be,' James answered. 'A plump young one,' he added.

Toothless, Moses grinned and, waving goodbye, roared off in his inflatable.

Sure enough, two hours later a young woman, generous in all her proportions, was rowed out to *Sorcerer* for James' approval.

'You her pimp?' James asked Moses.

'Nah, man, she's my daughter,' he said proudly.

'Hi, big boy. My name's Trixie!'

'Come on board, Trixie.' His eyes greedily devoured her ripe, round body. 'That's an unusual name for a local girl,' he added.

'Well,' started Trixie, 'my name in God is Mary but I'm called Trix, cos that's what I pull—a lotta trix—and mister, I mean T-R-I-X. Man is you in fer a good time!' She grinned happily, obviously pleased with her skills. 'D'you want to take a little shag-snack now?'

Jeeesus, thought James. *This is going a bit fast.* 'Hang on there, Trix. I'll fix us a drink first. Rum okay for you?'

'Hey, man, Rum's my middle name!'

Must take some Viagra, said James to himself, reaching for the little blue pills that were stored in a tub in the galley. An hour later, he was in heaven. Trix had stripped him, and he lay back in total submission while she oiled, licked, sucked, then finally smacked him soundly—before submerging him in her charms.

'Wow,' he breathed. 'T-R-I-X indeed!'

A bond was struck between the unlikely pair. Rather than local dollars, James paid her forty in US dollars daily. As a result, Trix really looked after him, on all levels.

After four days, he invited her to come on board for the duration and, once again, he established a woman in the role of cook, cleaner, and for him most important of all, sex slave. James had started to find Trix addictive. Her menu was very varied with many 'specials' on offer!

After a week, he rang the hospital for a report on Prue. The staff, believing him to be alone and lonely for his very sweet wife who was now established among them as quite a favourite, consoled him with soothing words. In the knowledge that Prue was as well as possible and in good spirits, he felt he had done all he could to contribute to her well-being.

Now he could concentrate on the shag-fest. Trix was the prime mover, offering James a glimpse of something he had hitherto only dreamed as he became lost in her soft and ample arms.

Sorcerer had been in Cumberland Bay three weeks now. James had moved the boat out quite a distance so they were no longer close to the others. He was frankly embarrassed in front of other Europeans.

Trix was cheerful, outrageous, and very noisy! But she was fun, a fantastic fuck, and she looked after him well.

They went on shore one day, and she took him by rickety local bus to Kingstown, the capital of St Vincent, where she introduced him to her friends as 'my big white boy.' In the evening they went to a Jump-up and both got so stoned on reefers and rum they could only stagger down to the beach and sleep there like a couple of hobos.

One month on, and seven weeks from Prue's accident, James decided that he and Trix should move on to Grenada. 'What do you think, Trix?' he asked her.

'Well, I like you, big boy. This is fun. But to leave the shore, man, I jes dunno bout that.'

Eventually and predictably, James persuaded Trix to sail with him. After a long phone conference with Prue and her doctors, he set a course for Grenada.

Prue slowly mended, but she still looked ill and weak. Extensive bruising was now visible over her entire body, and she had to endure painful sessions of daily physiotherapy. Progress was slow because of so much tissue damage, and the pain she experienced with minor exercise made her very weary. But there was much to occupy her mind!

On Tuesdays and Thursdays, she ran a literary circle and discussion group in the hospital grounds, for which the local library provided the books she requested. Thinking ahead to when Prue would be stronger, Treasure had arranged for her to be picked up, taken to the library, and then brought back to the hospital.

Feeling quite pleased with herself, she joined Prue who was sitting in her usual spot on the hospital verandah. With her usual rush of words, she launched into conversation. 'Good thing I remembered to fix the library run. It'll be much better for you to choose your own books. But heavens, there are so many family events at the moment, and I need to visit my cousin on Montserrat in a couple of weeks, or did I tell you that already?' She flopped down on an easy chair and, extracting a cane fan from her bag, started fanning herself vigorously.

'Yes,' smiled Prue. 'That's fine. I repeat myself all the time. I'm just sorry you have so much to do. Thank you for arranging for me to visit the library, that will be such a treat. Here, have some juice.'

The two women lapsed into shared silence.

This would be a good moment to introduce the Talisman, thought Prue and, without further ado, she picked up her carry-all type bag. 'Treasure, there's a saying that if you want something done, ask a busy person.' She paused as Treasure looked up enquiringly. 'Here, take this please.' Prue gave the Talisman a gentle farewell squeeze.

Treasure loosened the pouch ties and gently shook out the Talisman. She gasped as it lay in her hands . . . ivory on ebony. The deepening shadows of late afternoon guided the last shafts of sunlight to catch its colours. For a few moments she rotated it slowly, watching the shifting lights. 'Oh, Prue. This is real special.'

She fell quiet again, stroking the silken surface that appeared to shine even more brightly than usual against her own glowing skin. Spotting the label, she read it aloud. Then she asked, 'How did it come to you, Prue?'

'Well, it was strange really.' Prue paused. 'We had sailed into Graciosa, one of the Canary Islands, and were invited to supper on a British yacht. The Talisman was given to me by Daz, a lovely young person who'd been given it in London by a Russian man, who was a friend of the potter. Treasure, this may sound strange but I have very much enjoyed being its keeper. It has a sort of charisma, a lure, but I feel it's time for it to move on. Apparently Daz felt the same thing at the right moment, and maybe for you, there'll be someone you will want to give it to.'

'Thank you, I feel honoured. And I agree. Already there is a feeling, a warmth, I can't put words to it...' her voice faded.

Prue filled the gap. 'Would you mind wheeling me inside please, Treasure? I think the evening bugs are starting to bite.'

'Sure. You look tired. Take it easy now.'

'I seem to do nothing else these days,' Prue sighed.

Once back in her room, they smiled warmly at each other and said goodnight. Carefully stretching back on her bed, Prue relaxed into the pillows and, with a little smile playing on her lips, closed her eyes and reflected on her situation. She was surprised and gratified how many of the hospital staff and members of their families seemed to thirst for access to literature, and they joined the literary groups whenever they could. They also welcomed her to their social events.

Every Sunday, she was collected and taken to a beach party or a picnic. Her wheelchair was parked in the shade of the trees where she sat with a borrowed hat protecting her fair skin. Now she recalled how only last weekend, Roland, one of the young men, had made her a new sun hat. He had whipped it together in front of her, using stripped green palm leaves. The jaunty little figure of a bird, made from thinner fronds, was tied to the side of the crown.

'Thank you, dear,' Prue had said to Roland. 'This is a truly lovely hat, and I shall have great pleasure wearing it.'

Taking her hand, Roland kissed it. 'Don't you realise, Prue, that it's you who gives pleasure to everyone? Why don't you stay here and teach in our big high school in Bridgetown? I never had a teacher as nice as you!' With that, he smiled, waved, and went off to join his cousins.

But a tiny seed had been sown in Prue's mind.

During her first evening as *Guardian of the Talisman*—Treasure, who loved grandiose titles—could not stop looking at it. She put it up on the mantle shelf where she could see it from every angle.

Settling into her favourite rocker, an over-fed black cat by her side, she pondered on recent events in her life.

Though outwardly not unhappy, a tight lump of despair remained stuck in the region of her heart. It was five months ago that Errol had left her. He had run away with Hyacinth, a thirty-year-old waitress at a local restaurant. To smother the hurt, Treasure had made up a story and told it with such conviction that her family believed it—she almost believed it herself! Anyway, it filled that gaping wound of rejection. She had said that Errol had been offered the chance to buy a franchise operating an internet café in Barbados. He had accepted, and had gone to the States for training in all aspects of running the business.

Time to face the truth. I'll tell the family tomorrow. As she made her painful pledge, the knot eased, just a little, and Treasure felt a tiny surge of energy . . . of light. She felt her eyes drawn to the Talisman. Was it actually glowing with a sort of translucence around it? She shook her head and laughed at herself. *No wonder he left me. I'm seeing things, possibly going senile.*

But the Talisman glowed on, regardless. With a little snort of laughter, she pushed herself out of the chair and headed for a tot of rum!

Chapter 9

Taylor's restaurant in Deltaville was buzzing. It was early for dinner by European standards, but here in Virginia it was full of happy punters, ordering and enjoying the excellent food. Erika and Sven were no exception. They had been working hard this Saturday on the yacht that was the realisation of a dream, a 42ft Island Packet, in preparation for the Big Off in two days time. A farewell party was scheduled the following day. Folk would gather at Stingray Point Marina and Yacht Club to wish them well, which of course meant lots of alcohol and food—plus much *bonhomie* in the swimming pool. Sven was very conversant with *bonhomie* having spent his working life on contracts away from home.

He had been a consultant for the Department of Transportation for his whole career and had become an integral part of the system in all areas east of Washington. Employed as a troubleshooter, he had given his all, both in his work and in the motels he frequented. An aesthetic looking man of average height with deep brooding eyes that appeared to reach into the depths of a person, Sven never lacked female companions...

After forty years of dedication to her work as a health therapist, it didn't take much persuasion for Erika to agree to cruise the Caribbean, for however long it took. With some humour, they christened their yacht *Packet of Dreams*. Erika, a tall woman of sixty, still had a magnificent body, which she worked hard to maintain. In addition to her daily aerobics, she ate sparingly, and then only foods that were nourishing. She practised yoga asanas for an hour each morning. Obsessive about her own health, she was prone to give unsolicited advice to anyone she thought would benefit. Her relationship with Sven was one of mutual tolerance in most things, and occasionally, affection.

A love of the sea and sailing was their joint passion. They had always maintained a small sailing boat and would spend available weekends cruising Chesapeake Bay. They had worked out a good system, using both cars and the boat so they could visit different places around the huge bay while maintaining their small but serviceable apartment in Richmond. While they were away this time, their home was to be occupied by Erika's niece, Marie, a mature and sensible woman who worked for an agency that looked after the homeless. She would keep the apartment in good order in exchange for free accommodation.

Both Sven and Erika had parents who emigrated from Sweden to America just before World War Two so their children would be born US citizens. Like most new Americans they were fiercely patriotic, in spite of the Swedish influence during childhood. Apart from their rather typical pale Swedish looks and colouring, little remained that made them different from their fellow Americans, whose backgrounds varied in a wonderful potpourri of cultures.

Sunday dawned bright and clear, which was the norm for a midsummers day in Virginia. Sven and Erika had a cup of aromatic Javan coffee. They were in total agreement about their dislike of coffee served in this area and vowed they would always use freshly ground—precious fridge space always being allocated to the cause! A bagel each, with ham for Sven and homemade cottage cheese for Erika, completed their breakfast. They closed up the boat and, carrying rugs, headed for that special section of forest at Stingray Point where the weekly service was held. Folk passed them in cars and on bicycles, all heading for the same event. They arrived at 8.15am, spread their rugs, and watched the small three-piece band tuning their instruments. A fifty-metre cable provided power from the nearest house, and the lead guitarist tested the speakers while Johnny, the local lay preacher, checked his programme.

Fifteen minutes later, around a hundred and fifty men, women, and children, waited—some on chairs or rugs and a few standing. The sun dappled through the trees, gently warming the day. A strip of the bay at Stingray Point could be seen behind the band where the water sparkled and danced in the early morning sun. The whole setting was idyllic and peaceful. It was easy to imagine, and many of the congregation did, that God was indeed here!

Johnny picked up the microphone, raised his hand high, and described a broad sweep of the whole. His eyes raised to the treetops and then to the people. 'God's Country,' he said clearly into the mike.

The congregation came to their feet as one, clapping and cheering.

At the end of the service, many locals headed into Deltaville for a huge buffet breakfast always served at Taylor's on Sunday.

Erika stayed under the trees to do a little yoga practice. The air cool and sweet, she spread her rug over the pine needles, and did a few salutes to the sun—as a tribute to the lovely morning. Then she packed up her things and walked briskly back to the boat.

Sven strolled to the boat and sat at the chart table. He made one last check through the navigation plans, then made sure plenty of log sheets were printed out. Flares were all in date and life jackets accessible. He checked the life raft and other safety equipment before making a large mug of coffee. Donning his baseball cap with *Packet of Dreams* emblazoned across the crown, he moved up onto the foredeck to relax. As the delicious aroma of coffee assailed his nostrils, he sniffed with appreciation and felt a small kernel of excitement stirring around the area of his solar plexus. This was to be a huge adventure. At last they would be sailing out of Chesapeake Bay, down to Hampton, and then the ocean passage to Bermuda and the Virgin Islands.

Erika joined him, and they both felt the buzz in anticipation of their plans coming to fruition. Soon they would join their friends in the marina clubhouse and party, secure in the knowledge that homework had been well done. The boat was gleaming and in perfect order, and their sailing skills were competent and well up to the task ahead.

~~~~~~~~~~~~~~~~~~~~~~~~~~~~~
~~~~~~~~~~~~~~~~~~~~~~~~~~~~~

A few days later, Sven hailed the Hampton Yacht Club on the VHF. They were given a warm welcome by the club secretary and were able to enjoy three nights moored up to the club's pontoon while awaiting a good forecast for their onward passage to Bermuda.

On their first evening in the clubhouse, they met two other cruising couples also waiting for a favourable weather report and, in the tradition of cruisers, information and stories were exchanged. During that evening, they all decided to buddy-boat the passage, which was renowned for being difficult and testing. Knowing others were close just gave them all a little more confidence, though of course out loud, they based their decision on social grounds! It wasn't until 3rd December that they were able to leave Hampton, and they were relieved the passage was easy and without incident. Just one week later, the three yachts arrived and anchored in Bermuda within a few hours of each other.

Erika and Sven were delighted with this stunning little island in the middle of the north Atlantic Ocean—so much more than just the up-market tourist trap they had previously visualised—and their first country to visit outside the US.

They decided to take a local bus to the naval base and dockyard. The journey was fascinating. From the higher vantage point of the bus, they could easily observe the island's traditional system of collecting rainwater. Whether the building was a school, hotel or private house, all the roofs had drain channels built into the slope, so the rainwater could go straight into the storage tanks. It was clever in its simplicity. They discussed its merits, as the idea was not dissimilar to the rainwater collection plan Sven had engineered on the boat, with a filter fitted just before the water entered the ship's tanks. Erika observed that probably only visiting sailors would be so aware of the need for water collection and conservation on such an island.

The buildings of the navel base and dockyard were spectacular. It was a beautifully maintained complex. They wandered round the museum, totally absorbed in the many historical records of nineteenth century life that were so carefully preserved. They found it impossible though to imagine that this base was used up to and even during World War Two. It was all so incredibly ancient!

On the journey back to the harbour, Sven took photos of the lovely homes they could see from the bus—many from another era—with wide verandahs, long sloping lawns, and trees with shady branches.

Feeling very hot and weary, they were glad to be back on the yacht in order to shower and change. After a short rest, they headed for shore where they met their new friends for dinner. As they walked to the restaurant, they decided that because they liked Bermuda so much, they would stay on over Christmas. Many small boat jobs needed to be done, and they wanted to swim and explore some of the stunning beaches. They agreed that soon after Christmas, they would head for the US Virgin Islands in time for the New Year.

The group's plans differed too much to continue sailing together, but they agreed to keep in touch by ham radio and felt sure they would all meet up again in the coming months. Two days later, Sven and Erika woke to find the other cruisers had indeed sailed out in the early hours, on passage to St John in the US Virgin Islands.

There was a lot to do. Over the next ten days, they applied themselves to achieving a good balance between working on the boat and enjoying the island. Their most important job was to measure, cut, and sew spare sailcloth to hang off the bimini on three sides. These would form deep flaps that could be rolled up, but when down would give extra shade from the sun. Neither of them had totally realised the effects of the sun on these longer passages in the tropics. But with the aid of their sewing machine, the job was done in a couple of days, and they were well pleased with the result.

Every three days or so, they took time off to locate some of the beaches where they swam. Erika was able to do her yoga practice, and Sven walked for miles. They both felt refreshed by their time away from the boat.

Herb, a highly esteemed radio operator who advised the cruising community, was involved in their decision for passage making. They made contact with him every few hours and early on December 24th, he suddenly announced there would be a good weather window that evening. They swiftly provisioned the yacht with enough fresh food for a week. Then, with everything in readiness, they treated themselves to a Christmas-style lunch at a local restaurant.

It was during a very narrow weather window, between bad forecasts, that they slipped out from the anchorage with the usual adrenalin rush that accompanies a new passage—especially one that on occasion is known to be treacherous.

The evening was still sunny as they set sail. With great optimism they implemented a three-hour watch rotation, day and night. The next morning started fine, but the day deteriorated to rain with lumpy seas from the recent sub-tropical storm. Erika had pre-cooked a casserole so they were able to enjoy a good meal while maintaining contact with Herb.

On the second day, rough seas developed with waves up to twenty feet high. They were further dismayed to learn on the third day out, that a tropical storm, with possible near hurricane force winds, was three hundred miles southeast of Bermuda and moving in their direction.

By now both of them were feeling very queasy and unable to prepare or eat meals. Whoever felt less sick went below, quickly grabbed dry crackers, dried fruit, nuts, and bottles of water, which were then put in a carrier bag and passed up into the cockpit. Thus sustained they carried on, fighting the elements and their seasickness. Log keeping was done every few hours, and although it was essential, anyone who wrote at the chart table became very nauseated. Niceties such as washing ceased to be an option, as it was too unsettling to stand up and maintain balance in the heads. With safety harnesses clipping them onto the boat, wet wipes were the rule, and a system of 'bucket and chuck it' served their toilet needs. On top of feeling sick, they were scared. Being teased by a tropical storm was the most frightening thing they had ever encountered in their years of sailing, and nothing could have prepared them for it. *Packet of Dreams* corkscrewed on, a brave little yacht battling through heavy seas with a tropical storm moving slowly west towards them. To combat their seasickness, pressure point wristbands were strapped on. They realised how important it was that they were both able to work the boat during this foul weather.

On day four, they had the same big weather, but at least it was warmer and eventually the storm changed direction and moved away. At last they were able to thaw out, physically and mentally, and hope for better weather on day five. This did not happen and the three-hour watch system become a far less rigid arrangement. Whoever felt stronger stayed on watch and let the other sleep, but they were both exhausted from constant sail trimming and handling the helm manually—the weather being too severe for the auto pilot to function.

They were amazed their seasickness continued as they were such seasoned sailors and believed their sea legs were well established. The wristbands certainly helped, but they still felt slightly queasy. Day five brought more challenging and unpleasant sailing conditions with constant sail changes. The storm, though, had fizzled out. The three-hourly watch system was resumed. Erika was able to continue writing her journal by the light of the full moon when on night watch, and the ship's log was written up with less discomfort. The air was balmy at night as they entered the official tropics, but now there was no wind.

As they slopped around in the ocean, Erika suddenly said, 'Do you know, when I'm lying on the bunk, I feel as if I'm set on the wool wash cycle of the washing machine—being gently pulsed up and down and then patted sideways unremittingly.'

'Yup, good description,' Sven agreed, smiling.

But the weather was still erratic and unpredictable: warm sunshine and then black clouds followed by stormy squalls. During the squalls the wind gusted up to forty-five knots, and conditions on deck were treacherous. Being tall and supple, Erika did the deck work needed, while Sven worked the winches and clutches in the cockpit. The upside was that they were able to take many of nature's showers, stripping off and using the shampoo stored in the cockpit locker. It was unusual on a boat to be able to stand and let water run freely with no restriction, and after all the recent privations, they enjoyed this feeling of almost luxury!

The outline of St Thomas gradually came into view at 0300 on day seven. Four hours later, they dropped anchor, totally exhausted, but with a bit more than the usual sense of achievement.

Sven cooked up some oats with maple syrup, and they each had a cup of steaming hot chocolate before crashing onto their bunk. They slept for a full twelve hours, waking just in time to see the sun going down, and realised that the New Year had happened without them! After a swim and a shower, they decided to celebrate their arrival and the New Year by opening a bottle of wine and barbecuing steaks. Their seven day ordeal had drawn them closer to each other, and they spent a relaxed evening in companionable conversation. They decided to get another good sleep and leave cleaning the boat until the following day.

On the day after arrival at St Thomas, Sven woke early. He felt rested and content. Erika, still sleeping, looked youthful and attractive. He felt himself growing hard and wanted to make love to his wife. This was not a frequent occurrence and therefore a desire that took him by surprise. He touched her shoulder and stroked gently down her arm. It was the vitality of this woman, her sense of purpose, her general ability to do most things very well that kept him away from her most of the time. He often felt inadequate, but now in the relaxed aftermath of a shared trauma, he wanted her.

Erika opened her eyes and smiled at him. 'Come here,' she said . . .

St Thomas did not appeal to either of them so they decided to buy fresh food, then sail to St John and the other Virgin Islands. And this they did. Having never been outside the US, the idea had been especially interesting for them, but they were disappointed with the island chain as a whole. Everything was so costly, and they quickly realised they would not be eating out on shore. The other downside had to do with the hundreds of charter boats, many being sailed in a very amateurish fashion and often using haphazard anchoring techniques. More than once, they were enjoying a light lunch in a beautiful setting, when an anchor was dropped in such a way that the chain would eventually lie over their own. Of course, this meant they had to wait until the offending yacht raised its anchor first!

Occasional visits for drinks or a meal on another boat were their only diversions, and so far, they had only socialised with other Americans. They determined to spend more time with Europeans—people who had sailed from that little-known part of the world— the countries of their forebears. They were thirsty for information and knowledge from people living on the other side of the Atlantic. To that end, they decided to sail to the half-Dutch, half-French island of Sint Maarten/St Martin as soon as possible.

Chapter 10

S trains of Brahms Violin Concerto hung in the warm air as Sven pom-pommed in a fair tenor voice to the more rousing passages of the opening movement. Erika and Sven were now at Little Bay anchorage, off the British island of Anguilla.

When the music finished, Erika spoke, 'Let's go exploring by dinghy.'

'Good idea,' he agreed.

They put some food and water into a cool bag and climbed down into the dinghy. The island was sleepy and visually quite lovely. The beaches were stunning, nestled into rock faces, occasionally speckled with greenery that reached up to the light. And best of all, they were deserted as they were only accessible by a shallow bottom boat. The allure was such that they landed on two of the beaches and tried, unsuccessfully, to photograph a diving frigate bird. The speed of the dive was too fast to record, except by camcorder, which they didn't have. But the swimming and snorkelling opportunities were perfect, and both of them enjoyed these few days of rest.

Sven was content. He lay on the beach in the shade of a huge rock. Life was good and calm, but unexciting. He loved his wife and knew this to be mutual, but she was so precise in all things and strong in her views. There were no grey areas, and her habit was often tiring. He was far more tranquil in his *laissez-faire* attitude so the marriage worked most of the time.

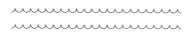

Unknown to Sven, Erika was having similar thoughts as she sunned herself. 'Must always use a high factor sun block in the tropics,' she had insisted. Now, as the warmth relaxed her usually controlled body—in spite of all the yoga—she felt a little scared of the future, and life with Sven. *The last third of my life with Sven, is not appealing. I want more excitement,* she acknowledged to herself. *But how can I have excitement on a boat all the time with him? Oh well, if it's not meant to be …* Erika believed deeply in destiny.

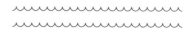

Sven suggested sailing to Marigot Bay, on the French side of the island. The supermarkets there were reputed to be well-stocked and excellent. However, once inside the store, wandering round with their trolley without any knowledge of French, they found themselves floundering. Choices were indeed wonderful but different from the food they were used to. They were confused and ended up buying chicken, salad and vegetables.

Erika observed that the freezers were full of strange, and often revolting-looking, creatures. 'Do they really eat snails in France?' she asked, after seeing a picture on a box in one freezer, and without waiting for an answer, 'Oh, how horrible!'

'But why not?' responded Sven. 'Obviously they cook them so it's no more horrible than eating tongue.'

'Yuck,' said Erika. 'I'm getting too much detail here. Let's get back to civilisation.'

They strolled to their boat, the cool bag slung between them.

'I found out something new from the supermarket,' said Sven, grinning.

'Yeah, what's that?' asked Erika.

'Well, Anguilla, the lovely island we've just left, is named for its eel-like shape, and that is *anguille* in French. I saw a picture of it on a freezer bag!'

'So now it's eels! Oh no, Sven, that's just too disgusting to contemplate.'

They took a bus to the Dutch part of the island and were immediately impressed by how friendly everyone was, and they all spoke English! The island, being only thirty-seven square miles, didn't take long to cross in any direction.

'Do you realise,' asked Sven, suddenly inspired by a leaflet he had picked up in the customs office, 'the French and Dutch actually signed a treaty of co-existence, and until the euro was introduced, two different currencies were used here? Also, sterling is accepted in a lot of places, maybe because Anguilla is the neighbouring island. Trust the Brits not to change their currency to euros and make it easier on everyone!' He paused. 'But I like it here. It's structured. Yet there is a sort of liberal attitude, like on so many of the Caribbean Islands. People seem to be more natural, have less convention.'

'Well,' Erika responded, 'I'm not so sure this over-liberal attitude is good. Women having babies with many lovers but no husband, it's not decent.'

'But does that matter, Erika, if the village structure is there to help support the mother and her children?'

Erika was not swayed. 'I think it's immoral. That's what makes America strong, their great strong family values.'

'Yup, plus incest, pædophilia and the brutalising of women—that's all swept under the carpet so the high moral front can stand up. A flimsy *façade*, that's what it is. I've seen and heard about women and children, in backwater places in America, suffering unimaginably while the family unit is promoted publicly.'

'I'm going for a swim.' Erika ended the argument suddenly and in a most infuriating way.

Sven poured himself a tot and sat on the foredeck. *Well, the more open attitude in the West Indies is healthier to my mind. Erika needs to loosen up a little.* As he watched the toned, tanned body of his wife striking through the water, he concluded to himself, yet again, how important it was to let folk live as they chose, to nurture the young and teach them solid guidelines within the rules of the culture in which they lived. *Difficult,* he mused, *to get all of it right.*

~~~~~~~~~~~~~~~~~~~~~~~~~~~~~~~~
~~~~~~~~~~~~~~~~~~~~~~~~~~~~~~~~

During the week on St Martin, they explored the island thoroughly, revelling in the colourful and noisy markets they had never before encountered and enjoying the whole Caribbean/European experience before deciding to move on to St Barts.

When they finally arrived at St Barts, there was another culture shock. They found it was a sophisticated island, patronised by 'the beautiful people' strolling round only partially covered by tiny bits of cloth or posing topless in gin palaces and on huge yachts. Erika was not impressed. Conversely and predictably, Sven was! But overall, it was not their type of place and, after only a day, they decided to leave.

The next tiny island was Saba. They were fascinated to recognise it from the cruising guide as a tall volcanic rock in the middle of the ocean. Choppy seas didn't permit landing, but they could see the landing area with steps cut into the vertical rock face. Apparently there were around two thousand inhabitants, but Erika commented that it was hard to see why anyone would want to live there.

'To get away from places like St Barts!' Sven offered.

After only one overnight stay in Saba's swelly anchorage, they were unanimous in their choice to move on to Sint Eustatius, another Dutch island.

On reaching the new anchorage, they hooked onto a fixed buoy, and then went for a walk on shore. Here they learned the horrifying history of the island, known locally as Statia. The museum was full of information, and there were records of the huge slave trade in the eighteenth century when the island had been a trade centre for legal, and illegal, commodities.

'Look, Erika,' called Sven. 'There's the slave road running from the dock up to the town. How did those poor souls survive after six weeks or so at sea, chained up, and then forced to walk this steep hill?' He felt hurt for them, those men, women and children, lying shackled together in the hold of a ship. 'And it was from here that guns were shipped to support the Revolutionary War, which caused Britain to declare war on Holland. God, what an appalling history!'

They were walking back to the dinghy dock when suddenly Erika stopped, shielding the sun from her eyes as she scanned the harbour more carefully. Then she shouted. 'Quick Sven, the boat is drifting!'

Both being slim and fit, they were able to race down the road, jump into their dinghy, and roar off. As they approached *Dreams*, their shortened name for the boat, they saw two figures on board, securing lines onto another buoy.

It happened that one of the men who came to the rescue was Danish and the other Dutch, both from yachts in the bay. They had noticed the Island Packet drifting, still attached to its trailing buoy, and had leapt into their dinghies and rushed to stop its progress towards the rocks. One had driven his dinghy in front, holding it there, while the other had boarded and found another line. Between them they managed to secure the yacht to a vacant buoy. Much relieved, everyone had a beer as they exchanged this information. Gustav said he would take the broken buoy, with its frayed and broken rope trailing, to the harbour authorities as proof that work needed to be done to the sea bed fixings. When it was discovered that they all planned to be in St Kitts and then Nevis in the next two weeks, Erika warmly invited Hans with his wife, Machteld, and Gustav who was sailing solo, to have dinner with them when they next met up.

Because of their huge fright, Sven and Erika decided to keep an anchor watch over the next few hours, and then sail at dawn to the marina at Porte Zante, St Kitts. They needed to refuel and fill up the water tanks before moving too much farther anyway.

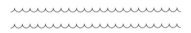

Porte Zante was a newly built harbour and marina. The old one had been damaged badly by Hurricane George, but Sven said he reckoned the steel reinforced walls and buildings should be safe from the next one. They left the boat and went into town for the morning only. Here they were interested to learn that St Kitts had very strict rules about couples displaying any form of affection in public. Even holding hands was outlawed!

'There you are,' said Erika. 'Isn't that better? No gross kissing in public. You see, it can be done.'

'There is a happy medium though,' responded Sven, ever the romantic. 'I enjoy seeing lovers focused on each other.' *But I don't suppose we'll ever agree on that one.*

However, they *were* agreed in their desire to get away from this bustling port with its cruise ships and tourists, and on to the quiet island of Nevis, which proved to be the complete antithesis to St Kitts.

Sven and Erika dropped anchor off Pinneys Beach. Then they had a swim in the warm, clean, water. After the usual brief fresh-water shower, they sat with their sundowners side by side in the cockpit, completely awestruck by the wonderful view. They were facing the shore—a deserted white beach fringed with palm trees. Behind that, a backdrop of volcanic rock covered with vegetation, appeared to touch the clouds, and a full moon was just rising and reflecting off an amazing foreground of blue, blue sea. In this moment they seemed united and very content.

After only four days, they were pleased to see the Danish and Dutch yachts being sailed into the anchorage. Much waving and calling to each other ensued. Sven and Erika learned the others had 'done' St Kitts, taking two days over it, and were now pleased to be away from the noise and sharing this gloriously serene place. Erika was able to offer the promised meal, and she and Sven, at last, were able to enjoy the company of real Europeans!

By chance, it appeared that Race Day was scheduled for the next Sunday so they all decided to put together a picnic and share a taxi to the race ground. As was usual, Sunday dawned bright and beautiful. Their taxi driver was happy as his day at the races was being paid for. It also gave him a good excuse to get away from the usual Sunday gathering of family and meet up with the young woman who had become a 'special' friend.

Everyone had a marvellous day, a day to remember always. After buying tickets for the one available stand with sun cover, they strolled round the surrounding area with its fairground atmosphere. None of them had ever seen anything like it. Large women in bright clothes and sun hats and under big umbrellas were selling food and goods of all types. They shouted cheerfully to each other, and the crowd, often trading insults! Their volume didn't vary . . . fortissimo!

It was hot so the sailors went to the stand for their picnic lunch. To their surprise, a party was already taking place! Rum flowed, and the large group of locals were enjoying themselves hugely. Someone had a transistor radio on, at full volume of course, and they were dancing.

'Hows about a bit of wucking up!' someone shouted

'Yeah man, do it!'

'Let's go!'

'C'mon!'

A man and woman started dancing to the music. They fitted closely, each to the other, spoon-like, with their pelvises bucking and grinding. The non-dancers screamed their approval, clapping and whistling, and when one particularly outrageous movement was performed, the audience was unanimous.

'More!' they yelled.

To non-Caribbean ears, the noise was immense, but so was the visual impact. All, but Erika, loved the spontaneity and sense of fun that emanated from the dancers. She was disgusted by the show of simulated sex and couldn't find any pleasure in such a display.

'Relax, honey,' whispered Sven in her ear. 'It's just fun, that's all—another culture, other customs.'

'I'll go for a walk,' she whispered back, leaving the stand.

When the racing started, they were again totally amazed by another sight. Rasta jockeys with hats perched on top of the dreadlocks, and another couple of jockeys with motorcycle helmets, in fact it seemed that any style of clothes was allowed. But they could ride! The group of visitors was held, almost breathless, by their daring, as they urged their horses ever faster, at terrifying speeds, round the track.

'Now I understand why the British call it breakneck speed,' commented Machteld. 'What a show! Nee, we don't have anything like that in Holland!'

Chapter 11

Montserrat—what a name. Sven said that for him the very words conjured up enchanted castles and wizardry! Sadly, there were no abandoned castles to explore, but there were many abandoned homes…

They dropped anchor at Little Bay and went on shore to check in. But checking in proved to be difficult. Here was yet another West Indies island drowned in bureaucracy, a simple event taking two hours. The only means of transport was a taxi so they negotiated a price for the day and then relaxed in their chauffeur-driven jeep.

Their driver, Sam, was voluble and from him they learned of the island's troubles. It seemed shocking that this was the first time they had heard the details in such a graphic and real way.

Sam, in his element now, talked expansively. 'My island is supported by the British Government, and they helped in our last crisis—we had a lot of help from America too. It was in 1995 when this mother of volcanoes erupted. It had been dormant for two hundred years so no one suspected impending disaster. Intact houses are still standing on the surrounding hills, deserted. Many retired people had their dream homes here and were ordered to leave quickly.' He sighed. 'So very sad. Such a trauma.'

'Were there many casualties, Sam?' Erika asked.

'Mercifully no. Only nine souls died and that was because they went back, against all warnings, to get livestock or goods. But for the aid from England and America, we would all have starved to death or died from lack of medicine. Nowadays, everyone lives on the southern part of the island only.'

Sam drove them round to see pathetically bare places, with naked ashen tree trunks and no vegetation or animals. Places where pastureland and industry had been sited were all swept away by the torrent of lava surging down the mountain. The capital, Plymouth, was totally destroyed and now in the land exclusion zone. This meant the visitors were unable to see the ruined city, but for Sven and Erika, what they had seen so far was more than enough!

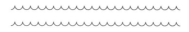

Mabel's restaurant was the lunchtime stop, and they enjoyed a magnificent chicken dish accompanied by homegrown vegetables. After lunch, Mabel introduced her cousin, Treasure, who was visiting from Barbados, and the two women joined them for coffee and chocolate cake.

They all looked at Sam's photos that he kept stored in a box in the car boot. He had witnessed the eruption and, even with a relatively simple camera, had been able to record some gruesome but excellent shots of the event. Subsequently, he sold the pictures to newspapers and was able to make enough money to upgrade his camera and buy a new computer.

He talked them through each photo as it was passed around. 'Under pressure, flames shot up from the crater. Molten lava with shafts of fire in it came rolling down the mountain. Trees and animals were ash encrusted and this was a truly horrible sight. People raced to get away, carrying all they could and then camped in a church hall. It just goes on and on.'

They were all very moved by the scenes in Sam's photos, and it was Sven who broke the silence that followed. 'Terrible! Shocking!' he said.

Suddenly Treasure spoke up. 'You seem such sensitive folks, just like my new friend, Prue. She had a terrible accident a few weeks ago and is in our hospital. As a matter of fact, she comes from Britain too!'

Sven smiled at her. 'Thank you for your kind words, Treasure, but we are American, not British. Tell us more about Prue.'

Treasure, suddenly realising that she was in danger of saying more than she should, replied, 'I can't do that, but be assured we are caring for her, and we all love her, she is a real beautiful person.'

She paused, looking at Mabel. 'Do you mind if I talk to your guests a bit more?'

'Carry on, honey, no problems.'

Sam nodded his acceptance too. They were always pleased to hear what outsiders had to say. This, he must have sensed, would give them new conversation for months!

'Okay folks. I'm not a fanciful or crazy woman but I feel drawn to you two. A few weeks ago, I was given a beautiful piece of artwork that seemed to hold its own special charm, and now I want to give it to you, Erika. I hope you enjoy it.'

Erika looked mystified but intrigued.

Treasure rummaged in her large bag and produced the Talisman. Sliding it out of the pouch she stroked it, a big smile on her face the whole time. 'Goodbye, my friend. God go with you.' She extended her hand to Erika and gave her the Talisman.

Erika, although startled by the speed of events, took it. Her face transformed immediately to one of delight. 'Wow! Treasure, this is beautiful.' Like many before her, Erika stroked the silky surface and wondered at the tiny exquisite birds. 'Look, Sven. Isn't this just lovely?'

'Awesome!' agreed Sven.

Perhaps sensing that Erika might want to keep the Talisman in her hands, Sven didn't seek to hold it. Mabel and Sam came over to admire and touch it briefly, and then Erika read out the words on the label. They all fell silent again. For these recently traumatised islanders, thinking of someone else who suffered was not difficult. Treasure's involvement came from holding the Talisman for two weeks. Sven and Erika, travelling close to nature, were aware of unexplainable events. And so it was that the Montserrat Islanders, the two Americans, and the Bajan woman, all sent their loving thoughts to the Russian girl.

A soft shaft of sunlight sliced through the cane-covered roof of the verandah and touched the Talisman as it lay on the table. Briefly, the light transfixed it, almost as if it was a source of power itself. *Was it a trick of the light or a trick of their senses,* Treasure wondered. Certainly, she had felt compelled to pass the Talisman to Erika, and now she felt deep happiness and energy within herself because she did so.

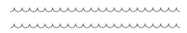

The group continued to talk, but now with a common bond.

Sam produced his new digital camera, saying, 'Erika, may I take a photo of you with the Talisman? While she is here, Treasure can send it to Russia in an email, telling Lana the story so far.'

Erika was delighted. Not because of the photo, but because for once she had been chosen to be part of a special mission. Folk seldom approached her in such an open way. Usually it was Sven who attracted warmth. She sensed something unique, and felt enormously proud yet humble too to be the new keeper of the Talisman. The photo Sam had taken showed a softer-looking woman, handling the Talisman with what could only be described as tenderness.

It had been a fascinating day, at times sad beyond belief but uplifting too. Sam had been a marvellous guide, giving information with the passion of a native islander who cared deeply. In the giving and receiving of the Talisman, a depth of warmth had been found between them all, something deeper than any of them could express in words. They all resolved to keep in touch and, with thanks given and hugs all round, Sven and Erika eventually went back to their boat.

That evening Erika joined Sven in a glass of wine, and they spent a happy and companionable few hours. There were times, she had to admit, when yoga simply didn't do it for her!

After spending the night at the same anchorage, they decided next day to sail round to the northern part of the island and anchor off Old Road Bay just outside the marine exclusion zone. From here the lava trails were clear, and they could see where new land had been formed in the ocean. Now there were still little pockets of fire on the hillside, and huge thick clouds spewed from the top of the volcano in a constant rain of filthy ash. The houses inside the safe zone were subject to being covered in this ash when an unfriendly wind blew.

'Must be a serious health risk for respiratory disease and all that,' said Erika, deeply shocked.

'It's ghastly! Unbelievable . . . awesome!' For the second time, Sven responded strongly on the subject. 'And to think we knew so little about it, that too is very shocking. '

Overnight it rained, and they woke to find *Packet of Dreams* covered in volcanic ash. This they could not remove as it smeared into stained strips when they tried to rub it off.

'Let's leave it until we get to Guadeloupe. It'd be better to scrub the boat with detergent and fresh water, I reckon,' suggested Sven.

'Agreed,' responded Erika, not really concentrating, the events of the day having had a huge impact on her. At this moment, unusual feelings of self-worth, unconnected with ego, absorbed her for the first time in her life.

Chapter 12

I t was happy hour. Freddy Muller leaned against the bar at the Royal Capetown Yacht Club enjoying his beer. *Bit of a misnomer, happy hour,* he thought. *Drinks are not offered at special prices in this establishment.* He supposed the name had drifted in with the American and Australian visitors. He remembered the last time he was in the club and how the world had changed since.

It had been September 11th 2001. On that evening, the members were gathered round two televisions, watching the ghastly news as it came through from New York. The visiting and resident Americans drew together as a silent and horrified group. Renowned for their patriotism, they held each other's hands in unashamed anguish as they watched the result of the attacks on the World Trade Center— and now the awful digging for survivors in tons of choking, hot, rubble. Manhattan's spectacular and famous skyline was disfigured, and Freddy was aware that to many New Yorkers, the World Trade Center had been as much a symbol of power and security as the Statue of Liberty itself. Their lives had been violated, their world shaken. Why? That was the word being shared with the tears at that time, and in fact, the question was still being asked.

But events in New York and Washington D.C. were of no interest to him. His life revolved around himself. People who touched his life were chosen according to how useful they might be. Freddy had driven to Capetown from Namibia, his place of birth, in readiness for leaving South Africa for the Caribbean. Three years earlier, he had bought a 42ft Van der Stadt ketch from the bereaved and heartbroken widow of a colleague. *And for an excellent price,* he remembered with satisfaction. Now he was nearly ready to leave.

Normally a loner, his nephew, George, would accompany him on the long ocean passage to Trinidad, and he had decided to wait for George's arrival before doing the last minute shopping.

Freddy watched the tanned, healthy-looking women sip their sundowners and chirrup to each other. The men tended to be in a separate group, and he could understand why. Freddy didn't like women—in fact, he didn't really like people—and this feeling was reciprocated by those he met. His sullen demeanour, lack of communication skills, and very tatty clothes gave the impression of a disappointed man . . . a loser. In fact he was very wealthy, having inherited the major shareholding of a South African gold mine. Profits were safely stashed away in the Caymans. After considerable research, when he came to create his portfolio, he found the rand to US dollar exchange rate was better than investing in euros or sterling.

Freddy had a three-year-old black and tan mongrel called Dog, acquired at the same time as the boat. Dog was as antisocial as his owner so they understood each other. George, an intense young man of twenty-six, was tolerated by them both.

George had landed a research project funded by the World Health Organisation as a marine biologist, and this enabled him to finish his PhD thesis. The subject for research was reef life in general and, more specifically, ciguatoxin—the poison carried in some reef fish. He had already been to Japan, spending three months diving, taking samples, and writing up results. His sponsors were pleased with his work, and valuable equipment was supplied to him for use in the Caribbean.

The idea of sharing the boat was a good one for them both. George, being a bit of a boffin, seemed unfazed by Freddy's normal state of *incommunicado*. The fact was, he didn't even seem to notice it! George was also a keen sailor and someone to share the work and expenses was attractive to Freddy.

George had been able to convert the forepeak as a study and computer area. A single bunk was fitted down the starboard side, and a well was created on the port side where a bunk would normally be. He fitted the computer and research equipment into this well. Information gathered could be stored easily and safely. When under sail, the whole area was covered tightly by a special padded wrap that clipped onto the base.

His uncle didn't mind the conversion as he was interested in George's research, and its results. Marine life in general, and coral reefs in particular, had always held a fascination for Freddy. These days he couldn't dive, as his eardrums had been perforated in a diving accident so being the support team suited him well.

~~~~~~~~~~~~~~~~~~~~~~~~~~~
~~~~~~~~~~~~~~~~~~~~~~~~~~~

It was with great relief that Freddy finally sailed *Ducky Do* into Chagueramas Bay, Trinidad. The relief was so great Freddy even failed to be embarrassed about the boat's name, though earlier at Ascension Island, he had resolved to change it, bad luck or not. He had emailed ahead to book a berth at Powerboats Marina. There were eight marinas within the huge bay, and this one had been recommended by other sailors for its good repair facilities and fair prices.

After confirming their arrival at the marina office, they had a stressful time with bureaucracy at the Customs and Immigration offices. George's diving and laboratory equipment, with all its accompanying official licences, posed a new situation for the officials who didn't seem to know what to do with them, and certainly didn't want to lose face in any way. In addition, Dog's papers had to be presented and stamped. It was nearly three hours later when they emerged, feeling very hot and disenchanted with everything, and with the officials in particular.

'Bloody coconut republic,' exploded Freddy just outside the customs shed door, much to George's embarrassment.

'Let's get a beer,' said George. 'I saw a place within this complex. Yes, there it is!' He guided Freddy into the air-conditioned bar and ordered drinks.

They were able to relax at last.

Halfway through the second beer, Freddy suddenly became aware that they both were in need of a shower. He stood up as he drained his glass. 'Perils of passage-making, George. We smell terrible. Marina showers, here we come,' he added with a wry smile.

Two hours later Freddy and George walked to a marina restaurant called Bail Out.

'Unfortunate name for an eatery,' observed George.

Tired as they both were, a local place seemed a good idea on their first evening in Trinidad. The menu was not inspiring, and everything was 'with fries.' But they agreed that char-grilled chicken drumsticks would be fine and could not be ruined in the cooking. They were wrong on both counts and decided the place was well named after all!

They walked back to *Ducky Do,* and by ten o'clock both were fast asleep in their bunks, rocked by a gentle swell.

Chapter 13

There had already been much discussion following the eye-opening visit to Montserrat. Sven and Erika agreed that life was for living and would seize every opportunity to have adventures and take calculated risks.

'It would be different,' said Sven, 'to go through the centre of Guadeloupe.'

'What d'you mean?' asked Erika.

'Well, think about this. Guadeloupe is shaped like a butterfly, with a large wing on each side, and the Rivière Sallée, the body down the middle.'

'Oh, I see now.' Erika was studying the charts.

The cruising guide enabled them to plan the whole trip that would take them eventually to the capital, Pointe à Pitre. They decided to set sail for Guadeloupe the next day.

As they approached the entrance to the river, Sven stood in the bow giving hand signals about direction while Erika gently steered round the treacherous reefs.

It was Sunday afternoon, and the cruising guide said the two bridges opened one hour apart just twice a week, Saturday and Monday. From their vantage point, they could see the huge mangrove swamps on each side of the river. Once clear of the reefs, they swapped places. Sven took the helm while Erika sped over the boat, covering it with a couple of huge mosquito nets. Then she went below deck and opened the two main overhead hatches to allow some air circulation. They would be under power now and going very slowly, so they decided it was safe enough to travel with the hatches open. The boat protected, they then sprayed insect repellent liberally on their bodies. Both hated doing this. They had read the label on the aerosol that showed a skull and crossbones with warnings in large red letters stating that skin must be washed before going to bed!

Just by the first bridge there were three mooring buoys. The first two were already occupied. One yacht carried the red British ensign but the other caused them to consult the flag book.

'Ha!' exclaimed Erika, triumphantly. 'It's South African, and I'm sure the sailboat is a Van der Stadt.'

Sven responded warmly, 'Well done.'

They waved at the South African yacht and two men waved back. A large black and tan mongrel appeared, wagging his tail but growling ferociously at the same time, just in case! The two couples exchanged pleasantries, and then Sven and Erika went below to escape the bugs and have a meal in peace. There was very little evidence of life on board the British yacht, but clearly they were at home and must have been sweltering down below to avoid the biting bugs.

At exactly 0420 the next morning, a horn sounded, and traffic approaching the bridge was stopped. The bridge opened at 0430, and the three waiting vessels progressed through the major part of the river.

Erika was impressed with all the slick timing. 'What an adventure! How majestic we all must look to anyone watching from the road—three yachts moving very slowly in single file up the river.'

'Yes, as long as they don't know we're going so slowly in order to pick up the directional transit lights. They're the very devil to see,' Sven countered, laughing.

As soon as the two other yachts reached the bay outside Bas du Fort Marina, they anchored quickly, and the occupants disappeared below.

'Well that was different, but boy am I tired.' Sven yawned .

'Yeah, let's sleep,' Erika replied. 'I think I'll just grab some cockpit cushions and stretch out right here.'

The two self-declared adventurers were soon in a deep sleep. Around noon they surfaced, had some lunch, and decided to motor into the marina, which was the largest in Guadeloupe. Bas du Fort was reputed to have excellent facilities as well as being close to the capital, Pointe à Pitre. After checking in, always a tolerable procedure in the French Caribbean islands, an afternoon of boat scrubbing was scheduled! But it wasn't until three weeks later that the final volcanic ash stains were gone, and during those weeks, they discussed many times the horror of living, but not really living, under the veil of choking ash.

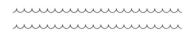

After that impromptu but memorable evening on *Green Flash*, Henry called their host on the VHF next day, thanking them, and saying, '*Au revoir.*'

Adam, who took the call, responded warmly. 'Henry, it's we who should thank you both, well Daz especially. Knockout performance. Lucky man!'

Setting sail for Dominica, Henry and Daz relaxed, glad to be alone at last. But as they raised the Dominican courtesy flag, about two and a half miles offshore, their peace was disturbed by the roar of three competing outboard motors—boat boys vying for the exclusivity of being appointed to the boat as it entered Dominican waters—a totally unofficial but customary event.

A broadly grinning young man in a dinghy, rather lightweight for the power of the engine, pulled alongside first. He introduced himself as Byron. Although his services weren't really needed, as they had their own landing transport, Henry realised this probably was an important income for the family so he agreed Byron could look after them. First of all, they were taken to the Customs and Immigrations Office, a shack in a dirt yard. It was arranged that Byron would take them on the River Pagua, in two days time. The Indian River, as it was known locally, was on Daz's 'must see' list so the arrangement was useful to them all. Then they bought some local bread and fresh fish from another boat boy, Tennyson, who was Byron's cousin. Henry and Daz enjoyed the colourful names, unaware that these two were only the start!

The day for the river trip arrived. They were being rowed quietly upriver in a large wooden boat— no engines were allowed in this environment.

Byron hailed Milton who was on another boat. 'He's my big brother and young Wordsworth is with him. Wordsworth is my half-brother. I have another half brother too,' he continued, 'his name is Shakespeare.' Byron then explained that his mother had children by three different husbands. 'Well,' he added, 'not exactly husbands . . . '

He grinned very broadly—one of Byron's supposedly endearing ploys—and Henry commented dryly that the family seemed to have stitched up the river business pretty well!

Their boat was shared by two South African men, Freddy and George. The former was not very communicative but George seemed happy enough to chat about life on his uncle's yacht, until it became clear that silence was better. This enabled them to hear the subtle sounds of land and water creatures.

The River Pagua was stunning. It flowed through a tropical rainforest, rich in wildlife, and was particularly well known for its birds and land crabs. The sun occasionally dappled the ground beneath the trees that joined overhead to form a green protective canopy. The water was translucent. It was a fantastic subject for photos, but George had his notebook and sketched quickly with great accuracy. He sketched

Byron too and gave him the drawing, to the young man's great delight.

At the head of the river was a very basic bar and restaurant where they enjoyed strong rum punches, and a meal of rice and vegetables. It seemed to be the custom to buy lunch for their boat boy, and although no one objected, the attitude of 'gimme, gimme' left a slightly nasty taste! After a short siesta in the homemade, slightly dodgy-looking hammocks, the group returned to the boat for their trip downriver and onward to their yachts.

Once back home, Daz suggested they invite Freddy and George over for a beer the next day, and Henry said, 'Sick of me already, my sweet?'

'You are so silly, Hen. You know how we both enjoy other peoples' stories.'

Daz had chosen to take his words seriously.

Freddy and George seemed happy to join them, and the following evening, the four of them enjoyed chilled beer, cheesey pasta and garlic bread.

'Thank God for the microwave,' said Daz. 'Henry is the cook. Not me!'

Attracted by the write-up in the cruising guide and the name, Daz and Henry planned to anchor off Castaways Beach the next day. To their surprise, *Ducky Do* was already there.

As they waved hello, Henry commented, 'What a dreadful name. How could anyone choose such a silly name for a boat? It sounds more suitable for one of those tiny dinghies children learn to sail on.'

The following day, Freddy and George disappeared for hours in their inflatable, presumably fishing, and leaving Dog in charge—a role he took very seriously, snarling at anyone coming near the boat. But on the way back, they hailed Henry and Daz, inviting them to dinner.

That evening, Dog stayed in the background but after an hour or so, came over to Daz who cooed at him and gently scratched behind his ears. Twenty minutes later he was lying at Daz's feet, looking up in adoration!

'Typical,' said Henry, grinning. 'Eventually all males, even male dogs, are devotedly at your feet!'

'With reason,' said George, smiling.

Freddy cooked a delicious fish meal with local plantain *sautéed* with garlic and served mashed, a new experience for the guests. They ate salad as a starter and finished with coconut ice cream, George's speciality, with fine white rum poured over it. South African wine, which was stowed in every available space on the boat, flowed liberally, and they were all interested to learn more of each other's background and the motivation for this trip.

George's story gripped Daz and Henry. He told them about the months of reef-diving: taking samples, labelling, analysing and writing up results. He was due to fly home soon—currently being on a brief holiday after this compelling project—to make his presentation to the boffins at the World Health Organisation.

'World Health Organisation,' repeated Henry, his head snapping up. 'We've spent a lot of time recently in the company of Eva and Adam Pitman. In fact, we did the transat with them. She is the British liaison officer for the WHO, presently taking time out but on emergency call.'

'Yes,' George replied, 'I've heard of her. She's more in the troubleshooting arena. I am strictly research.'

Daz, sounding young and enthusiastic, interjected. 'They're on a 44ft Contest, *Green Flash*. They're a really lovely couple, especially Eva who is clever, incredibly articulate, and my good friend—our good friend.'

Dog thumped the floor with his tail and had a brief fondle as a reward.

'That's quite some tribute,' said Freddy, smiling at Daz. 'I hope we'll meet them.'

After being side-tracked by Daz, Freddy gave a brief account of their sailing experiences to date, plus George's diving in the Venezuelan islands, the ABC islands, Jamaica, and Cuba. When George was asked the subject of his research, he talked fluently about the project, and with some passion, about the need to find an answer.

'Do you know,' he told them, 'Ciguatera sickens and kills thousands of people worldwide each year. Usually it's the locals in poor fishing communities, but it also affects others—outsiders, business people, and those travelling to these areas.

'Ciguatera, but what is it?' asked Daz.

George continued with his story. 'Ciguatera poisoning comes from a toxin, ciguatoxin, found in reef fish. There is no natural immunity to it, and there is a need to isolate the toxin and find an antidote—

or maybe even provide immunisation—as soon as possible.'

Daz and Henry were horrified and fascinated at the same time. 'Tell us more, please.'

'Well, ciguatera poisoning is often terminal, seemingly unrelated to the health and strength of the individual—acute diarrhoea and vomiting, severe pain, convulsions, and appalling dehydration are the symptoms. There is no antidote or cure at this time.' George promised to fax them an information sheet, but in the meantime, urged them to eat no reef fish larger than an average forearm. 'So far, the toxin appears only in the larger fish,' he told them.

The informative evening ended. As they left, the guests felt they had much to consider.'

There you are,' Daz said to Henry. 'Wasn't that interesting? It's good to talk to other yachties, isn't it?'

As they got ready for bed, Henry said, 'I'll send the fax to the others about ciga-whatsit. Sounds horrendous.'

Later, as he gathered Daz into his arms, he murmured, 'Do you fancy visiting the Venezuelan islands? They sound magic, don't you think?'

'Mmm, cool!'

Chapter 14

Freddy was at the helm as *Ducky Do* motored into the marina at Pointe à Pitre. With the practice of years, George attached warps to the cleats on shore, tied off all the fenders, and waited for Freddy to join him for checking in.

Apart from the usual documentation, other papers had to be presented to the customs and immigration officials to prove Dog's microchip was in place and that his rabies jabs were valid. This enabled the animal to go on shore. They went back to the boat to collect Dog. As usual, he went mad with excitement, racing flat out with his head thrown up, sucking in extra air, tongue lolling through the side of his mouth. After the exercise, he left his mark on as many places as possible over the next fifteen minutes.

George was due to fly to Geneva in four days. He planned to rejoin Freddy in Grenada for a three-week holiday during August, but for now, his work was finished. He needed to pack all his research files and specimens in special cases designed to carry sensitive material on the flight. He elected to complete the packing right away—then, as a reward to himself, he could justify a few extra days in Guadeloupe, visiting the places that really beckoned. A small Fiat was rented for a week so they could have the freedom to drive round the island—it was also essential to have a car to get to the airport.

'Guadeloupe!' exclaimed George. 'The country of exotic stamps for child philatelists, but when we collected them, no one really knew where it was!'

'How true,' agreed Freddy. 'I wasn't aware where Guadeloupe was until I decided to sail to the Caribbean. Fancy admitting such ignorance.'

Rainforests abounded, and the pair enjoyed treking through these preserved areas, now national parks, with thousands of birds making a huge racket. The endangered Guadeloupe wren was much in evidence and clearly making a good comeback. As strong conservationists, this delighted both Freddy and George.

However, they didn't see one raccoon, although the animal had been promoted as the official symbol of the national park. But they agreed the whole experience was well organised, with the minimum of interference from the park rangers, and they particularly enjoyed identifying the wildlife, which was so different from their own homeland. Being from Southern Africa, they both knew about covering legs and arms against mosquitoes and biting bugs and had about them a certain smugness as they observed the red weals and lumps on the legs of European tourists!

It was at the volcanic summit of La Soufrière, the island's highest point, that George suddenly called out to a couple standing nearby. 'Hi there! Didn't we meet going down the Rivière Salée?' Putting out his hand he said, 'I'm George Muller and this is my Uncle Freddy.'

'Sven Pedersen and my wife, Erika, from the States.'

The four of them shook hands. Then, chatting amiably, they found a shack selling drinks. They were weary as it had been a challenging hike so they decided to eat and rest before the homeward trek.

The scenery was stunning! The lush, wet, variegated greens of the rainforest provided a magnificent backdrop to a waterfall. They were silent, absorbing the view.

'Must be the reason why the natives chose Karukera as the name for Guadeloupe—it means *island of beautiful waters*,' Freddy supplied.

The others looked at him, well impressed!

After a short pause, Erika said, 'Anyway, it's worth being a little weary in order to see all this fabulous nature.' With that she stretched her limbs in a series of complex moves.

'Yoga!' informed Sven, nodding with the acceptance born of a long marriage.

The tiring but pleasant day ended with a sundowner on *Ducky Do* before Sven and Erika climbed into their dinghy to return to the boat.

George revived and went back on shore with Dog for a stroll in the quickly fading light of dusk. They sat together, young man and dog, looking out at the bay. Each was content, in his way, about a task well done—Dog's successful marking of territory no less important than George's ciguatera research! His thoughts drifted to the sail from South Africa. *It was amazing,* he reflected, *how well Freddy and I co-existed on this trip. A mutual respect for each other's privacy seemed to work well.*

The WHO had gained top priority clearance for George, his research material and supporting paperwork, so he was able to relax prior to his longhaul flight, knowing that after many months his collated work was secure.

It was with regret that the two men gave each other a hug at the airport, now looking forward to their next meeting in Grenada.

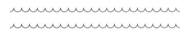

Freddy sat in the airport coffee bar, sad at losing his companion. *Reckon I've changed a bit. Must have to to do with the constant awareness of the sea being the boss—things out of my control for a change—maybe also seeing a different type of poverty in these islands where the ancestors of the people hailed mostly from the African continent.*

But he had acknowledged that the black West Indians had a far better life than their cousins in South Africa. These people governed their own islands and, especially in the case of the French and Dutch West Indies, enjoyed an input of skills from Europe in addition to a high standard of education that included a chance to go to university. Most of the islanders had only a little knowledge of their African roots but forged ahead in the present time, trying to move on from the agony their forbears suffered at the hands of European slave traders.

Freddy suddenly realised that he was interested in other people and their *raison d'être*. He smiled at this

French connection as his knowledge of the language was minimal, German being his other fluent tongue.

His smile was noticed by a mature, rather voluptuous, woman at an adjacent table. She noted a stockily-built middle-aged man, clean but as scruffy as the mongrel lying at his feet.

Freddy looked up and caught her eye, feeling rather foolish at his self-smile being witnessed. He smiled nervously at her and she nodded her acknowledgment. She noticed his piercing blue eyes with shaggy grey brows topping them and the full but hard mouth.

The mouth spoke. 'C'mon Dog.' it said.

The woman understood. The words said a lot about the man!

A couple of days later, Freddy sat at a marina restaurant, studying his cruising guides and reduced charts. A shadow fell across the table, and he looked up to see the attractive, dark haired woman from the airport coffee bar.

'*Bonjour, Monsieur,*' she said. 'Welcome to my restaurant.'

'Wonderful food,' he replied, feeling flustered and confused.

'My name is Lily Trampton.'

He was taken by the musical voice with its slight French accent. Light brown skin and pale eyes showed a handsome mix of ethnicity. *Attractive? No, stunning,* he thought. She wore no makeup, and had a body that hinted at earthiness. 'Please join me,' Freddy said, surprising himself.

Lily sat down and for the next two hours they sipped wine, told of their lives, discussed the world, and enjoyed doing so.

'Can we meet again soon?' asked Freddy.

'Yes,' replied Lily. She, fortunately, had the assurance Freddy lacked. 'Would you like to join me for dinner, as my guest, tomorrow evening?'

'Thank you, I'd like that.'

As he left the restaurant, he suddenly saw himself mirrored in a shop window and realised he looked a total mess—he also knew his clothes on board were no better. In a small panic, he toured the marina shops, Dog anxiously at his side, not understanding his master's sudden need for retail therapy. Dog was commanded to 'stay' outside the chosen shop, which he implicitly did while eyeing up the local talent trotting past—each at the end of a swanky lead or a piece of rope.

'Dress me!' Freddy ordered the startled salesman. 'I need clothes. I've just arrived off a boat and need decent clothes to socialise in.'

Marcel, the salesman, recovered quickly, probably anticipating the good commission that could result from this customer's request. An hour later, Freddy left the shop some fifteen hundred euros poorer, but satisfied with his purchases. However, he drew the line at poncing about with carrier bags so Marcel promised to deliver them to the boat that evening before going home.

For the dinner date, Freddy selected biscuit-coloured slacks with a light blue shirt and fawn deck shoes. He had asked Marcel to put each combination of clothes in separate bags. Their contents were now transferred onto hangers—shirts, light sweaters, shorts and trousers—hangers tied together with a bit of string, each in a group of co-ordinated clothes!

He looked well, and when he arrived at the restaurant the next evening, Lily hardly recognised him. '*Mon dieu*, you look *très élégant . . . fantastique*,' she said warmly, grasping his hand and offering her cheek for the traditional French greeting.

Freddy complied equally warmly. Lily, Freddy noted with approval, wore a copper-brown silk dress that swirled around her curves—touching, then not touching! Her feet were prettily clad in strappy sandals, again no makeup and no nail polish, nor did she need it!

Her dark hair was dressed away from her face accentuating the high cheekbones of her ancestry.

'You are marvellous,' enthused Freddy. 'Absolutely everything a woman should be.'

'Thank you.' Lily accepted his compliment with a smile. She sat down and their evening started.

Lily's grandmother, she told him, was a Carib Indian, and her parents were from equally mixed origins. They had first opened Le Jardin, which Lily later expanded into Le Jardinière Creole, and the business thrived. Her son, Pierre, was the chef. He had trained in Paris, but had been born in Guadeloupe and those credentials assured the best of French-Creole cooking. Pierre was highly thought of, and other restaurant owners often tried to lure him away. Lily left it at that. She was wise enough to know when not to talk about her progeny too much!

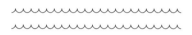

After catching up on sleep, Sven and Erika decided to check out Guadeloupe. They talked to other cruisers and picked up some leaflets.

'Well, I think we could spend at least a week here. What do you think, Erika?'

'Sure. There are masses of nature walks, museums, and places to explore. Let's stay for a while.'

They were fascinated at what they learned, having had only minimal history and geography lessons in school. As they wandered round museums, they read how the inhabitants of Guadeloupe had changed from Carib to Spanish after Columbus discovered it. Fierce fighting followed as the Caribs fought for their land, ending up being driven off the island or being used as slaves. France and England then fought over the island, a bloody history, and the two Americans were amazed how domination see-sawed between France and England. In the mid-eighteenth century, the two governments had worked out a deal. Britain took over Canada and France colonised Guadeloupe. Slavery, they discovered, lasted for another one hundred years before it was finally abolished in 1848, following a campaign led by Victor Schoelcher.

'Surely,' questioned Erika, 'that's a German or Dutch name?'

'No, he was a French politician. I read it somewhere, no idea where.'

They loved Guadeloupe and, on their wedding anniversary evening, treated themselves to a meal at

Le Jardinière Creole in the marina at Pointe à Pitre.

Erika, spotting a man she recognised, whispered to Sven, 'Isn't that Freddy? Didn't we meet him at the Rivière Salée and La Soufrière?'

'Yes, I believe it is,' replied Sven, 'but he looks so different—sort of cleaned up!'

'Something to do with the attractive woman with him!' Erika suggested.

Freddy looked up and caught them looking his way. They all smiled and raised their hands in greeting. Lily turned round, and they were struck by her uncontrived mature allure.

'Not exactly beautiful,' Sven said. 'But something more than beauty. She has an element of...' he paused, lost for words.

'Earth Mother. Timeless, calm . . . magnetic,' Erika supplied.

'That's it! You're smart in your observations, Erika. Particularly about people.'

They smiled at each other with the ease of two people who'd been married a long time and were good friends. That evening, after their excellent chicken creole, they checked their sail plan to Dominica, Martinique and finally Grenada where they planned to sit out the hurricane season.

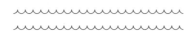

Freddy was enjoying himself. Lily was the first woman he had spent much time with since he was a young man. She was not silly. Not at all. She was cultured and smart, yet she did not display any of the aggressive feminist characteristics he usually noticed. She was informed on political issues and was able to discuss subjects objectively, another unique characteristic, in his limited experience. In passing, it occurred to Freddy that maybe it was something in him that caused so many women to react aggressively...

Over the next three weeks, Lily and Freddy became close friends and sought each other's company on a daily basis. He explained that he and George had only visited Guadeloupe for its hub airport—that he had always planned to sail back to Dominica and then on to Martinique—until he met her!

'I wonder if you can spare the time, would you be interested in joining me in Martinique,' Freddy asked one morning over coffee.

'Freddy, I'd love to,' responded Lily. 'I can arrange time away if I have plenty of notice. Are you thinking of four days or so?'

'Why not a week?' he suggested. *This will be a good test of our friendship,* he thought. But aloud he said, 'Now that George has left the boat, you will have the whole forepeak to yourself.'

The friendship had remained warm, yet no moves towards intimacy had been made. When they parted that morning with the knowledge of further time together, just the two of them, Freddy wrapped his arms round Lily in a huge warm hug.

'What's a forepeak, Freddy?' she asked, with just a hint of coquetry.

He laughed. 'Sweet Lily, it's the pointy bit at the front end of a boat! As a cabin, it's large and roomy as the boat broadens out quite quickly,' he explained.

'I'll look forward to it then,' she replied, laughing!

It was in Dominica that Sven and Erika spotted the now familiar lines of the Van der Stadt. They hailed Freddy on the VHF, and invited him and George over for a meal. Freddy told them that George was now in Geneva and that he was travelling solo *en route* to Martinique. He accepted the invitation, saying that he would be very pleased to have an evening with them. He particularly liked Erika—a woman of definite views, physically strong, a real sailor, and in no way a deck babe!

During the evening he told them, rather shyly, that Lily would be joining him in Martinique for a few days. Sensing a reticence here, Sven and Erika nodded and wished them a happy time.

Changing the subject, Freddy said, 'While you're here, be sure to visit the capital, Roseau, and go by local bus. It's an experience you won't forget!' He wouldn't be pressed to give more detail, adding, 'Trafalgar Falls is also a must. But sadly for me, having canoed and treked to the Angel Falls in Venezuela, all others can only measure poorly. But here in Dominica, you can hike round the whole area and bathe in the hot sulphur springs.'

'Brilliant!' said Erika. 'I'm sure we'll do that. And we'd love to hear about the Angel Falls trip sometime. That's definitely on our itinerary, such as it is.' It was at this moment that Erika had a feeling so powerful, she gasped. The two men looked at her with concern but quickly realized that she was all right when she reached for her bag.

'Freddy, a very strange thing happened to us in Montserrat—well to me, really.' She pulled out the Talisman, still in its pouch. 'We met a Bajan woman who'd been given this very beautiful, and somehow mystical, Talisman. It had been given to her by an Englishwoman, a sailor who'd been injured. She paused. 'You should have it now, Freddy.' Erika took the Talisman out of its pouch and held it out to Freddy.

All this time Sven had been watching expressions of *déjà vu* fleeting across the older man's face—surprise, slight suspicion, curiosity, and now as he held the Talisman, love. Nothing more or less. It was love!

Freddy couldn't speak. His eyes were soft as he stroked it. Eventually, all he said was, 'Thank you.' His voice was hoarse.

Erika continued to tell him the background story as far as she knew it.

Then Freddy read the label, and his hands shook as he whispered, 'My friends, this is no co-incidence. I had a child once. She was a gifted artist and potter. She made beautiful porcelain objects that she painted with tiny exquisite birds...' Freddy's voice cracked. He stopped as his eyes welled up.

'What happened, Freddy?' Erika's voice was as gentle as a soft breeze.

'She was killed by a hit and run driver—and my life stopped.'

Sven and Erika supported Freddy's silence, sharing his grief, feeling his pain.

After several minutes he put the Talisman back in its pouch, and then into the bag strapped round his body, under his shirt. His action brought a conclusion to the episode, his meaning couldn't be clearer.

Erika poured them each a small Schnapps. 'What are your plans after Martinique?'

'George will be flying over to Grenada for a few weeks holiday in August.'

'That's wonderful news,' she replied, warmly. 'There'll be quite a reunion in Grenada as we've met a few cruisers who plan to spend the hurricane season there, as we do.'

'I'm so happy to hear that.' Clearly, Freddy was struggling now and wanted to leave. But not before they exchanged warm hugs. As he climbed down to his dinghy, he called back to them. 'Erika, I'll sort out a photo and send it with an email. Travel safe!'

'Thank you, Freddy. Fair winds to you and see you soon.'

Sven undid the painter from the bigger boat and passed it down. 'What a great guy,' he said. 'What an extraordinary but wonderful evening!'

'Certainly was. I'm glad we'll be meeting up again, with Lily too maybe. He seems very sweet on her.'

Sven laughed. 'You're so right.' He put his arm round his wife and kissed her cheek but with more affection than he could remember feeling for years.

After ten days on Dominica, Sven and Erika decided to move on to Martinique, and there they experienced the more sophisticated atmosphere of Fort de France and, again, the very distinct French-Creole culture.

Coming from the US, they were particularly seduced by the French colonial architecture of the capital and its ruined fortifications. They spent days out visiting the birthplace of the Empress Josephine, the tragic ruins of St Pierre, and treking through more rainforests. The only downside for them was the language.

'How difficult it is to communicate in a deeper way,' Erika said. 'At home, we really should offer more foreign language skills and make them easily available. There's so much I'd like to ask local people here, but there's no way I can, and we Americans are judged insular because of this. How about we spend some time on one of the French islands and learn the language?'

'That sounds like an interesting idea, Erika. Let's research it.' Sven's memory of trying to learn French bothered him. He had found it impossible to pronounce, and his smattering of Swedish words was useless here.

They loved Martinique, but after two weeks, the time had come to sail to St Vincent and the Grenadines.

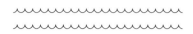

At St Vincent, entry procedures again were conducted officiously, so different from the friendly and easy manner of the French islands. They decided to anchor at Wallilabou Bay where the filming of *Pirates of the Caribbean* had taken place. Buildings from the film were still standing and being used. Markets selling fish, fruit, vegetables, livestock, and clothes used the space during the day. Each night much rum, and who knows what else, flowed alongside the partying and dancing. They found the St Vincent islanders to be friendly, hospitable, and wanting to chat—charmingly less sophisticated and worldly than on neighbouring Martinique—but best of all for them, they spoke English! Another plus, meals on shore were much cheaper than in the French West Indies so they were also able to enjoy some local cooking.

There were many small islands around the mainland of St Vincent, and they spent two weeks sailing into different anchorages then taking the dinghy to shore.

On one such island, Erika was in a tiny local shop, hardly more than a shack, buying some banana bread.

The shopkeeper introduced herself as Betty. 'Hi ya, honey—where you from?'

'I'm from Virginia in the US.'

'That's nice, hon. What's your name?'

'Erika.'

'You married?'

'Yes, my husband is Sven.'

'You stayin' here, honey?'

'Well, we're here on a sailboat.'

'A sailboat! You're real brave. I tell you what, hon. Tonight I'll cook you an' your hubby some real good local food. You like that, honey?'

Erika was beginning to feel she'd lost control of events—unusual for her! A little fascinated and sort of drawn to this ebullient woman, she said she'd discuss it with Sven and let Betty know by mid afternoon. 'Oh, by the way, how much would the meal cost?'

'Okay, honey. Three courses and the main dish is fish. For you, honey, twenty dollars each.'

'Oh no,' said Erika. 'We can't afford that sort of money for a meal.'

Betty, who'd met many Americans, felt that very few would admit to not having money—money meant success. Wasn't that part of the American dream? She backtracked and reduced the cost by half!

Erika, starting to get the drift of things, said, 'Thank you, Betty. We would not pay more than fifteen for both of us to eat out. We travel on a budget, and the occasional meal out is a treat.'

'All right, honey,' responded Betty. 'I like you an' I bet your hubby's somethin' else so I'll cook you a real delicious dinner for fifteen US dollars. How 'bout that?'

'I'll confirm later after speaking to Sven. Thank you, Betty. It was good to meet you.' She left the shop, and Betty waved goodbye from the door.

Betty proved to be an excellent cook! That evening they enjoyed callaloo, a traditional soup made from dasheen leaves, coconut milk and herbs. Next came bul jol, a delicious local dish consisting of roasted breadfruit and salt fish, made with tomatoes and onions. The meal ended with homemade coconut and banana ice cream, followed by coffee and a tot of rum so rough that Erika choked as the powerful liquor burnt all the way down!

'My, you is real soft, honey,' laughed Betty, as she swallowed her second shot.

Sven was very red in the face, and his eyes watered, but he was determined not to show what would be unmanly weakness in Betty's eyes. *How ridiculous I am,* he told himself. *How unimportant. And for this show of ego, I suffer actual pain!*

Their hostess, after a short display of modesty, was persuaded to write down her recipe for bul jol. Then, with promises made to send photos they had taken of her and her simply constructed wooden home, they all shook hands and parted company.

During their weeks sailing round St Vincent and the Grenadines, Sven and Erika had many such meals in local homes, sometimes eating with the family and sometimes being served on their own. Eventually, they had twelve photos of jolly hostesses, posing proudly with their family or with Sven and Erika but always on their front doorstep!

'Wonder if *National Geographic* would be interested in all this,' Erika said, half seriously. 'I don't see why not. "Hostess Cookery in the Caribbean" or "Caribbean Home Cooking"—that sort of thing but with a story. I'm impressed how these women use only island produce to create such delicious food. High cholesterol in the coconut though,' she added.

'Time to move on to our hurricane hole,' Sven said. Then he suddenly asked, 'What do you think about flying home for a few weeks and leaving the boat in Grenada?'

'Mmm sounds good, but let's wait and see how things go,' she replied. 'By the way, did you know that Grenada is known as Spice Island? They produce and export enormous quantities of nutmeg, mace, cloves, cinnamon—and cocoa too, I think.'

Presuming her question to be largely rhetorical, Sven did not respond.

Chapter 15

The cockpit of the Fountaine Pajot is almost too big for comfort, but when in an anchorage or marina, Henry managed to fill it in a comfortable way. Cushions for the built-in *banquettes*, sun loungers, directors' chairs and table were normally stowed in a starboard hull locker, but this day Henry had taken them out. He had designed and built a removable table that screwed onto a pedestal, and that in turn screwed into a fitting on the sole. When under sail, a neat cover clipped over the hole. The cockpit now looked colourful and attractive; a relaxing place in which to eat and to lounge and, justifiably, Henry felt proud of the result.

The smell of coffee drifted out, while Daz, a dab hand at cooking unhealthy food, was preparing waffles. While having breakfast and chatting, Henry wanted to discuss their more immediate plans. 'I reckon Dominica would be fine for a week. Shall we just poddle around?'

'Perhaps there'll be a Jump-up somewhere.'

'What on earth's a Jump-up?' asked Henry, already dreading the answer!

'It's a sort of Caribbean party with lots of dancing.'

'Oh,' groaned Henry. 'Not my sort of thing at all.'

'Dearest Hen, couldn't we go, just for a couple of hours'?

'How selfish I am, my sweet. Of course you shall go to the Ball!' He took Daz's hand, turned it over and pressed soft kisses into the palm. Daz came over and sat astride Henry's knees, wrapping slender arms round his neck, kissing him with such love that Henry was breathless with emotion. 'You are the most important thing in my life, Daz.'

'Me too,' responded Daz, holding Henry in a huge close bear hug.

That morning they went into Roseau and found the Tourist Information Office. Their time had been loosely planned, but they were both always happy to go with the flow on new ideas. Daz sweet-talked a young man in the office, and found out *the* place to go for a Jump-up. 'Fridays and Saturdays are the keen nights. Shall we go, Hen, this Friday?'

'Of course, Daz, I'm already looking forward to it.' Henry's eyes rolled up as he made a helpless gesture of submission with his shoulders and arms. Daz hugged him and, with an arm slipped through his, they walked out into the blisteringly hot midday sun, while the young man in the tourist office grinned widely as his eyes followed them.

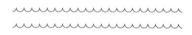

The Jump-up was wild! There seemed to be an endless river of rum, so the few remaining inhibitions among the partygoers were abandoned. As usual, Daz soon became the focus of attention—imitating the moves of the local dancers—spinning, swinging hips, gyrating, and posturing. Daz loved the attention, and the other dancers loved Daz. But when Henry wanted to leave, there was no sense of loss, just the feeling of going home; keeping a pact with a beloved soul mate.

Back in the bay, a very smart Hallberg Rassy circled five times and eventually dropped anchor. 'That's supposed to be the crème de la crème of yachts,' explained Henry, 'though personally I wouldn't have one.'

'Well, this cat is purrfect,' drawled Daz.

'How original,' said Henry. 'I've never heard that one before.'

Daz blushed, feeling foolish. 'Sorry, Hen, just a bit of fun.'

'Anyway, my point is not the boat, it's the occupants. Old duffer, much older than me, well actually, probably around my age!' Henry had the grace to grin. And his young bit of stuff, what is she, trophy wife? Totty? That's okay but it's his pompous demeanour that gets me. And, predictably, he flies a blue ensign. That's unnecessary in my book, a bit elitist. Also, I saw him in town—white trousers, I ask you, a navy jacket, and a peaked cap—not real sailing gear.

Daz took Henry's arm and with eyes open wide, gazed up at him in a mock sycophantic pose. 'Hen, am I your almost trophy wife?'

'Oh yes, definitely,' he retorted, laughing hard. 'Daz, you know you lighten my life, in so many ways…'

They headed south and spotted a yacht leaving a mooring buoy in Soufrière Bay. As a protected marine reserve there were only a few buoys available, so they waited. 'It's the old duffer with his totty!' exclaimed Daz.

'And look at that,' Henry laughed. 'His ensign is flying upside down, that's supposed to be a sign of distress.' Henry appeared to be delighted and explained to Daz that it was always good fun to spot someone else's error, especially if the someone was a poser. Clearly the yacht was not in trouble, and it was with amusement that they waved to the couple as the Hallberg Rassy sailed past them.

As a snorkelling site, Soufrière Bay was reputed to be marvellous, so the next two hours were spent swimming. But this time Henry was the poser as he tried out his new underwater camera! Daz, wearing a teeshirt for protection from the vicious sun, swam round in circles, finding new hidey holes for marine life, and then racing back to Henry, pointing excitedly.

After doing all the tourist things on shore over the next few days, they fished, lazed in the sun, and loved each other.

'Not worth doing any boat jobs here,' pronounced Henry. 'It's easier done in the marina at Martinique.'

It was five days before Christmas, so they decided to head south into the Martinique Channel, and then on to Martinique itself. Henry made contact with the marina, but found there was no space until 23rd December, the date from which Adam had already reserved the berths. They motored round to the very pretty anchorage at Anse Mitan, and were content to stay there for the three waiting days, making one sortie to a supermarket on shore. The priority, according to Daz, who'd been conferring with Eva on the SSB, was food shopping. Together they planned a Christmas Day reunion and feast!

On the day after hosting that extraordinary evening in Guadeloupe, Adam and Eva had discussed what to do next. They decided that, en route to Martinique, they would explore La Desirade, Marie Galante and Iles de Saintes. Going only to French dependencies, avoided the chore of having to check in and out of the islands they visited, a fact they found very appealing.

'I'd love to visit Pigeon Island,' said Eva. 'I realise it's in the wrong direction for our sail plan now, but maybe one day we'll come back.'

'Isn't that the Reserve Cousteau—a protected marine area—oh, and didn't Jacques Cousteau publicise it first about twenty years ago, as one of the world's greatest dive centres?'

'You've got it,' replied Eva. 'It's known as an underwater park and is apparently fabulous for reef marine life.'

'Sounds like it definitely should be on the list of places to visit sometime,' he agreed.

Waving to Margreet and Warner, and calling out 'See you in Martinique,' they left Bas du Fort Marina and set sail for La Desirade. Anchoring off a lee shore they went in by dinghy. They tied up on the jetty for small boats, but after two days, concluded that the tiny island sounded better and more interesting than it was in reality. The chapel and cemetery of the leprosarium still stood, but Eva felt a grim energy around the area—not surprising, as for over two hundred years, from the early eighteenth century, lepers were forced to go there on a one-way ticket. The colony closed in 1955, but there were no more historic details about the place.

Marie Galante was their next stop. An island mostly dedicated to sugar cane production and rum distilleries. They met no one who spoke English and, here again, Eva came up trumps. Adam, less fluent, did his best, but cheered up when he found he could follow the French conversation, if not actively participate.

They visited the distilleries and bought three different styles of fine rum. Again, restaurant food was French-Creole, and always delicious. They decided, like many other cruisers, that as it was so inexpensive to eat out, it wasn't worth cooking at home!

On to Iles de Saintes, they beached the dinghy on Terre de Haut, and walked through the main town of Bourg des Saintes. They found the folk friendly enough, and bought a bag of *tourment d'amour*— sweet, coconut filled cakes. These were often eaten for breakfast, and sold by young women carrying baskets of this traditional island delicacy.

Walking away from the town centre, they suddenly happened on a shop called Maogany, a shop that was totally different. Outside its frontage, on the pavement, fine mahogany racks displayed silk or cotton scarves, shawls and *pareos*, dyed in all the luxuriant shades of nature. Each piece was knotted loosely, and the whole effect was a seductive abundance of colour. Eva was excited! She was definitely not a shopaholic, so Adam was happy to accompany her, and indeed, he too found the clothing inside the shop very attractive.

Eva went through the racks of garments and picked out a selection. She modelled several and finally chose a pair of silk harem pants in rich gold silk, shimmery and slightly transparent, with a matching gold scarf transforming the outfit to *haute couture*; two silk sarongs in diffused colours, one of the changing sea, the other in the greens of a rainforest. And finally, a dress in soft blue shades that set off her colouring and tan, its delicate and feminine skirt was especially stunning and Eva felt the very female upsurge of a woman who knows she looks fabulous! 'Oh, how I wish Daz and Henry were here. We'd have such a good time, and these colours would be just perfect for Daz.'

Eva's comment was overheard and an attractive man of middle years bowed slightly to her. '*Bonjour,*

Madame! Excuse my English please. Your friend, she can order from my catalogue. Email or phone me with choices, and sizes, and we will send.'

'Oh, how wonderful!' exclaimed Eva. 'What a good idea, and yes I'd like a catalogue. I'll pass it on.'

'Yves Cohen, *Madame. Enchantée*! Welcome to my shop.'

'Eva and Adam Pitman, from London. We sailed here.'

'Ah, sailors,' breathed Yves. Yes, I too sailed here thirty years ago, and never left.'

'How did that come about?' asked Adam. 'Sounds as it there's a story to tell.'

'Please, have a glass of wine with me.' Yves indicated a room at the back of the shop. Easy cane chairs, covered with fabric that complemented the colours of the clothes, provided a welcoming atmosphere. They were all seated, with glasses of island-bred fine wine, when he started.

'I arrived here from Paris in 1973, desperately seeking Life. I wanted to live in a different, non-city way, maybe on a boat but certainly to sail. A fisherman gave me a Santoise boat, his father's. We repaired it, and then I made new sails, by hand. At that time, I used the boat at night for fishing, and by day I painted, I had to earn a living after all.'

Adam and Eva were fascinated and smiled encouragingly.

Yves continued. '*Maogany* is the Indian name for mahogany, the wood used traditionally for boat building here. This shop started in the early eighties, first of all just selling shirts and then, a few years on, we expanded into selling clothes for men and women.

The materials we use are tough and, although often elegant in design, many of the clothes will improve with age—like fine French wine!'

'What a romantic story,' said Eva, warmly. 'And you bring it to life so well. It all must have been such a lot of hard work.'

'It was, but now I have a successful business. The staff are like our family, and I have a wife who is a clever businesswoman. She runs the administration. Also she is *très chic,* and can do the modelling when necessary.'

'Wonderful!' Adam said. 'Thank you so much for telling us.'

Eva collected her purchases. Each garment was neatly folded, beautifully wrapped, and presented in a natural cotton bag, with Maogany printed on the front. So with feelings of time well spent, they finally took their leave, amid many handshakes and good wishes for their future sailing.

'The rainforest sarong is for Daz and the grey/ blue shirt will look great on Henry,' she told Adam, smiling broadly. 'Christmas presents!' She sounded triumphant, but kept quiet about her gift for Adam— a cotton shirt in shades of autumn leaves falling on sand, teamed with smart beige trousers.

Quite apart from the interesting time spent at Maogany, they loved Bourg des Saintes and spent a few more days exploring and enjoying the island, which, typical of many French Caribbean islands, displayed a strange dichotomy of sophistication and simplicity.

Finally setting sail for Martinique, they were passing Dominica when Adam suddenly said, 'We have time on our side. Let's drop the anchor here overnight, perhaps do some fishing *etcetera,* have a good rest, and sail on to Martinique tomorrow, or the day after.'

'That's breaking the law. What if the Coastguard checks up, and catches us not checking in to Dominica'?

'Well, we'll say we have a sudden engine problem that necessitates a stopover,' Adam said. 'It's not unusual you know. Many cruisers in the Caribbean islands spin stories. If the authorities in general were not so greedy, visitors would not seek to evade the stress of checking in, and being fleeced financially for the privilege!'

'OK you win,' said Eva. 'But if we're caught, you can do the lying. Now tell me about those *etceteras* you mentioned…'

No coastguards appeared, and they used the overnight stay to enjoy simply being at home and, unusually for them, they spent the following day swimming, lying on the foredeck, and reading. They were in a perfect place. On shore was an attractive beach with picturesque shacks; a green covered hillside was dotted with homes between the trees and, of course, the warm sea of the Caribbean surrounded them.

Adam had sent an email to Pointe du Bout Marina in Martinique, confirming two berths, and the arrival of *Green Flash* and *Wild Foxes* around 23rd December. It suddenly occurred to him that he had completely forgotten a Christmas present for Eva. *Oh God! What to do? A woman, who anyway has everything, now topped up with clothes as well. An idea will come to me, it always does.*

Disaster struck! Just short of the entrance to Pointe du Bout Marina, the engine spluttered, stopped, and would not be persuaded to start again. Eva ran up the foresail to steady the boat, while Adam climbed into the engine room and ferreted around. 'It's beyond me,' he called out. 'Certainly overdue for an oil change, but this total failure is strange, and it's a hell-hole down here. Why don't engine rooms have aircon?'

When he emerged—sweaty, oily and irritated—it was hard to imagine the usual suave sophisticate! He called for help on the VHF. In less than fifteen minutes, the Harbour Master came out, and also the tender from *Wild Foxes,* driven by a grinning Henry. Tow lines were attached, and *Green Flash* made its ignominious entrance to the marina, then, with the help of many willing hands, berthed safely.

'What a way to meet new people,' declared Adam.

But for the cruising community, this attitude of helping whenever needed, was part of the unspoken code—it simply happened that way. Once safely tied up, they both showered, then walked over to *Wild Foxes,* where long cool drinks were waiting for them. 'Not a natural grease monkey I'm afraid,' Adam confessed.

Next day, Christmas Eve, Adam rushed off to get advice about hiring an engineer to attend to the engine. The Harbour Master, Giles, recommended a local man, but after leaving the office, he was approached by another Brit who had overheard the exchange. He suggested that Adam may like to meet a young Aussie itinerant engineer who had 'the touch', and had done an efficient and excellent job on his boat. 'Giles is a good enough chap, but of course he recommends local people for jobs, probably a relative.'

Contact was made with Aussie Steve and he was booked for 28th December.

'Should be over the hangovers by then, mate,' he said cheerfully. 'Til the New Year anyway.'

The marina shops were still open, and Adam scoured them for Eva's present. He struck luck when he found a strong and attractive hammock—*just the job*—he thought, and then decided it would be unsociable for her to sleep alone, so bought a matching one for himself!

Chapter 16

The remainder of the short sail back to Dominica was achieved in a day, and Freddy anchored for two nights, giving himself a good rest. Although a competent sailor, he recognised how different it was and the extra level of concentration needed to sail single-handed.

He manoeuvred into the anchorage at St Anne's, Martinique. It was exactly a week since he had invited Lily to join him and, as soon as the boat was safely anchored, he rang her. They planned her flight from Guadeloupe for the following weekend. That gave him three days to clean the boat, buy provisions, and rent a car. By Thursday evening, everything was ready on board *Ducky Do*.

Damn silly name. I must change it, he said to himself for the hundredth time!

Freddy was, frankly, nervous. He realised Lily was important to him but felt inadequate to be a good host. He also knew she would be able to create ease just by her presence so he tried to relax the last few hours before her plane landed. *Chic* yet natural was how Freddy thought of Lily . . . and approachable.

With great delight, he saw her walking towards the arrivals area, immaculate in white trousers and a navy cotton top with epaulettes across the shoulders. A peaked skipper-type hat, set at a distinct angle, was the very French touch to her nautical ensemble.

Lord, I hope she has remembered it's a sailboat and not a gin palace with big engines...

He needn't have worried as Lily was more than capable of teasing him, and her big grin confirmed this as she saluted, then kissed him warmly on each cheek. Arm in arm they went to the car and drove back to the harbour at St Anne's.

Lily was not at all happy about the dinghy. In fact she was terrified! Freddy drove it slowly, noticing how she gripped the handles with her knuckles showing white. But the boat looked wonderful, floating calmly on a smooth sea with the sun setting behind it. In fact, it was a scene of alluring tranquillity.

'*Mon dieu!*' exclaimed Lily. 'How absolutely lovely.'

Her appreciation warmed Freddy as he steered towards the Van der Stadt, and he reminded himself how lucky he was to have such a marvellous companion on board for a few days. He was also very aware that he must take her introduction to sailing very slowly.

They ate on board the first evening.

While Freddy barbecued two steaks, he said, jokingly, 'In South Africa, everyone's middle name is *Braai.*'

Of course, Lily didn't understand until he explained that this was the Afrikaans word for barbecue.

As before, they enjoyed their days together, walking round the small towns of St Anne's and

Marin and visiting the capital, Fort de France. They were especially fascinated by the ruins of St Pierre. In the Tourist Information Office, they learned how, in 1902, the governor was warned of the imminent eruption of Mont Pelée, but he and the plantation owners didn't want to disrupt the tending of crops so they ignored the warning. The entire town was wiped out! There was only one survivor, a prisoner in a stone cell awaiting trial, and he suffered only minor burns. The town had preserved the ruins as a reminder.

'Reminder of what?' asked Lily. 'Man's greed or stupidity—or perhaps the tragic loss of thousands of lives, both slaves and masters. Somehow nothing changes, does it?'

They had dinner on shore that last evening and were shocked how quickly the week had gone. It had been a close and happy time. As they retired, Lily, dressed in a peacock blue sarong, knocked on Freddy's cabin door. She moved into his arms, and for the first time in thirty years, Freddy knew the magic of a woman's touch.

Lily flew home to Guadeloupe leaving Freddy in very reflective mood. He wanted more of this woman! They kept in close touch by phone, and Freddy decided to sail *Ducky Do* straight to Grenada on his own. He didn't want to frighten Lily at this early stage, and it would be simple enough for her to fly.

She was planning to join him again in a few weeks. They both had experienced a meeting of minds and were very easy in the other's company, each of them trying not to have expectations, but knowing at the same time that here was something special.

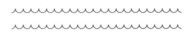

Just twenty-four hours after leaving Martinique, Freddy anchored off St Lucia overnight. Then he set off on the longer passage to St Vincent. This time, the Grenadian island of Carriacou allowed him to check in. Now Grenada itself was only one day away. He was again feeling the strain of sailing solo so it was with great relief on the following day that he was able to anchor in Prickly Bay, and allow himself to fall into a dreamless and exhausted sleep.

On shore the next day, Freddy treated himself to a couple of chilled lagers and a meal. He planned boat jobs while he was alone, and in just two and a half weeks from when they'd parted, Lily flew into Grenada. This time there was no denying their joint delight as they walked towards each other—into a long mutual hug!

He had moved the boat to the town dock of St Georges. It was easier to get taxis to the airport from there. It also involved fewer dinghy trips. The only downside was the unsolicited exhortations from the minister in a nearby church, who roared at his parishioners each evening.

'We'll move on in a day or two,' Freddy said. 'Can you stand the voice 'til then?'

'Of course,' said Lily. 'I'm just grateful we're not sitting in front of him!'

Together they strolled through the markets of the capital, sampling the sickly sweet sugar cane syrup that was on tap from a barrel, and sharing the pleasure of dining in some excellent restaurants, though of course none of them ever quite came up to the standard of Le Jardiniere! One lunchtime on shore, Lily asked Freddy if he'd ever eaten a roti.

'No, what's a roti?'

'Come with me!' They settled on a wooden bench next to a table made of a couple of planks of wood, and Lily ordered two chicken rotis and two lagers.

Freddy took a bite and started chewing. 'Oh God, no,' he said. 'That's just revolting.' He swallowed with an effort and quickly drank some lager.

Lily was appalled. 'Surely it's not that bad? It's just a cheap local dish eaten in most of the islands.'

'What on earth is it?' asked Freddy. 'Tastes like uncooked dough.'

'That's not too wrong,' responded Lily. 'It's a sort of tortilla flatbread with curried meat and vegetables wrapped inside. Maybe the flatbread is rather thick, and you don't like that style.'

'The words *style* and *roti* cannot be used in the same sentence,' retorted Freddy. 'Truly this is the worst food I've eaten in years. I can't believe that a top restauranteur, such as yourself, would eat such muck.'

'Well, Freddy, maybe I don't think it's muck. But then being an islander, perhaps I'm more accustomed to eating muck than you—you with your refined taste buds.'

Lily gave no quarter, and this was a new experience for Freddy. She was a calm and very articulate woman who made him squirm at the memory of his poorly chosen words.

'I'm going for a walk,' he said, stomping away and stopping briefly to grab a pizza from a take-away hut. *Why did I react like that? So I didn't like the roti. So what? Why offend someone I'm fond of just because of a piece of food?*

After an hour or so he walked back and found Lily dozing near the roti hut, stretched out on a sun lounger under a palm tree. She looked wonderful, untroubled and relaxed.

He bent down to her. 'I'm sorry,' he mumbled.

Lily held up her hand to stop him. 'Freddy, I suggested you experience a local dish, that's all. I don't much like flatbread myself. But why did you get so nasty and personal?'

'Misunderstanding,' he said. 'Sorry.'

But Lily was not impressed, and an unease between them remained. *Misunderstanding? Crap! It was the hissy-fit of a spoilt child—nothing more, nothing less.*

They went back to the yacht, mostly in silence. Each had a brief shower and joined up for a drink prior to the meal of parrot fish that Lily had planned to cook. They were sipping their second punch, Freddy's recipe of rum, coconut, pineapple juice, and a tiny slug of cream—when he produced little strips of something on a plate.

'What is that?' Lily asked.

'Biltong. It's a South African delicacy, something that is eaten for a bit of nutrition when out on safari for days.'

Lily took a strip and started chewing. She almost gagged and was quite unable to swallow the strong, very tough, coarse meat. 'That,' she declared, 'is the most foul thing I have ever tried to eat.' She spat it into a tissue and disappeared below decks.

When she reappeared, they took one look at each other and burst into gales of laughter. 'Never, ever, give me biltong, and I shall never, ever, give you roti. *Touché mon amour!*'

They fell into each other's arms and kissed away the hurt of their first row.

Chapter 17

Christmas that year included an abundance of eating, drinking, and the *camaraderie* of good friends. Margreet and Warner eventually arrived in the marina on Christmas Eve. They had been delayed in Guadeloupe by unreliable workmen who did half the job before disappearing for eight days. They had even wondered if they would be able to leave in time for their first British Christmas—in the French West Indies!

Daz and Henry invited everyone on board *Wild Foxes* for Christmas Day. In this situation the air-conditioner was a huge advantage, and the larger than usual galley was a welcome sight to the cooks. Henry provided *canapés* and Champagne, plus wines and brandy. Eva and Adam brought the turkey, ham, and plum pudding. And mince pies that had been deep frozen emerged, looking only a little weary. All through Christmas Eve, Daz had prepared and pre-cooked bread sauce, gravy, chestnut stuffing, sage, onion and plantain stuffing—the plantain being a little Caribbean extra that Daz thought would 'go'—cranberry sauce, custard, and brandy butter. Then, in addition, garlic bread and soup for later in the evening. It was a fiddly and mammoth task for a novice cook, but Daz was determined, and everyone said the results were well worth the effort.

As they sat down to eat at the groaning table, Eva apologized, 'Sorry guys, no sprouts!' Hoots of laughter followed her words, but no one was quite able to explain the joke to their Dutch friends!

Margreet and Warner were bowled over by the generosity of their hosts and were glad they'd had time in Guadeloupe to buy some thoughtful presents. They gave Daz a hand-crafted brooch of a tree frog in climbing mode. Henry received a bottle of the finest quality rum. Eva was given an illustrated book, *'Birds of the Caribbean'* and Adam also had a finely illustrated book, *'Diesel Engine Repair Manual for Dummies!'*

'Excellent,' he said wryly. 'Thank you both very much for that.'

The sarong was a big success. Daz loved it so Eva was well pleased. Henry immediately changed into his new shirt, and they made plans to meet again soon to study the catalogue from Maogany with Eva guiding their selections.

'Boxing Day brunch on *Matador,'* announced Margreet much later as Henry helped her off the boat.

Warner received her onto the pontoon and supported his wife's unsteady walk back to their boat, with Margreet giving an enthusiastic rendition of 'Silent Night' in Dutch.

'Not before noon though!' Henry called back, laughing.

They all agreed that staying in Martinique to celebrate New Year's Day seemed a good idea. On 28th December, Daz and Henry sailed to the anchorage at St

Pierre, and the Dutch couple joined them a day later, but Adam and Eva had to wait for Steve to complete the engine repairs. They didn't arrive until the afternoon of New Year's Eve, so were glad the others had found and booked a lively-looking place on shore, in which to frolic. 2004 came in with an explosion of fireworks, and the fun went on all night.

They had breakfast on shore and then wearily returned to their boats and flaked out in total exhaustion. The level of partying took its toll on everyone except Daz who simply slept in until the following afternoon, and then woke, looking and feeling refreshed.

Margreet put the situation very well. 'We can still do everything we used to do, only now it takes a couple of days to recover!'

Eva agreed, contributing, 'It's like after making love. A young person has gentle smudges under the eyes, but middle-age produces a sort of shagged-out look. Very unattractive . . . so unfair!'

After the festivities, the three couples had a sail plan meeting. They all got along so well it seemed natural to continue sailing together.

Adam started the ball rolling. 'Eva and I would like to leave Martinique around the end of January. I need to spend a few days catching up on some ideas being discussed in London, and this island seems to have a lot to offer as a base for Eva while I'm away, then on to St Lucia. In fact I have a proposition!'

Hoots and chuckles from his expectant friends.

'After St Lucia, how about we sail direct to Trinidad and Tobago, then back to Grenada, by June. We could even sail to the Venezuelan islands from

Trinidad. During the hurricane season we could visit the Windward Islands we missed on the way down. With plenty of warning we can race for shelter. What d'you think?'

'Well,' said Eva quickly. 'I think I don't want to be in the position of outrunning a hurricane, but the rest of the idea is fine.'

Henry nodded, knowing Daz would be in agreement. But Warner said that he and Margreet had discussed visiting the island chain between St Lucia and Grenada and then seeing the Venezuelan islands after the hurricane season. He suggested maybe they could do the first bit together, then meet up in Grenada.

Henry and Daz were easy. They enjoyed the company of Adam and Eva so much, it seemed a good idea to buddy-boat. Sailing always had the advantages of being together, just the two of them if they chose, or socialising with their friends. Adam and Eva were the sort of people who understood this.

∿∿∿∿∿∿∿∿∿∿∿∿∿∿∿∿∿∿
∿∿∿∿∿∿∿∿∿∿∿∿∿∿∿∿∿∿

The little flotilla left Martinique and set off for St Lucia. The group was happy to be under sail again, the sort of feeling that cannot be described to landlubbers!

Eva tried writing about it in her journal and, on the evening after their arrival in St Lucia, she read it out. 'There is a sense of freedom that accompanies windswept hair, possibly also associated with wearing very little, bodies normally presented in appropriate attire, now freed. The mind is freed too. It's difficult to concentrate on other problems when sailing, as there are no problems. The elements are so dynamic and huge, we realise we cannot control anything. We are here as tolerated guests. Helpless! Unable to change anything, except maybe our direction. It can also be living on the edge where every human resource has to be summoned to survive. But for me, the greatest thing is being your real self. There is no room or time for posing. True sailing demands that.' She paused.

'Go on,' urged Daz. 'It's wonderful.'

'Well, I read a quote recently, by Renan, that sums it all up: *Les marins, vois-tu, ne resemblent pas au reste du monde!'*

Adam nodded his agreement.

'Translate, please,' said Henry.

'Well, in a nutshell, *Sailors are not like other people!'*

'How true,' Daz said. 'Would you mind printing it out for me . . . all of it?'

'Not at all,' promised Eva warmly.

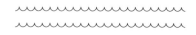

They were now in Gros Islet, an anchorage on the northwest coast of St Lucia, and planned to sail down that coast of the Caribbean sea and visit the less hospitable Atlantic coast by hire car.

In the meantime and shortly after arriving, Daz discovered that there was a well-known site for a Friday night Jump-up and persuaded the whole group to give it a whirl. With some trepidation, Henry tried to act positive prior to the event. In fact, he found that in a group, he actually enjoyed the evening! They did indeed jump up and down and around in circles, ably assisted by the rum! Daz, as usual, was the star and enjoyed showing off in splendid form, accompanied by whistles, shouts and clapping . . .

The few weeks on St Lucia were memorable. They visited the sulphur springs and the Diamond Botanical Gardens, and were surprised to learn that the mineral baths had been used around 1784 by the troops of Louis XVI. It was early enough in the year to be able to visit the two nature sanctuaries: Maria Islands, famous for lizards, rare grass snakes and sea birds—and the Frigate Islands, specialising in frigate birds, herons, boa constrictors and the dangerous fer-de-lance pit viper. They had a guide on the second trail! During the summer, the islands were closed to visitors to preserve the breeding grounds and leave the creatures in peace. They were glad to have arrived in time, before this happened.

Interspersed with social evenings, the yachties made their way to Marigot Bay, a stunningly beautiful deep inlet fringed with green hills that dropped down to white beaches, backed by palm trees. They took adjacent mooring buoys for three nights and spent time on their boats, catching up on chores.

'Hey!' called Adam to his friends. 'Today I just read that the whole British fleet laid low here to escape French warships. They covered their masts with coconut fronds, and the French navy sailed straight past the inlet. How amazing is that.'

'Must have been bloody big coconut fronds!' remarked Henry.

The weekend was approaching, and the anchorage started filling up to an uncomfortably crowded level. They decided this was the time to move on, and a visit to the Pitons provided a two-day trip, staying in the hotel between the two peaks. The Pitons, emerald green with overgrowth, stunning and very photo-friendly, gave them all a wonderful memory.

Warner and Margreet had opted out of the Piton trip, and at breakfast, Daz commented on this. 'I think our Dutch friends may have a tighter budget than us. Why else wouldn't they visit this glorious place? Also, I have noticed that they quite often cut back on lots of little things.'

The others took this observation on board as Eva responded, 'Well spotted, Daz. I hadn't noticed, but now you come to mention it ….'

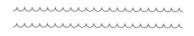

Adam had to take a couple of days to sort out some London office problems and asked Eva to check out flights back to the UK.

She searched the net and came back saying, 'British West Indian Airways seems to be a good option. I used them a couple of times for work, and they were always efficient and friendly. They certainly didn't deserve the acronym that was put about.'

'What was that?' asked Adam.

'B-W-I-A. *But Will It Arrive?* The phrase was probably spread around by a competitor. Their safety record is excellent so maybe it's because they have been known to divert unexpectedly for a local VIP who is flying with them. Still, I suppose that's more eco-friendly than using another aircraft for just one person.'

'Damn nuisance for everyone else though,' countered Adam. 'Frankly I'd rather pay more and be sure the airline goes where it's scheduled to go. Stuff the local VIPs. I think that's outrageous.'

'Okay, okay. Keep your hair on! I was only giving some local info—MEN!'

As it happened, a trip to the UK was avoided for the time being. The Dutch couple left for the Grenadines, planning to spend at least two months cruising there and, as they sailed away, the usual farewells were called out.

'See you in Grenada in June!'

'Keep in touch—SSB 1800.'

'Will do!'

'Take care!'

'Bye!'

During the next few days both *Green Flash* and *Wild Foxes* went into the Rodney Bay Marina to check out the boats, stock up with food, and buy fuel. Henry also had the nasty job of doing an oil change. This was an ideal opportunity as there were good facilities for dirty oil disposal.

They decided to do the fairly long ocean passage to Tobago first. That way the final stretch to Trinidad would be with the wind. The passage itself was without problem, and Englishman's Bay was their landfall. From there, they caught a bus to Scarborough to check in.

The journey was tough. They were pitched and buffeted by potholes in the road and suspect bus springs. They were certainly not prepared for the bureaucratic and officious manner of the staff in the Customs and Immigration office, who seemed to delight in making the visiting cruisers suffer by delaying them for hours. Fortunately, the two couples had gone together. This enabled them to take it in turn to sit in the smelly, airless room, waiting for their numbers to come up.

Once free, they walked round the noisy, bustling, town. Ghetto blasters at full volume made them wince, and in fact, the only thing they found amusing about Scarborough, Tobago, was the name!

Another bone-shaking journey back to the boats concluded an unpleasant day, exacerbated by a lone Englishman on the bus. Typical of many of his type his odour was choking so he sat at the back in isolation.

'What is it about some older Englishmen that they won't use deodorant?' wondered Eva out loud. She was sitting next to Henry. 'Can't they smell it? Or do they think it's attractive or sexy? I find it gagging!'

Henry agreed, and leaning over to Daz, repeated their exchange.

'Absolutely gross, un-cool,' was the response. 'Young men don't stink. Their partners wouldn't tolerate it.'

At this point Adam chipped in, having listened to part of the conversation. 'There's a joke about it used in sales training seminars. I can't remember the details, but it has something to do with the smell when Englishmen take their jackets off in an aircraft.'

'Yuck!' Daz said, grimacing. 'Even grosser!'

After the Scarborough experience, as it became known, the two couples spent a few days swimming and relaxing in the beautiful anchorage. Eva and Daz went on shore for a spot of beachcombing but found only some broken conch shells.

Their next move was to sail to Plymouth. They wandered round the town and its fort, but they all felt they wanted to explore more rural places so went into a bar for a bit of forward planning.

The Bay of Buccoo generated more interest. They left the yachts at anchor and chartered a glass-bottomed boat; this way they could enjoy the stunning coral reefs that extended to Pigeon Point on the southwest end of the island. They all agreed that Tobago was a lovely place and the local people seemed relaxed and friendly. Deciding they really would like to see more of the coastal villages—but with the memory of the bone-shaking bus still fresh—they rented a car and stayed in little guesthouses along the way.

The next two days brought them to Speyside, a small fishing village, and from there they visited the Little Tobago Bird Sanctuary. Many birds bred there, including red-billed tropic birds, red-footed boobies, brown boobies, shearwaters and noddies.

Henry was in a private heaven. He loved birds and always aspired to having a large aviary. *Perhaps when I retire*, he told himself!

After a scenic mountain drive, they reached Charlotteville and stayed overnight in the charming village with local families. Eva and Adam spent hours in the library, which was impressive with its stock of books, sailing magazines, and newspapers. They were able to catch up on world events and were shocked at how out of touch they were.

In the early evening, they all walked along the road by Man of War Bay, another glorious place, then to Pirate's Bay just round the point, which they suspected had gathered even more drama over the years. Apparently the bay had been a staging ground for pirate attacks on Spanish and British vessels. It was also rumoured that treasure was still buried there, and while the tourists knocked back a few rum punches, ever more exaggerated plans were drawn up to find it! It wasn't long before two frigate birds caught their attention.

'Would you look at that,' said Henry. 'They're attacking the terns and gulls in mid-air in order to steal the food they are carrying. That is amazing, and considering this is Pirate's Bay, it's very appropriate!'

It had been a happy and compatible few days, but they were all keen to get to Trinidad. Henry had done a first-class public relations job, praising the beauty of that island and the many places to visit. They had enjoyed Tobago immensely, apart from the Scarborough experience. Its peace, great natural beauty, and wildlife put it way up in the list of favourites. But now they were ready to move on.

Chapter 18

Only seventy miles away, Trinidad was just a day-sail from Tobago. The two yachts took berths in Peaks Marina in the huge Chagueramas Bay, and they found the facilities good. The marina restaurant turned out excellent meals in a welcoming atmosphere, and because of this, people from other marinas walked over to eat. A balcony overlooking the sea, with easy chairs dotted around, provided a congenial place for cruisers to meet. It was here that many friendships were formed and new crew members found.

No time was wasted in checking out options for a trip to a turtle-laying beach. The two couples were interested to hear Annette Trump of Trump Tours on the cruisers' net, a daily VHF broadcast for visiting sailors. She gave an informative talk about her business and, having dangled the carrot, left her contact details.

That morning, they all went over to the Trump Tours office to discuss what was on offer, then booked a three-night stay at Mt Plasir Hotel and Spa in the northern mountain range.

They left Chagueramas on Wednesday, arriving at Mt Plasir during the afternoon, after a gruelling five-hour drive on more dreadful pot-holed roads. The return drive was booked for Saturday afternoon.

The beach cabins were perfect for this type of visit. Very basic accommodation, but comfortable enough, with good mosquito netting and an adequate bathroom en suite. Stable-type doors separated the cabins from the sandy beach of Grand Rivière.

On the first evening they met in the bar for drinks, and during their meal, a local guide came to their table. 'Hi guys! My name is Leon. I think you are booked on the turtle watch tonight.'

The group nodded.

'If you wait in the hotel lounge, I'll come to meet you at 2200.'

~~~~~~~~~~~~~~~~~~~~~~~~~~~~~~~~
~~~~~~~~~~~~~~~~~~~~~~~~~~~~~~~~

There was an air of anticipation, of excitement, as they waited in the lounge.

Leon arrived and seated himself in front of the group. 'Before we go, there are a few rules designed to protect the turtles. Please listen carefully, it is vital you remember.' Leon paused and looked at them before continuing. 'No flashlights—you Brits call them torches. These disturb the females and frighten them away. For the same reason, no cameras with flash. We will use infrared flashlights only and please be very quiet.'

'How close can we get?' Henry was completely fascinated by this whole event.

'When we watch the chosen turtle, it will be from several metres. You will see her scoop out a hole for her eggs. She then goes into a trance for the laying, which takes about twenty minutes, and she lays up to eighty eggs.'

Eva gasped. 'Poor soul, no wonder she needs to go into a trance to lay that number!'

Leon continued his talk. 'During the laying period we can go up close, even touch her, and she will not notice. But no flash photos. She will cover her eggs, creating a decoy in the way she spreads the sand, and then crawl, exhausted, to the sea and swim away. The only time it is possible to take photos is if you wish to rise at dawn and see a few of the stragglers.'

He guided them onto the beach and they stood in amazement. The enormous area that had been so deserted earlier now had hundreds of huge leather-back turtles on it. Some were on their way to the sea after laying, others were actually laying, and the rest were moving onto the beach to begin their ritual. Led by Leon, the visitors walked quietly across the sand and stood outside the laying area of the first turtle. She dug her hole, and the watchers were almost as mesmerised as the female going into a trance! She was intent on her task, ensuring the future survival of her species by this exhausting role. Those watching found the whole experience unforgettable. They stayed on the beach for another two hours, finding the ritual of each laying breathtaking. When they went back to the hotel bar, each sat quietly, deep in thought. Speech was somehow too much.

Leon joined them, sipping his nightcap. 'You will see the vultures tomorrow at dawn. There are hundreds of them too, watching and waiting. They will eat many eggs now and, in a few months, catch the hatchlings as they race to the ocean. As you know, the laying season is March to August, and the first batch of eggs hatch soon after the last laying. Sadly, only a small percentage of the hatchlings ever reach the water, and many of those who survive are then eaten by predators in the sea. Because of this high mortality, we catch quite a number, let them grow, and then we release them into the ocean when they are bigger and stronger.'

'Thank you so much. It's been an amazing and unique experience. I feel privileged to have been part of it, even if only passively.' Eva felt uplifted, and when the others nodded agreement, realised it was a mutual feeling.

It was equally moving to observe the greater scene the next morning. Now they could clearly see the remaining females laying and the vultures watching, greedily. Adam stood behind Eva, holding her in his arms. But Henry, for once, stood alone, wrapped in the depth of his emotions.

The turtle beach was available to use during the day, but they all walked very carefully! The sea was inviting and they decided to swim—Daz, as usual, wearing a large teeshirt over bikini shorts. Eva and Daz were quickly sucked out by the strength of the ebb, then picked up bodily, and rolled onto the beach. They both struggled to their feet and ran from the water, rubbing their bruises. Henry and Adam dived into the big breaking waves as they came in. It had been some time since they had exerted their bodies in this way, and they enjoyed it.

Daz and Eva strolled down the beach to where the river came in and walked into the fresh water. A row of vultures sat on the beach end of the river and watched them!

'Isn't this great,' called Daz, 'to be able to swim and mess about in fresh water?'

'Certainly is,' responded Eva. 'But I'd feel more comfortable without the audience!'

They both laughed and, climbing out of the river, walked back to their cabins.

Over the next few days they talked and analysed their feelings about the turtle experience. Daz was impressed by the largeness of it all. Eva and Adam were deeply moved. But Henry, in a rare burst of eloquence, said that he felt this annual ritual, showing the continuum of life and the certainty of nature, to be utterly mind-blowing.

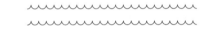

The famed Asa Wright Nature Reserve was another place to visit in Trinidad, and this time, they chose Honest John Tours. True to his name they reached the centre, as scheduled, for a modest price.

Looking forward to another three-day break, the two couples went to their rooms, taking with them all the centre leaflets informing them of the various options available. It was here they learned that Trinidad was known to the Amerindians as Lere, land of the hummingbird. There were many different nature walks to choose from, an overnight bird watch, and advertised feeding times for the various protected species in the acres of rainforest.

While settling in, Adam called to Eva, 'Hey sweetheart, listen to this. It seems that Asa Wright was a Swedish woman. She bequeathed her plantation home and its grounds to the nation so that lovers of nature could visit and enjoy the estate.'

Eva gave Adam a saucy look. 'Lovers of nature, eh? Well, that's certainly us!' She gave a little jiggle and blew him a kiss before returning to the leaflet she was studying.

The complex was set in the rainforest with eight double cabins available for residential guests. There were four large rooms to a house, simply furnished but containing everything needed for such a break. Henry and Daz were relieved to see anti-bug screens outside all the windows. The catamaran, because of air-conditioning, was very efficient in insect control so they were accustomed to high living standards.

Daz, wearing charcoal grey long trousers rolled up at the hem, a skimpy top, and with a denim jacket swinging from one finger, gave Henry a big hug. 'Hen, darling, I'm dying to get over to the main house to photograph the hummingbirds. Can we meet there?'

'Anything you want, my sweet,' responded Henry, just a little disappointed.

When the other three arrived on the verandah— a construction out of the 1930s—they were fascinated to see Daz rushing round photographing the birdwatchers, instead of the birds. It soon became apparent why.

'Just look at them,' said Eva as she sank into a large cane chair. 'Men and women in safari suits of green or beige with Crocodile Dundee style hats. And they are all so intense.'

Amused, Adam and Henry followed her gaze.

'Look,' she added. 'Daz seems to be getting submerged.'

At that very moment, one of the twitchers called out in a stage whisper, 'I've got a fork-tailed flycatcher in the scope.'

A tidal wave of khaki and beige overtook Daz, who escaped unscathed, camera still in hand. Binoculars poised, the enthusiasts focused and held their combined breaths, as they scanned the foreground.

Daz raced back to the group, almost incoherent with delight and excitement. 'Look at these frames.'

The digital camera showed the event.

'Just look at them! Little books, pencils, and binoculars, suspended from white scrawny necks. No one has a suntan, and they wear big boots with thick socks. They all have large or sharp noses and receding chins and they're so terribly excited!'

'And so are you, my sweet,' observed Henry. 'And you know what they say about mens' noses!' He raised his chin, and his aqualine nose became a subject of admiration and conjecture…

At this stage the twitchers lowered their binoculars and started scribbling in their little books.

Adam stood up and casually strolled to the edge of the verandah. Turning round, he called out to everyone in general, 'Look! Quick! There's a rare greater-spotted, yellow-breasted, marine knee trembler in my sights.'

Pencils and notebooks were dropped as the group surged to the rail, binoculars at the ready.

Adam rejoined his friends, and the four of them collapsed in a heap of mirth. Henry had tears rolling down his cheeks!

A very tall thin man with an impressive lapel badge walked towards them. Looking at Adam, he spoke in an injured tone. 'I don't think that's very funny.'

But by now Eva and Daz were helpless, hanging onto each other, and unable to speak, like a couple of children with the giggles.

The twitchers were called to lunch. As they filed past, baleful looks were thrown in the direction of the group who tried, unsuccessfully, to control themselves. By the time the birdwatchers reached the dining room, they could still hear howls of mirth behind them. One or two of them grinned at having been set up, but the majority were not amused, not at all!

Chapter 19

The two British couples had been in Trinidad for three weeks now, and felt they really had explored the island thoroughly, hiking through rainforests and visiting deserted coves from their dinghies. In addition, they'd frolicked at a beach party given in honour of Eva's birthday with local guys playing tin pan. Port of Spain, with all its noise and colour, was walked exhaustively. The Asa Wright Centre still made them all grin conspiratorially, and the turtle beach was simply one of those never-to-be-forgotten events.

Eva had found the turtle-laying event the most magical experience she'd ever had, possibly only comparable with swimming in Dingle Bay with Fungi, the dolphin who had been adopted by that Irish town. She paused in her thoughts, remembering the fragile colleague she had taken there. Following years of abuse, Ann had finally opened up after swimming with Fungi, and this had enabled healing to take place. That was another amazing and humbling experience she could never quantify.

The group met for coffee and discussed where to go next.

'How about visiting the former leper colony island before we leave Trini?' Daz proposed. 'It's called Chacachacare. That's where lepers were taken. It was a whole colony, complete with medical staff and nuns who served as nurses.'

'Where is it? I've never heard of it! Did you read about it?' Henry was often surprised how Daz was so well-informed.

The others looked interested. Daz's ideas were always entertaining.

'Well, I was chatting to this German woman in the marina store, and she told me about the island. It's only five miles off the northwest tip of the mainland, and apparently well worth a visit.'

They looked up the island on the chart and decided to sail there for a few days before replenishing stocks and sailing on to Grenada.

~~~~~~~~~~~~~~~~~~~~~~~~~~~~~
~~~~~~~~~~~~~~~~~~~~~~~~~~~~~

During the short sail to Chacachacare, both yachts were treated to hundreds of dolphins racing them and bow leaping. Cameras and camcorders were kept very busy as the spectacle was quite breathtaking. Then a Royal Navy destroyer passed them, heading towards Port of Spain. Adam saluted the senior vessel by lowering the ensign and, to their delight, the huge ship dipped its ensign in response! Adam and Eva were very chuffed, and Henry later commented on such a rare exchange, congratulating Adam for even thinking of saluting them.

As they entered the very pretty anchorage, they could see a group of houses on the right that had been lived in by the medical staff. Farther along the shore, other buildings could just be seen, though most were swallowed up by vegetation.

'Presumably those buildings housed the lepers, and on the opposite shore, must have been the nunnery.' Adam pointed to the Gothic-like buildings with a small chapel adjacent.

'It's a bit bizarre, isn't it? There are abandoned buildings all around us.' Eva spoke with feeling.

They could just make out the Swedish ensigns on two yachts at anchor in front of the nuns' quarters. This prompted her to comment, 'I do like Swedish people. Those I've met at the World Health Organisation are so genuine, never two-faced or acquisitive.

'Perhaps, my sweet, most people who work for the WHO are genuinely decent and caring people. Had that occurred to you?'

'Well, no it hadn't. And yes, probably you're right. Anyway, they are also very competent sailors.'

Adam smiled, thinking how he loved her grasshopper mind!

Daz and Henry anchored without hassle so it especially irritated Adam and Eva that their anchor just wouldn't dig in. It was not until the fifth attempt that they were finally able to feel satisfied the boat was secure.

The sea was clear and inviting so they enjoyed skinny-dipping and cooling off. Eva swam towards the anchor chain and Adam called her. She turned towards him, treading water. Her breasts were bobbing up and down with the movement.

'You look so sexy.' His meaning was clear as he eyed her with appreciation.

She laughed at him. Flirting! Inviting! They both reached the anchor chain and grabbed it, then caught each other with a spare arm. Their lips met, each absorbing the taste of the other.

Within minutes Adam was moving inside her. 'Just going with the flow, my love.' he whispered in her ear.

Next day they all joined up to visit the island and explore the buildings. Trying to beat the heat, it was only 0800 when they landed on the dilapidated old jetty in front of the fairly well-preserved intake building. It was easy to imagine lepers being interviewed and logged in as they landed in boats from the mainland.

Eva had researched the history of the island, and Adam, knowing this, suggested she might fill them in on what she had learned.

'Are you sure? Preachy people are always a bit of a pain.'

'Come on, Eva, you could never be boring. I'll buy you a drink later!' Henry spoke for them all as he secured the dinghy, and with big grins, they arranged themselves schoolroom style on a low crumbling wall in front of Eva.

Always an interesting orator, but also having a good sense of humour, she sat on a tree stump facing them in teacher mode. Enjoying the gentle early sun, Eva started to recount her understanding of events that had taken place on Chacachacare. 'It seems that Chaca, as the locals call it, was the leper colony for Trinidad. It was started in 1922, and during its existence, over two thousand sufferers were treated. Once here, the patients stayed for life. Two good-hearted doctors and other staff lived in separate buildings, but well away from the hospital area. Nuns provided the nursing care. They travelled to the hospital either by boat or truck on a dirt road that connected the two areas, a road that is now overgrown. The convent with its small chapel and cemetery is on the shore opposite the hospital, as you will have seen. Strangely, only the nuns were buried in the cemetery, and there is no record of what happened to the remains of the lepers who died here. Quite a lively community was built up, and the patients who were well enough, organised cricket matches and other forms of entertainment. There were also two churches and a school. A few patients built small dwellings, and sometimes a wife and children would join a sick man, but of course they were never able to go back to the mainland again. Very few men came to Chaca to join a sick wife!' At this, Eva gave a wry smile, and paused before she continued. 'It seems that a cure for leprosy was found in the sixties, and the historical records simply stop there. The discovery of an antibiotic for the bacillus was quickly followed by a mass exodus of all the patients, staff, and the nuns. Just like that!'

'Wow! What a story.'

'Thanks, Eva.'

They all were glad to have such a vivid background history of the place. Adam simply took Eva's hand and squeezed it.

The four of them walked in single file along an overgrown path, with Henry in front, chopping back the vegetation with a small sharp hatchet. Adam brought up the rear. All of them were dressed in long-sleeve shirts, long trousers, and walking boots with socks protecting lower legs. To complete the picture, each wore a sturdy hat and gloves and a thick layer of insect repellant, and they were very glad Eva had advised these precautions. Huge spider webs stretched across the track, making them wonder about the revenge that might be sought by a spider whose home had just been destroyed. Mosquitoes carrying dengue fever whined overhead, and they saw a sleeping anaconda curled up in a tight grey ball.

They arrived at a church but decided the broken steps were too dangerous to negotiate. The building next to that was the hospital, but the floor was in such poor condition, they had to walk very carefully over split or missing boards and hold hands for added safety. The first room was a hospital ward. Iron beds were still there, narrow and uncomfortable looking. They walked through several such sleeping areas into what must have been an operating theatre and examination room, with an obsolete x-ray machine and a disintegrating leather chair beside it. There were even a few rusty instruments in evidence.

'How gruesome,' Daz said. 'I wonder why the table is so short. What are the drop-down trays for?'

'Designed for amputating limbs, I think,' offered Eva.

The four of them had good imaginations and found this idea overwhelming, revealing the awful level of suffering that was part of the deterioration of a human body.

They moved into the next room, a kitchen, with dirty plates and cutlery from forty years earlier, sitting in the large sink and on the table. This led into an office, and a dispensary where there was a cupboard still containing some medicines. To their horror, there were patients' case notes—complete with names and personal details, treatments given, and results. Often the dates of death were written on thick yellow cards. They recorded how the lepers had their wounds scraped and dressed with sulphur powder. Here was the most intimate information about real people scattered all over the floor. It was very shocking! An office in total disarray. Confidential data abandoned as if everyone just suddenly left, vanished, interrupted in the middle of doing something, leaving behind a skeleton of real lives and events.

The group walked on, carefully picking their way through jungle and debris. Broken masonry and split shafts of wood making it more like an assault course, they gingerly crept to the next building. Clearly this was a film theatre, with a screen, rows of seats, and a projector with a film still inside! Outside, a few small broken-down wooden buildings could be seen through the trees.

'Married quarters?' Adam suggested.

Now, in a state of heightened awareness, they noticed a large flock of vultures circling overhead.

'I wonder why so many vultures live and breed on a deserted island?' Daz voiced.

But no one felt willing or able to explore that thought. The whole area was grim and surreal. Unanimously, they decided to leave the ghost town with its overpowering feeling of sad memories and eerie abandonment.

That evening they met up and discussed their day. Based on today's standards of confidentiality, they agreed the seemingly callous betrayal of patients' trust was very disturbing, quite apart from all the other bizarre scenes.

'Why didn't the government repair and preserve the complex as a museum, a testament to medical research, or something?' Henry wondered out loud.

'I don't know,' replied Eva. 'But I aim to find out. It's all too weird and awful!'

Her friends, recognising the tone of Eva's voice when she took on a project sorting out yet another cause or injustice, realised there was nothing more to be said!

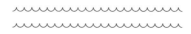

As planned, the two couples went back to the mainland supermarkets to do their shopping. Then they checked out of Trinidad and set sail for Grenada. Daz and Henry arrived first, and with their shallow draft, had no problem entering the anchorage at Hog Island, but Adam and Eva, with their six-foot draft, dropped anchor only after making a slow and careful entry through the treacherous reefs.

'Here at last, safe in Grenada at the start of the hurricane season,' breathed Daz, leaning back on a comfy chair in the cockpit, relaxed and smiling. 'I just don't believe life can get any better!'

Chapter 20

On the day following their 'roti versus biltong' row, Freddy told Lily he'd like to sail round to the Hog Island anchorage because it was sheltered but also picturesque. It was almost the start of the hurricane season, and he preferred to be prepared, especially with a very novice sailor on board.

'What can I do to help?'

Freddy felt this was a very positive question that showed interest. 'Thanks, Lily. But for now I'll do the anchor work from the cockpit. That's because there are a lot of boats to avoid!' He talked through what he was doing, and Lily observed intently, occasionally asking questions. 'It's not far,' Freddy told her. 'I think we'll just have a gentle sail round.'

It was early afternoon when he took in the sails and prepared to motor into the bay at Hog Island. 'Lily, we have to go between the reefs that protect this anchorage. Can you go forward and stand at the highest point? Would you double check to see if I'm steering right in the middle?'

'Lord!' said Lily. 'Am I up to this?'

'It's okay. This is only a backup observation thing, but you'll be a great help. Oh, and Lily, hold on tight!'

With her confidence boosted, Lily scanned the water as Freddy directed, and they entered the anchorage. Once inside, Freddy motored round it before choosing a place to drop the anchor.

'This is lovely,' exclaimed Lily with delight. 'It has everything—beaches, shallows, palm trees and woods. Shall we explore later?'

As she finished speaking, two children, aged around ten, sailed slowly past the yacht, each child on a plank of wood with a very homemade-looking mast and an old piece of cloth for a sail. Lily and Freddy laughed and waved.

'How good to see children enjoying themselves in such a simple way, quite old fashioned, *très charmant*.' Lily was thrilled with the whole *ambiance* of the place.

Suddenly, a large wooden boat painted red and yellow and powered by a huge outboard motor, roared to the entrance of Hog Island Bay. The driver cut the engine right back and motored in more slowly, eventually making a beach landing. He tied up his boat, then unloaded bags and boxes onto the shore.

'Smuggler?' suggested Lily.

They dinghied to shore with Dog standing in the front like a figurehead. He had accepted Lily and seemed to enjoy feminine company, something unknown when they were in South Africa. Another couple in an inflatable dinghy were also heading towards shore. Presumably on the same mission, it became clear they knew the ropes. Greetings were shouted to the shore, and they secured their dinghy with the ease of experience.

The rasta from the red and yellow wooden boat ceased his unloading and, wading out, took the dinghy painter from Lily. 'Welcome to Hog, folks! I'm Roger. and the bar will be open for sundowners in half an hour!'

Lily and Freddy looked at each other and with rare humour, Freddy whispered to her, 'Roger the Rasta?' Then, turning to Roger, he said, 'I've no money with me.'

'No worries man. Put it on the slate 'til I see you next!'

They had a couple of rum punches.

'Not as good as yours,' Lily commented.

As dusk started to fall, the man from the Island Packet came over to introduce himself, and then, recognising them, smiled with pleasure and extended his hand. 'Oh, hi there, it's you! We've been here just a few hours and thought we saw you arriving. How are you?'

'Just fine, thanks. And you?' Freddy introduced Lily.

She remembered the two of them in her restaurant—just part of the skills needed in her business. Sven seemed impressed at her memory.

Sven told them how they had spent a couple of weeks sailing round the mainland and returning to Hog Island. 'Did your nephew get back to Europe safely?' he asked.

'Thank you, yes. As a matter of fact, George will be joining us later this month.' They all smiled companionably as they sat down on logs, sipping their punches.

All his life, Freddy suddenly thought, he'd had problems remembering faces and loathed social occasions. Now he realised he must have changed, and this surprised him a lot. He really *was* enjoying himself!

Erika arrived back from her walk and joined the group. She seemed glad to see different faces, and also was pleased that Freddy and Lily appeared to be so happy together. Two more couples came on shore to have a drink, and the children on the raft landed. Dog, after an initial stand-off, acted like he enjoyed their attention, and they all raced round with the mad excess of energy so often displayed by children and canines. It was a pleasant enough evening. Roger told them he did a cook-up on Sundays and opened his beach bar most evenings from 1800. Obviously used to sailors, he quoted the international clock.

The beach bar, though very basic, had the usual nautical gimmicks: postcards, and small flags from all over the world, an old hurricane lamp, and a couple of fenders that had washed ashore. The unique touch was a huge old fishing net covering the whole—Roger simply rolled up the net and raised the Grenadian flag when opening the bar!

As everyone started to leave, the tropical darkness fell suddenly. It was like the change of a cloth backdrop on a stage. Tired children on rafts were towed back home by their parents. Dog, taking up his usual position on the front of the dinghy, looked towards the disappearing figures, tail wagging, tongue lolling.

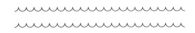

Of course Trix had been persuaded to stay on the boat with James, and they sailed to Bequia first. As a citizen of St Vincent, she was able to travel freely within the Grenadine islands, and all this was a source of enormous excitement for her, having never left her home island before.

They anchored off Princess Margaret Beach, and James, thinking out loud, said, 'I wonder why it's called Princess Margaret Beach?'

'Ha, I know the answer to that! My cousin Jon says that's where Mick Jagger shagged her.' Trix was delighted with herself, especially seeing James's face and his expression.

He grinned. 'And X marks the spot I suppose?'

A bit puzzled, Trix thought about that. 'Nah, there was too many places. They did an awful lotta shaggin', so it's said.' Then, getting into her stride, she added, 'My cousin Jon was one of the beach cleaners at the time. They called Mick Jagger her *Playboy on Toast!* Those two did the whole biz, oral numbers, and he has one big mouth—know what I mean?'

Visualisation was James' speciality, and having digested this information, grabbed Trix's hand and made her feel his growing erection moving hard against her.

'Man, I think you is good an' ready for an oral number yourself...'

'Yes! Quick! Wrap those gorgeous juicy lips round me and suck me, baby, suck. Oh yes, that's it! Oh, yes . . . YES!'

~~~~~~~~~~~~~~~~~~~~~~~
~~~~~~~~~~~~~~~~~~~~~~~

Trix spent the next morning shopping in the market. She carried on the usual noisy haggling while buying fruit and veg. She had her hair braided and bought a dress.

'Well, nearly a dress,' James commented, as his eyes feasted on the two glowing brown orbs, struggling to escape the top. 'Turn around,' he ordered.

Trix twirled and rocked her pelvis.

'Your bottom looks like two dogs humping under a pelmet. Dear God, what a wonderful sight!'

'I think I feel a little siesta comin' on,' she said, giving a very licentious wink and slowly licking her lips.

~~~~~~~~~~~~~~~~~~~~~~~
~~~~~~~~~~~~~~~~~~~~~~~

The next island, Canouan, was just twenty miles away. Here they discovered few people, but a lot of goats! The beaches were deserted and lovely, but neither James nor Trixie favoured beachcombing or sunbathing so they stayed for just two days.

Following that, they sailed to the stunningly lovely Tobago Cays. Clear blue water, sandy sea bed, and tiny islands dotted the view . . . perfect! The anchorages were not too crowded so they enjoyed eating freshly caught fish, and local vegetables that they bought from boat boys on rafts. Trix's banter with the boys almost paralysed James with embarrassment, and he hoped the cruisers on the nearest yacht hadn't heard. It wasn't just the volume, but the content, frequently interspersed with screams of bawdy laughter.

They also overdosed on sex. James felt exhausted, but under Trix's skilled attention with her soft hands, he also felt rejuvenated! After a few days, more yachts arrived, and the area became crowded so James decided to sail to Meyreau. They anchored in the picturesque Salt Whistle Bay, but there was nothing much there to attract either of them. James preferred to save his energy for Trix's erotic and inventive sexathons rather than climbing the one steep hill with a view, and certainly *she* was not interested in views.

They sailed on to Palm Island where it was reputed some steamy filming had been done, and looking at the palm trees on the deserted white sandy beaches, it was clear why such a location had been chosen. James was concerned that Trix may become bored, but she had found books! When rummaging through lockers, she found *Jane Eyre* beneath Prue's knickers, and this she read slowly, whenever there was an opportunity. Many things in the novel puzzled her—not least of all, the lack of sexual action—so she asked James to explain. And he was much too fascinated by her ingenuousness to wonder where she had found the book . . .

They stopped off at Union Island to buy provisions and check out of the Grenadines before the onward sail to Grenada. Trixie stayed on board as she would now be travelling without a passport. James told her she would have to lie low in the meantime, but eventually he would pay a fisherman to take her home to St Vincent.

He rang the hospital from each island, and it was with mixed feelings he learnt Prue was no longer in pain and a discharge date was in sight. But the idea of losing his lively, sexy, young companion filled him with dread. *Life will never be the same again*, he thought.

Taking a big chance with the law, James identified himself to the island's customs and immigration authority as the sole visitor. He and Trixie then kept a low profile, staying only at isolated anchorages before finally leaving for Grenada.

Once at Grenada, James again avoided the main town anchorage. By this time, Trix was totally enamoured of the cruising lifestyle and enjoyed a freedom hitherto unknown. Sex with only one man in six weeks was unique for her, and all she had to do was what she did anyway for a living wage. But now there were many fringe benefits! Free food, accommodation, booze and occasional gifts, even if these were added to the shopping list by herself so her wages would remain untouched. This could be a good future business venture, giving comfort to lonely yachtsmen . . .

James and Trix went on shore together just once, but found they attracted too much attention, spiced with adverse comments. Subsequently, they separated when they reached the landing area, and Trix went off to do the food shopping. She was forbidden by James to speak to any men, and she had given her word on this.

When they returned to the dinghy, James was very pleased with information he had picked up in a bar in the capital, St Georges.

'Trix, there's an island here called Hog. It's protected by reefs and has limited room for boats. It sounds like a perfect hideaway.'

'Wow!' said Trix. 'How exciting—a hideaway!'

He carefully studied the charts in order to work out the safest course for entering the anchorage. At noon, with Trix reef-spotting, hanging over the pulpit like an exotic black Brunhilde, James slowly motored through the narrow entrance between the reefs.

Their arrival did not go unnoticed among the cruising community already anchored, but James was having far too much fun to care!

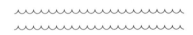

Sven was reading in the cockpit when he heard the yacht. Suddenly he was riveted, not at the sight of the Crealock motoring into the anchorage, but rather the vision hanging off its bow—a plump young black woman in a minimalist bikini, presenting her breasts to the world as she leaned over to release the pin that restrained the anchor. 'Phew!' he exclaimed as they swung, generous and almost unhindered. 'Tits ahoy!' he called.

Erika came running up on deck. Eva also appeared from below on *Green Flash* after hearing his call. She looked over to see what was happening.

'Did you say, 'It's a buoy?' Erika asked.

Sven laughed out loud. 'No. I said, tits ahoy!' Sven pointed out the vision.

Erika grinned. These days she seemed a lot more relaxed, less judgmental. As they watched Trix and her amplitude, she laughed. 'A perfect description, Sven, I must agree.'

On *Ducky Do*, Freddy and Lily were enjoying a pre-lunch drink when they too heard Sven's call.

'Wow!' said Freddy, his eyes popping out on stalks. 'Wow!'

'Down boy,' Lily commented mildly, but quite unable not to laugh.

Adam was hull-scraping so he missed the event.

Eva had been repairing a cockpit cushion and, sensing this manoeuvre may get interesting, muttered to herself, 'He'll never believe me. That is one amazing sight.' She reached for the camcorder.

As *Sorcerer* drew closer, Trix hailed everyone in her usual uninhibited fashion.

'Hi, everyone!' She raised both her arms high and waved them excitedly, at which point the bikini top gave up the struggle and flew off. Unencumbered, her liberated breasts frolicked briefly before she gave a little shriek and, with plump hands inadequately covering each one, subsided onto the deck.

The onlookers were speechless with amazement and laughter, but Eva was jubilant. She'd just had time to preface her recording with the words 'Island Charms'. So much easier now, rather than faffing about later with editing.'

'That was too funny to even be erotic,' commented Freddy as he and Lily returned to their drinks.

But peace was short-lived. Late in the afternoon, the sea around *Sorcerer* became turbulent. The yacht swung violently from side to side.

Trix's voice could clearly be heard, ringing out through the anchorage. 'Giddy-up! C'mon! C'mon! Ride me hard, baby!'

Then a very explicit and prolonged scream erupted.

Birds looked alarmed and stopped preening, fish swam for cover. Dog started howling, and as the bass shout joined the soprano, humans rushed to their various vantage points. Within minutes, VHFs buzzed and loaded messages went over the air on Channel 16.

'*Ducky Do, Ducky Do—Green Flash*—over'

'*Green Flash*—hello there, *Ducky Do*. Try channel 68—over'

'Usual place 1800—over'

'Wilco—out.'

The same message was heard by those on *Wild Foxes* and *Packet of Dreams*.

That evening, Daz and Henry picked up Adam and Eva and motored to shore. George and Lily went in their dinghy. Sven and Erika swam. They all met on the beach and, after buying drinks and bags of nuts, settled themselves on logs. Anti-bug smoke coils burned and the pungent aroma swirled around their legs.

'Well, what do you think of them?' started Sven.

'Hilarious!'

'Amazing!'

'An eye-full!'

'You mean an ear-full!'

'Too much.' They all contributed to the list.

'But seriously.' Sven was taking an unusual moral stand. 'In my opinion, that's taking freedom of expression too far. It's inappropriate and intrusive behaviour.'

'Sadly, I have to say I agree.' Eva nodded to Erika. 'Siesta fun is fun, and as a one-off it's fine, but somehow I don't think it will be a one-off.'

'Wonder where he picked her up. She is outrageous and so young,' added Erika.

'And so noisy.' Lily spoke with feeling. 'Is everyone's glassware intact?'

They all laughed, and the conversation batted back and forth until it was agreed, many drinks later, that Adam would have a word—man to man! The group had decided that it may come better from another Brit rather than from an American or South African. Henry and Daz were in agreement, but due to the industry in which they worked, it seemed wiser for them to steer clear. They had been on shore earlier and missed the voluptuous busty display. Now they were filled in with a hilarious mime performed, surprisingly, by Lily.

She had them all in fits of laughter at her posturing and mimicry, ending up with a shriek, dainty hands cupping supposed enormous breasts as she sank to the ground! Everyone clapped and cheered.

'Such talent,' murmured Freddy to Lily. 'You should be on the stage.'

Daz, Henry and Adam certainly got the message, and wished they'd witnessed the actual event—such was the inspiration from Lily's performance!

'Well, guess what? I've got the video,' claimed Eva. 'Should be a good party centrepiece when there's nothing new to distract us. Maybe I should re-title it *How to Carry on Sailing!*'

It was agreed to invite the newcomers to the usual *Welcome to Hog Island beach party*. Overall it was a success. It was certainly different…

At the beginning of the evening, Trix was shy outside her own environment, and even her dress was almost respectable. Her breasts bobbed around inside a pale pink halter-neck sarong which fell down at the back, barely covering her massive bottom. Braids were tied back in loops with pink ribbon, giving a rather wacky-topsy-type appearance. But she was understated beside James' lurid shirt, covered in palm trees, dancing girls and donkeys.

'Why donkeys?' asked Erika.

'I think it's symbolic,' answered Eva

'How so?'

'Well, hung like one!' Eva suggested.

'No,' said James. 'Actually I bought it from a club in Barbados where the speciality of the house included dancing girls and a donkey stallion. The donkey had been teased until he was ready to . . . '

'No,' shouted Freddy loudly interrupting James. 'Not a good idea. There are ladies here.'

James apologized, and Trix defused the situation by suggesting a limbo competition. She rushed off and came back with a broken off lightweight branch. 'There's nothing to hold it in place so here you are.'

She organised Adam and Sven to rest each end lightly on their hands. Daz, quickly getting into the idea, switched the CD player to Salsa, then Daz and Trix shimmied to the music, wriggling their hips and shoulders and bending backwards to go under the pole. Though both were around the same age, there couldn't have been a greater difference. Daz—slender and lithe, elegant, and sexily suggestive—slithered gracefully under the pole. Trix—plump and bouncy, basic, earthily and explicitly sexual—gyrated under the pole in little stamping jumps, legs wide apart, breasts rolling!

Henry tried next but was totally useless, his physique and level of fitness not being trained to backward bends. Freddy had a go, but suffused with embarrassment, immediately knocked the pole off.

Lily gave him a quick hug before having her turn, and he stood by the pole to catch her, as she also felt the impossibility of her spine bending to that extent. 'I save my backward curves for you,' she whispered softly to Freddy, who smiled back at her conspiratorially.

Branch holders were changed so everyone could have a turn. Erika executed a perfect limbo, technically controlled, but lacking any raunchiness. However, Sven was good. His slender frame writhed under the pole and drew whistles of appreciation from the women. Adam and James were not pliant enough, and Eva went straight onto her back, gracefully, and then lay there like a startled deer that had tripped up.

Adam hauled her up and gave her a quick hug. 'Must get in some practice and do this again when Paul and Frances join us.'

Adam's voice tailed off as he, with all the others, focused on Daz and Trix, now dancing a wonderful, crazy, sexy, duo. Full of admiration, the group watched as the limbo took on an earthy freedom, with the performers dipping and stomping under the lowered pole.

Daz went under easily but Trix's breasts only just cleared it.

Hooting with laughter she stood up, saying, 'Jeeesus, I'll have to strap 'em down next time.'

The dancing continued as Adam spoke quietly to James, inviting him for a quick word away from the others.

It was as if James had been in a hypnotic trance, and Adam's words returned him to reality. He apologised and explained his situation a little. 'My wife had a terrible accident in Barbados and will be flying here to convalesce soon. Our daughter is joining us too. In the meantime, this girl is, well…'

James stopped talking. Adam patted his shoulder, not really understanding but keen to keep the peace.

They rejoined the group, but the point had been taken. Next morning *Sorcerer* motored back through the reefs and anchored round the point in Mt Hartman Bay.

Chapter 21

E va and Adam rented a car and met their son and daughter at the airport. Paul and Frances were glad to be spending a few weeks with their parents in the Caribbean, their time together was usually harmonious.

The four of them, plus luggage, balanced precariously in the tiny dinghy. As they motored out to *Green Flash*, they saw *Sorcerer* returning through the reef, but on this occasion, Trix was not adorning the foredeck!

That evening, a much-subdued James joined the welcome party for Paul and Frances. He drank too much, and the group felt a little sorry for him. He announced that Prue would be flying in from Barbados in two days and would need much care while she gathered her strength. Their daughter, Harriet, would be joining her parents and had managed to arrange an extended leave to help care for her mother. In the tradition of cruising folk, they all offered their support, but their thoughts differed greatly, each remembering the outrageous Trixie.

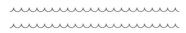

Amidst all the changes, Lily had to return home. Freddy agreed he would stay and meet George, who was returning for his holiday. He would spend a couple of days with him, and then fly to Guadeloupe to be with Lily. They both found they couldn't bear to be apart for long so she would return to the boat with him as soon as business allowed.

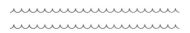

Then Prue flew in. When she and James arrived at her welcome party on shore, it became apparent just how frail she was. She still needed to use crutches. Three of the men lifted her carefully out of the dinghy and carried her onto the beach where she sat on the only proper chair. The evening was gentle and sociable, and Erika's heart immediately went out to this pale and hurt woman. Then, remembering James saying he couldn't cook, she suggested that Prue might enjoy a little time on *Dreams* until Harriet arrived. Prue's lit up face said it all, but she deferred to James.

He agreed, with great relief. 'It makes perfect sense, thank you, Erika—just until Harriet arrives in a few days.'

'Come back with us tonight,' said Sven. 'Saves you having to take two dinghy rides. I'm sure Erika can lend you anything you might need, and we have a spare toothbrush for sure. Perhaps James can bring over some things for you tomorrow.'

'You are kind. Thank you both so much,' Prue responded. She was looking exhausted now so James and Sven carried her to Henry's tender, this being the most comfortable method of transport available.

Carefully, they supported her up onto the deck of *Dreams,* and then Erika took over, settling their guest in the comfortable aft cabin, which was separate and complete with its own facilities.

She brought Prue a small cup of hot chocolate with a shot of brandy in it and a bottle of water for the night. 'Sleep well, Prue. And please remember this is your home.' With that she kissed her on the cheek and left her cabin.

How very lucky I am, thought Prue, as she snuggled down and slept soundly.

∿∿∿∿∿∿∿∿∿∿∿∿∿∿∿∿∿
∿∿∿∿∿∿∿∿∿∿∿∿∿∿∿∿∿

The flight arrival times for George and Harriet, both travelling from the UK, were only one hour apart so Freddy elected to pick them both up. George was greeting his uncle when the arrivals board flashed up a message that Harriet's Virgin Atlantic flight would be delayed by fifty minutes.

'Sod's law,' said Freddy. But he did not seem too bothered because they had much to talk about.

George was in a buoyant mood. His research work had been well received. Samples of the toxin were being graded and then grown in varying conditions. But best of all, his thesis was complete, and he had it with him in draft, for editing.

Freddy was delighted for him. 'Well done, well done! You deserve success after all that hard graft and dedication.' He put out his hand and patted George's shoulder. 'I too have some news!'

George looked up at Freddy and waited.

'I've met a woman!'

George was now seriously surprised. 'Tell me more, Uncle.'

Freddy gave a quirky smile at the epithet. 'Her name is Lily. She is a restaurant owner in Guadeloupe—wise, clever, and beautiful. You'll meet her soon.'

'What's the plan?'

'Well, in a few days, I'll be flying to Guadeloupe to join her, and then we'll fly back together for the remainder of the summer. How long are you in Grenada?'

'My flight back is to be confirmed. This is an open-ended holiday, paid for by the WHO. They probably want some more information from here after the results of the lab tests are logged. But as it is a holiday, it will take around four weeks. Is that okay? I won't be in the way?' He looked at Freddy, eyebrows raised.

'You're very welcome. *'Ducky Do*—really must change that bloody awful name—is big enough for us all, and we have very separate quarters.'

George grinned at the implication. 'I'm pleased for you, really. Can't wait to meet her.'

Freddy checked his watch yet again. 'Stay here with the bags, will you, George? I'll be looking out for this stunner!' He had a photo Prue had given him, and showed it briefly to his nephew.

'Cool!' George agreed.

Harriet, looking elegant and remarkably fresh, walked with purpose into the arrivals area. Well primed by her mother, she recognised Freddy immediately—sandy grey hair, shaggy brows, but above all, amazingly blue eyes. 'Freddy?'

He nodded.

'Hello, I'm Harriet.'

He took her hand and shook it hard. 'Welcome to Grenada!'

They walked over to George and, introductions completed, headed towards the car park. *She's a cracker*, thought George. *At last, an unattached female in the sailing community.*

Harriet took longer over her assessment. *Not bad—nice open face, bright blue eyes—must be a family feature—short dark hair, neat bum, good legs. Needs a bit of lightening up, maybe.* Harriet was an inveterate fixer-of-people, which she achieved with charm and ease, before moving on. *Fancy meeting talent on arrival . . . excellent!* She grinned to herself, speculatively.

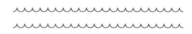

A few days later, Harriet walked back through the trees on a well-worn dirt track, keeping a sharp look out for any Caribbean nasties that might be lurking on the ground. Suddenly she saw the boy on the beach. So young and slender, not yet filled out. Fair hair and golden body. So beautiful. Laughing, as he threw a stick for the dog.

She moved towards the boy. He saw her and stopped. Unlike his peers he was innocent, knew the principle of the thing, but a virgin nonetheless. Harriet's lightly tanned body in a small green bikini was ripe and firm—a body that would confuse most men—a body that taunted as it strained the pieces of material. Her dark hair was coiled on top of her head, and brown eyes gazed back at him in appreciation.

Taking control, she walked up to the boy, hand outstretched. 'Harriet, known as Harrie, from *Sorcerer*.'

The boy blushed as his swimming trunks bulged. 'I'm Paul, from *Green Flash*,' he responded.

Harrie, seeing his erection and his embarrassment, took pity on him. 'Let's sit down in the shade, I'm not acclimatised yet.'

He sat on a log, part of the beach furniture Roger had dragged there.

Harrie felt stirred by Paul's youth. She was surprised at the strong pull she felt towards this near-man so different from her usual sophisticated male companions. She let her eyes dwell on him, and then suddenly became aware that her breasts felt heavy, and there was a distinct aching warmth in her crotch. *What now?* she wondered. 'Are you at Uni? Tell me about yourself.' Another surprise, she found she really wanted to know.

'I left school a few weeks ago. My A grades should be fine, and I've applied to Trinity in London.'

'Ah, music,' breathed Harrie.

'Yes,' Paul became more animated as he talked of his music. 'Violin is my first instrument, and I play piano, of course. I also love jazz. When Dad and I fell out a few months ago, he withheld funds—he controls me that way. Sorry, I shouldn't have said that. Well anyway, I'm sort of living with Claire, Aunt Claire really, Mum's sister. Sometimes I busk with three friends at Hays Galleria, which is quite close to her flat. We earn a lot of money.'

'Wonderful!' Harrie said warmly. 'But what is Hays Galleria? I've heard of it but can't think where it is.'

'Not my sort of place really,' said Paul. 'It's an old wharf on the river, just west of Tower Bridge. It's been reconstructed as an up-market shopping area with *cafés* and bars around it. Lots of small stands in the centre with arty-type goods for sale, a bit like Covent Garden, but less expensive. We played there at lunchtimes and sometimes during the early evening. On one occasion, the others were busy, so I took my violin and played popular sort of stuff. Claire, who is great fun, came along as moral support. She took the hat round! And I earned a lot more than Dad ever gave me.' Paul grinned, displaying white teeth, just a tiny bit crooked in front—but that added to his appeal. 'Gosh! You're so easy to talk to.'

You wouldn't say that if you knew what I'm thinking. Isn't life just full of surprises!

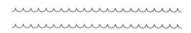

After giving Harriet and George a couple of days to settle in, it was time for their welcome party. The cruising community grew larger and got to know each other better so the shore events became more relaxed and friendly. During the beach parties especially, the younger element tended to group together, apart from Daz, who had a foot in both camps! Frances had long, deep conversations with George. As scientists they formed the more serious part of the gathering. Paul always found an easy companion in Daz, but throughout the whole evening, he watched Harriet. He felt electrically charged, with equal quantities of adrenaline and testosterone buzzing through his confused frame. The evening was pleasantly sociable, but it was unusually early after an extremely hot day when the participants drifted back to their boats, ready for sleep.

Prue was already much stronger. Erika's TLC had worked wonders and she was certainly glad to be away from James. Sven, for his part, found that his wife seemed happy and relaxed in such a caring role, and this spin-off effect ensured that *Packet of Dreams* was a happy boat!

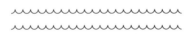

After just a few hours of being together on *Sorcerer*, Harriet and James were at loggerheads. It was she who turned angrily to her father. 'I'm thirty-eight years old, James. Don't correct or patronise me. I have a successful career, and am independent. Mum is far better off where she is so perhaps you and I can share the chores on this boat.'

James paled almost visibly. 'I can't cook. Not at all,' he confessed.

'Yes, I know. You've been spoilt by Mum since forever. I'll teach you to cook, just basic stuff. How about that?'

'Well all right then, just until your mother gets well.'

Harriet restrained herself from further comment. She felt that for the moment, enough ground had been made!

George felt a little lonely at the beginning, but as soon as he became more friendly with the other cruisers, his social skills grew. He enjoyed his time looking after *Ducky Do,* with Dog now his constant companion. He and Frances started to spend long hours together, arguing and hypothesising in the manner of young people, and they were both surprised at this turn of events. So unexpected!

Adam and Eva enjoyed having their offspring on board. Sometimes they even spent whole days together. It was reminiscent of old school holidays, only better.

Daz and Henry invited them all on board *Wild Foxes* for a short cruise round the island. 'It's easier to take the cat,' Henry told everyone. 'Bags of room. You can have the family cabin and the double cabin in the port hull, and there are two heads there so you'll be self-contained. Daz and I are in the starboard hull.' Then he added, almost as an afterthought, 'Why don't we invite Harriet and George too?'

The eight of them had a riotous time! Dog was invited along and being so close to Daz, he seemed to be in doggy heaven. When they went on shore, he fiercely guarded the whole boat, tearing up and down the decks barking hysterically when a dinghy strayed too close. The sleeping arrangements alone were fun. George and Paul slept in the forward space of the huge family cabin with cylindrical fenders separating them from Harriet and Frances, who slept in the remaining part of the double bunk. The four of them shared a bathroom. Adam and Eva occupied another double cabin, a few steps down from the main saloon. They too had their own bathroom.

They sailed by day, and when they found a good anchorage, stayed for twenty-four hours or so, swimming, snorkelling and sunbathing. In the evenings they played cards, danced, told stories and drank too much rum punch! On one such evening the younger group went on shore to a club. Henry hated it but knew he had to trust them and to let Daz go occasionally.

By pre-arrangement, the clubbers waited down on the jetty and were collected by Henry at 0100. The rum had taken its toll. Giggling and hanging onto each other, he ordered them to sit deep in the tender. He didn't trust their balance and there was certainly no commonsense around. One at a time, he helped each of them onto the cat and Adam hauled them up from the platform. The last one up was Paul and, perhaps inevitably, he lost his balance and fell into the water. Henry grabbed him by the collar as he came up, spluttering and gasping for air. The others, looking down, howled with laughter. Henry and Adam knew how dangerous it was to be drunk on deck so they shepherded the revellers below decks as quickly as possible. For at least another forty minutes after retiring, laughter, singing, and young voices were heard, until the excesses of the evening claimed them in sleep.

Next day, they all felt ill until late afternoon, resulting in amusement—and eventually sympathy from the others—even Henry, who said to Daz, 'Who am I to judge! I've been there too many times, my love. Tomorrow is another day after all.'

It had been a great week, but they decided to return to Hog. Adam and Eva didn't entirely trust leaving their yacht in the care of Dicky Bones. He kept himself in little luxuries, his words, by boat minding while the owners returned to their homes. Known as Tricky Dicky, he was thought to be light-fingered, though nothing was ever proved. Daz couldn't help remarking that it was a pity Dicky's little luxuries didn't extend to soap!

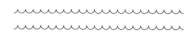

Harriet found a tiny cove, facing out to sea—a little beach sheltered by palm trees. She had packed a dry bag with a book, bottled water, an apple, and sunscreen. With this strapped to her back, she swam over the reef and round the corner of the island, hoping to find just such a place.

Paul was snorkelling over the reef, having swum there from behind the island. He spotted Harriet and swam towards her. As he grew nearer, he shouted out, 'May I join you?'

'Please do,' came the reply.

He walked out of the water, high stepping in an ungainly way with the flippers still attached to his feet. He looked ridiculous, and by the time he reached the beach, Harriet was grinning broadly. 'I never thought to take them off before walking,' he said. He sat himself on a log. 'Pretty reefs out there but nothing different, really.'

'How's it going?' she asked, closing her book.

'Good. Harrie, can I ask you something?'

'Fire away.'

'What are your parents like?'

'Well,' Harriet paused, thoughtfully. 'Mum is great, but to her detriment, non-assertive. We meet in town sometimes to do an art gallery or a film. Dad is well-meaning enough on one level, but a total control freak who believes a woman's place is one of servitude. Of course, we don't see eye to eye because of that. I haven't lived at home since I was eighteen. How about yours?'

Paul gave his answer quickly. 'Mum and Dad are the best. They've been married for at least twenty years now and are still wrapped up in each other, happiest when they are together, like now.'

'That's good. So is there a problem?'

'Well, it's not always so good for me because sometimes I need to discuss things or to talk. But they are both so pre-occupied they are a bit out of touch.'

Lord, thought Harriet, *I could be his mother. But taking the role of loco parentis is not so appealing!* 'Can I help?' she asked.

Paul blushed. 'No, it's okay really.'

Mmm, thought Harriet. She felt moved by this boy, remembering him from their first meeting, and smiled at him. 'Paul, would you mind putting some sunscreen on my back?'

Paul nodded and took the oil from her. As soon as he touched her, he had an erection.

Of course, Harriet was not unaware of it. She too was aroused by his touch. She reached up, took Paul's hand and pulled him down. 'Kiss me.'

Paul held her head and kissed her hard, ramming his tongue deep into her mouth.

Oh God, no. He kisses like he's cleaning my teeth— no, my whole mouth, it's awful. What can I say without offending him? She pulled away and said gently, 'Paul, have you kissed a girl before?'

'Of course,' he replied. 'At a Christmas party . . . was it all right?'

Oh, Harriet told herself. *This boy is so ready*. But aloud she said, 'Paul, I want to tell you something about women that you'll never forget. The senses of a highly sexual woman are tuned to very sensitive vibrations.' She continued, as she touched his face. 'Start off gently.' She demonstrated this by kissing him softly, her full lips slightly open, brushing his mouth with hers. Then she leaned back a little and drew a finger slowly across his mouth. Paul groaned. Harriet continued in a low voice, now husky with arousal. 'Tease me with your tongue but whatever you do with it, wherever you use it, be subtle.' She kissed him again, letting her tongue briefly tease his. 'Yes, that's delicious. You have a sexy mouth.'

The kiss became deeper as their mouths merged, their breath as one, and both became breathless with excitement.

Harriet drew back and stood up, unhooking her bikini top and stepping out of the pants. She stood there looking at him, her tanned body gleaming with oil, the white bikini parts, tempting and inviting. Paul gasped as Harriet knelt down and carefully eased off his boxers shorts. Then she lay down beside him, took his hands and guided them to her body.

'Look, Paul! See! Feel my nipples—gently, with your lips now. They're so sensitive. Oh yes, that's it. That's so good.' Her hands stroked his back, his buttocks, ever more urgently, and when he groaned again, she guided him inside her.

Paul gave one thrust . . . and came!

'Don't worry,' she reassured him. 'Each time will be better. We'll make love again soon. You have a great body and your hands, your wonderful fingers, will play me. As a musician, you will be a fantastic lover.' Her hands stroked his head and gently tugged his hair. She massaged and stroked his body, her fingertips seeking out and finding responses he didn't know were possible. She scratched his bottom, oh so lightly, and Paul was ready again.

Ah, youth, she thought, marvelling at his quick recovery. Then all real thought ceased as she enjoyed what he was doing, mirroring the way she had touched him. She moaned and let her body move. She took Paul's hands and let him explore her breasts and feel her now erect nipples, her stomach, and finally her outer lips and the moistness within. 'Oh yes,' breathed Harriet. 'I want you inside me now.'

Paul was there, inside her and moving sweetly, with Harriet moving in response.

It didn't take long, but this time—moving in harmony, she felt his strength and how he filled her—and she called to him, letting him be aware of her pleasure. 'Now, Paul. Oh now.'

Paul gave a joyful shout and came too, in this, his second coupling with a woman. They lay together, still joined until he subsided. Then they drifted off to sleep in the warm sunshine, shielded by the trees.

Harriet stirred first and looked at the beautiful young man beside her. She kissed his shoulder, and he opened an eye. 'C'mon lazy bones. Let's have a swim'.

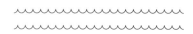

'Eva, there are problems in London. I'm afraid I'll have to fly home for a week or so.'

'Okay. Bring back some decent English marmalade, will you?'

'Oh, *sorry you're going, darling,* or *I'll miss you, Adam,* would be nice.'

An edge to his laughing tone snapped Eva to attention.

'Of course I'll miss you, darling. I'd come with you if the children were not here.'

Adam, feathers smoothed, held her in a hug. 'Children? They haven't been that for years. Seriously Eva, do you think our boy is no longer a virgin?'

'Definitely! I think Harriet has grown him up. From a woman's perspective that's good. All young men need an older woman to show them what's where and how.'

'Yes, sweetheart, you're right as usual. I remember as a young man being like a bull in a china shop. Poor girls, I was rough and fumbling. I honestly thought, if indeed I thought at all, that girls' clitty bits needed to be wanked like a boy's dick.' Reminiscing, he grinned wryly.

Eva looked a bit shocked at the revelation. 'Dirty talk so early in the day?'

'What a prissy missy!' Then as Eva rubbed up against him kneading his bottom, he said, 'Oh, okay, maybe not so prissy. Anyway, I like Harriet—it won't last, but I agree it's a terrific start for Paul. She is, how can I put it, such a modern woman. Back to business though. Will you be okay here?'

'Don't worry, Daz and Henry are close by. And Prue is with Erika and Sven—what a lovely person she is. Then there's George, Harriet, Paul, and Frances, so I won't be lonely.'

'Well, watch out for George. He looks about ripe for an adventure.'

'Oh no, darling. George is interested in Frances and she in him.'

'Really?' Adam was genuinely surprised. 'You are truly amazing. You pick up such a lot, intuitively.'

'Yes, I'm a woman! But please Adam, bring back some tasty marmalade. The overly sweet stuff we get here is the pits. Adding lime juice to it just doesn't quite do it. It's all in the peel I suppose.'

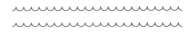

By now the number of cruisers had dwindled. Freddy, Lily and Adam were all due back at the end of the month, and now James had left too. He had given a weak excuse about needing some boat bits he'd seen in St Vincent.

'The only boat bits he's spotted,' said Eva quietly to Erika, 'are bosomy, plump, black, and about eighteen-years-old.'

Erika agreed. 'Yes, he's a pig of a man. I'm glad Prue is safe with us. And Harriet is so competent. She'll be fine on her own.'

'On her own? Not for long, I'll bet,' retorted Eva. 'Our boy and Harriet are, well…'

'Really? That's amazing. Do you mind?'

'Not at all,' replied Eva. 'Adam and I think it's the best thing for Paul!'

True enough, Paul was seen swimming over to *Sorcerer* daily. Or Harriet collected him to go on shore. After a few more days, he was away overnight.

Eva heard him climbing on board at dawn. Over breakfast and unusually serious, she addressed her son. 'Paul, you're an adult. What you choose to do, within reason, is fine. But do me the courtesy of telling me if you are away overnight. That's the rule at home, and here on a boat, it's even more important. What would happen if a storm blew in, and I didn't know where you were?'

'Sorry, Mum, point taken.'

'Tell you what Paul, here is a clothes peg. Put it in your pocket when you leave the boat, and then clip it onto the spice rack when you return. Easy. Then I'll know whether you're here or not.

'Mum, you're unreal, a total fruitcake.' Paul laughed so hard he didn't see Frances appear, scratching her head, and yawning.

'What's up? So much noise.'

Paul relayed the gist of events to his sister who shook her head in disbelief.

'A clothes peg? Okay then, perhaps I'd better have one too, pink for me, blue for Paul.' They both fell about, laughing.

'I don't think it's so funny,' said Eva crossly. 'And anyway, why d'you need a clothes peg too?'

'Just keeping my options open—sauce for the goose and all that! Why can't we leave notes like any normal family? But clothes pegs? Pur-lease Mum…!'

Chapter 22

Alone at home, home alone. *This is great!* For two days Eva enjoyed her own company, and Frances joined her for dinner. Paul had vanished! On day three, she called Erika and invited her and Prue over for lunch.

Eva lowered the more substantial swimming steps, and Prue managed to climb on board, carefully but unaided. 'You look marvellous.' Eva greeted Prue warmly. 'Welcome on board!'

Erika's strong, tanned body then appeared over the guard rail. She looked happy and relaxed. 'Thanks for this invite, Eva. Sometimes it's just great to be with other women.'

They all agreed, and Eva asked if Prue had heard from James.

'No, I haven't. And do you know, I'm quite happy about that. You two have been such good friends, I'd like to tell you a little of my plans.'

Eva nodded encouragingly. Erika nodded too but looked a bit startled.

'Well, it all started in Barbados. During my recovery programme, some of the locals, chiefly the well-named Treasure and her friends, formed the strong support group for the book club I started. To cut a long story short, I've been invited to live over there and teach adult education in literature and creative writing. Some of the Bajans, and ex-pat Brits living there, want to study—maybe do a sort of Arts Foundation. I'm so excited. The invitation came by email only this morning.'

'That's brilliant, Prue. What a plan, gosh that's amazing, well done!' Eva said.

Erika was shocked but managed to gather her wits quickly. 'I agree with Eva. That's fantastic news.' She touched Prue's arm lightly as she spoke.

'This calls for Champagne,' declared Eva, rushing off to get a bottle from its cold storage in the bilges. 'Could be cooler—freezer boost for fifteen minutes I reckon.'

'You are all so kind to me.' Prue was moved by the response of her friends. 'I've never experienced such warmth as here in the Caribbean. It must be the sunshine.'

'How about, it's *you*,' Erika countered firmly. 'You are a wonderful, warm woman. Everyone who meets you loves you. You have everything. You are in fact an awesome person.'

Prue blushed. 'You Americans, always so effusive and overstated. But thank you both so much.'

'To Friendship! Wonderful women! Personal Success!' they toasted.

By the end of their meal, the three women had sorted out world events and illuminated the meaning of life in general.

'Where are Daz and Henry?' Prue asked Eva.

'Gone on shore again. They tell me it's golf, then it's buying fine rum, then it's learning the Tin Pan. Now I hear they are planning to do week-long workshops in salsa and learning local dance—a sort of Caribbean Dirty Dancing, I expect.'

'Well Daz certainly keeps Henry young,' observed Prue. 'And they obviously adore each other.'

Eva smiled to herself, nursing a secret so deep and personal, she could only nod in affirmation!

~~~~~~~~~~~~~~~~~~~~~~
~~~~~~~~~~~~~~~~~~~~~~

Feeling very mellow, Erika suggested to Prue and Eva that they all take a stroll on shore. She was very aware that Prue needed gentle exercise to regain her strength. Her scars were terrible but totally healed now. What had not healed was the mental scarring from many years of abuse at home.

If she really did move to Barbados, what a fantastic step that would be for boosting her confidence, Erika affirmed to herself.

I'll take a rain check, thanks,' Eva told them. 'I'm reading such a good book.'

'What's that, Eva?' Prue always seemed to be interested in bookish matters.

'Well, you know the book on grammar, *Eats, Shoots & Leaves*?'

Prue nodded.

'Well, this is a parody on it. It's called *Eats, Shites & Leaves*. It's hilarious, in a literary sort of way. I'll lend it to you when I've finished it, if you like. I think you'll love it.'

Following hugs all round, Prue and Erika took their leave, and climbed into the dinghy.

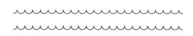

'I've a rug here, Prue. Shall we have a little siesta on shore and then a walk?'

Prue readily agreed. She needed to rest, her stamina still being low, and she liked the way this strong and warm American woman recognised her weakness without talking about it.

Erika rowed them to the shore and, after helping Prue out of the dinghy, spread the rug under the trees. As they stretched out, side by side, Erika spoke. 'Prue, tell me about that book, *Eats, Shoots & Leaves*. What is it?'

Prue laughed, but in her gentle way. 'Now you've got me. How can I explain a book on precise English grammar? Perhaps it would be easier if I show you the book—I found a copy in Barbados, and my group loved it! Must sleep now, Erika. So tired.' She took Erika's hand and squeezed it lightly.

Erika responded, and her hand stayed, holding Prue's as they both drifted into sleep.

About half an hour later they wakened, and Erika rolled up the rug. Taking a bottle of water, now warm, from the dinghy, she led the way on a path through the trees. After about fifteen minutes, Prue admitted her legs were aching.

'Let's stop here,' suggested Erika. 'Why not sit on this tree stump, and I'll massage them.'

Under her gentle fingers, the recently traumatised muscles relaxed, and Prue felt they could continue. She was still sitting there when Erika heard a rustle. She looked through the foliage and caught her breath, George and Frances were making love! Two young, naked bodies, entwined, deeply inside each other, moving slowly, and with tenderness.

Erika was stirred. 'Come here, Prue,' she whispered.

Prue joined her . . . and gasped. 'Wow, that's truly awesome,' she breathed, lapsing into an Americanism.

As they watched them, Erika put her arm round Prue who leaned into her. She stroked Prue's shoulders gently. 'So bruised, my poor sweet.'

Prue turned to look at Erika, surprised at her words. Erika stroked her face gently. She smoothed the hair back from her forehead in a gesture reminiscent of a mother soothing a sick child. Her fingers moved over Prue's face—tracing the curve of hairline, cheeks, jaw, then softly over her lips. Prue was mesmerised. She couldn't move. Emotions never before known were surging through her.

'Such a beautiful person,' Erika murmured as she tipped up Prue's chin and softly kissed her.

Prue's reaction, after her initial shock, was *yes*! Her arms crept round Erika, and they were locked together in a deep embrace. Erika took her lips away from Prue's, and gently deposited soft kisses round her neck and breasts. Prue gasped again as Erika gently pulled her down to the ground, carpeted with soft fallen foliage, and worshipped her body. She undid the shirt buttons and eased down her swimsuit, sliding it over her hips. Her hands caressed, her mouth kissed and nibbled gently, her tongue licked softly, and she went down on Prue.

'Oh God! Oh that's amazing!' Prue was loving it, no longer able to think, just loving it!

As Erika's magic moved over her, Prue's body started moving. 'Yes, my sweet, that's it. Move into my hands, into my mouth.' Erika sucked and licked, nibbled and kissed, always gentle and slow.

Prue moaned, a long, slow moan that encompassed her life and lack of love. Her recognition of tenderness, hitherto not experienced, heightened her pleasure. Her hips bucked as Erika guided her to a most fabulous orgasm and then held her close.

They lay for a long while. Prue cried and Erika soothed her. Gradually the tears stopped, and quietly, Prue told of her humiliation and degradation over the years. She told of her role-playing—Miss Blossom, stern teacher with her cane, and Lotus Blossom, gentle acquiescent female seeking only to please. Both roles always designed to give James pleasure. 'I've never been made love to . . . until now,' she whispered.

'Just fucked, eh?' enquired Erika, who by now was feeling savage towards James. Controlling herself, she said, 'You are moving on, sweet Prue, leaving the awful past behind. Your future is bright and your skills are within you.'

'Thanks Erika. You make me feel good about myself. That's a first. Now I don't even feel embarrassed at having a sexual encounter with a woman! Are you a lesbian?'

'No, darling, I'm bi. Shall we have a swim?' She helped Prue to her feet, and they walked to a deserted part of the beach. Taking off all their clothes, they walked into the warm sea, Prue revelling in her new-found freedom and sense of self worth.

Over the next few days, Prue started to remove her possessions from *Sorcerer* and arranged to meet her daughter—no mean feat as Harriet was always elsewhere!

~~~~~~~~~~~~~~~~~~~~~~~~~~
~~~~~~~~~~~~~~~~~~~~~~~

On the agreed date they got together for lunch. After a couple of glasses of wine, she told Harriet that she had accepted a teaching post in Barbados. She would be settling into a small house in October, and the job would start the following January.

Harriet was thrilled for her mother and spoke warmly. 'Mum, that's marvellous. I'm so glad you're getting out of this situation.' Her arm swept round, taking the whole boat into her words. 'Tell me all. Where will you live? What are you teaching? May I visit?'

Prue had always revered this talented and successful daughter who was now, to her surprise, addressing her as an equal. She told her of the offer and where she would live. 'And you will always be welcome to join me, Harrie, wherever I am.'

Harriet hugged her mother tightly. 'Look, I'll get your things from home and bring them to you.'

'Thank you, darling, only my personal things— books, photos, letters. No clothes. I'm turning my life around!'

Harriet looked at the woman in her mother. *Something's changed. She stands taller, with more confidence. There was even a sparkle about her.*

'There's something else,' added Prue. 'I'd like to remove the rest of my things from the boat as soon as possible. Erika and Sven have invited me to move into the aft cabin on *Dreams*. They even said they'd sail me to Barbados and see me settled into my new home.'

Over the next two hours, mother and daughter downed a bottle of wine, and became re-acquainted! Eventually Harriet brought up the subject of money, but Prue was adamant she wanted nothing from her husband or the family home.

'But Mum, you're entitled to money from James. Of course I don't know details but I know he is a horror. Actually, I loathe him!'

They both looked shocked at this announcement.

'Oh dear, *in vino veritas!*' Harrie added.

'Harriet, I don't want anything to do with him—no money, nothing.'

Her daughter responded. 'Okay, Mum, I'll respect that.' But she told herself that she would work on her father to make a legal settlement on Prue, without her knowing. Not now, but sometime in the future.

During his week in London, Adam contacted Eva and asked her to book them into one of the pleasant small hotels on shore and arrange a taxi to meet his flight. This she did, and the taxi delivered him to the hotel.

There were two shower cubicles in their room, equipped American-style for a whole family. Eva was already having a shower. She didn't hear him come into the room. He dropped his clothes and went into the other shower.

She came out just ahead of him and, with a mischievous smile and wearing just a towel, walked slowly towards him, stopping just in front. 'I missed you.'

Adam stretched out his hand and pulled her towel so it dropped to the floor. She mirrored his action. There was a brief pause, and then they were locked in a passionate, un-tender kiss as she tightened her arms round his neck and lightly lifted herself so her legs could wind around his waist. He was ready for her, as she knew he would be, so she lowered herself onto him. They both gasped with the intensity of their desire, and his legs felt weak as he walked her over to the bed with her moving on him. There was no subtlety when they reached the bed still coupled. His deep, strong thrusts made her moan with pleasure, and as he swelled more, her legs achieved a lightness, her feet on his back, her pelvis answering with urgency.

'Oh fuck me harder, harder,' she gasped. She dug her fingers into his back as her body bucked.

Adam felt himself squeezed as he pulsated and his breath was let out in a great shout. They lay together in the afterglow, looked at each other, and started laughing.

'That's quite some reunion,' he said.

They snuggled together and slept.

A little time later, Adam woke. He rolled over and let his eyes rest on Eva's naked, mature beauty as she lay on her back, still asleep. Her dark hair, slightly flecked with grey, looked wild but her lips looked innocent and were softly parted. His gaze rested on her breasts, not large but wonderfully alive. His hand moved towards her but then he controlled his need to touch. *Not just yet.* As if in defiance he swelled—a part of him almost of independent brain, aware that control did not feature in the appreciation of the possibilities! His eyes travelled over her rib cage, over her rounded belly, and lingered on the mons, still a little damp on its curly exterior . . . almost like dew. Rounded but taut thighs were the start of legs that seemed to go on forever, and he felt himself twitch as he remembered those legs wrapped round his body.

Adam rose to kneel at the side of the bed. Their coupling had been so fast they had hardly moved from their position of landing, he noted with a smile. He breathed on her feet, and gently sucked her big toe—one, then the other, sucking, sucking ... Eva stirred and sighed. Softly, he licked his way up her legs, lightly flicking his tongue on the underside of her knees—one, and then the other. The tongue lazily licked and flicked up the inside of her thighs and Eva, wide awake now, sighed again. Adam suddenly realised he could taste himself on her. Recognisable! Strange! As his senses absorbed this, he became very stimulated and his tongue explored her moistness. He teased her tiny pink pearl with his lips and she swelled in response. Eva groaned deeply, as if the sound was dragged out of her. She shuddered and cried out again, her legs opening, pelvis rocking.

Softly he sucked and rolled her with his tongue until, sensing she was beyond control, he thrust his tongue strongly into her. Eva's orgasm went on and on. He stayed there, holding her, breathing in her sex until her movements ceased.

Her hand stroked his head, and she relaxed. Adam moved up her body, his own need urgent now. His hands touched her breasts, the nipples instantly aroused as he nibbled and sucked them until she was once again ready for him. His mouth moved up to hers, and they kissed. 'I missed you, my love,' breathed Adam, without taking his mouth away.

Now her tongue was teasing his, mimicking his recent moves, gently catching *his* tongue with her teeth, softly, and with her lips, sucking. Her body started moving against him, undulating, touching, rubbing, then moving away. Without hurry, Adam grabbed a pillow and pushed it under her buttocks, raising her higher so he was able to reach her G spot with each thrust. Eva's fingertips softly scratched down his arms, into his head, over his bottom as his powerful strokes reached her, and then she quivered from head to feet with another voluptuous climax. Adam joined her as he felt and heard her pleasure, his deeper moan echoing hers as he finally released in a series of powerful comings. They stayed wrapped round each other, inside each other, lips close together, whispering their love, holding, loving, spent—as sleep overtook them.

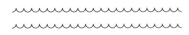

The anchorage was now almost full. It could never be overcrowded as the amount of anchor chain needed to swing safely kept the number of yachts to a minimum.

Margreet and Warner arrived, and those on the few boats left at the anchorage welcomed them in the traditional fashion. Then suddenly everyone was back at the anchorage, except James.

Lily took up residence on *Ducky Do,* and immediately she and George formed an attitude of restraint with each other, both being slightly embarrassed at the change in their roles on the boat.

Sven, Erika and Prue were, by their own admission, amazed at the development of events, but each in their way seemingly content to continue as they now were.

Daz and Henry had stopped wandering on shore and were once more at Hog Island, socialising with the other cruisers.

Adam had returned from the UK, and after their brief sojourn on shore, he and Eva were back on the boat. In triumph, he produced four pots of the best British marmalade, and the family was even reunited for breakfast!

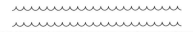

Paul was seldom on *Green Flash* these days as he and Harriet, completely engrossed in each other, spent most of their loving time on *Sorcerer*. It was, therefore, a shock to their summer idyll when an email arrived from James. He would be back in two days!

'Well, it took three weeks for him to buy boat bits . . . fancy that!' said Harrie.

Paul hadn't ever heard Harrie in deep sarcasm mode, and it chilled him.

Oh grow up, he told himself. His perspective had been altered in the last few weeks, and from a young man's point of view, both idealistic and romantic, he wondered why life couldn't just be full of love! 'Why do you dislike him so much?' he enquired.

'It's a long and not very pretty story. But he is a bully, especially to Mum, and he is so far up his own rectum, he's lost the light.'

Paul had enjoyed some marvellous talks with Prue and could only go along with her daughter's feelings on the subject. Anyone who could hurt Prue wasn't worth anything, he acknowledged. Putting his arm round Harrie, he nodded his understanding and support.

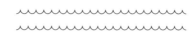

Dog was having the time of his life! He spent his Happy Hour digging. He had discovered that if he dug into the sand or in the woods, all sorts of tiny creatures would emerge, and try to scuttle away. Some he ate and some he tortured with his nose and paws, but none of this mattered if children appeared! Then Dog and the children ran through the wood, he chased sticks and enjoyed games with them. Never before having experienced this type of interaction with humans, big or small, he loved it. Sometimes they took him out on their rafts, but during the day he got too hot and had to jump into the water and swim for shore. This happened so often Roger kept a large can of water in the shade for him.

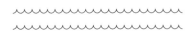

One evening, Freddy and Lily had been having a stroll, while Dog was appreciating and checking out the trees. Shortly before reaching Roger's bar, they met Eva and Adam, walking from another direction. They fell into step and chatted. Soon they were sitting on logs drinking chilled beer. Beside them, Dog was stretched out, twitching in the manner of sleeping dogs. A hurricane lamp threw a soft glow over the whole.

Adam and Lily were soon deep in conversation, exchanging information about their favourite haunts in Paris. Freddy and Eva talked about Namibia—how to teach villagers to plant and market paprika and how best to use the natural resources of the land. Then they fell silent, an easy silence.

Freddy became aware of an increasing warmth against his chest. 'Oh, there you are,' he acknowledged quietly. He reached into his breast pocket and took out the Talisman, handing it to Eva in a simple wordless gesture. She took it and looked at Freddy. She must have seen the strange expression on his face—mouth soft, eyes bright, but above all, a look of vulnerability.

'It's too dark, Freddy. I can't see much. But it has a wonderful feel. It's cool, yet warm, all at the same time. This sounds ridiculous but it feels sort of alive!'

Freddy reached over and picked up the hurricane lamp, throwing its light onto the Talisman.

Eva appeared enchanted when she saw the painting and read the label.

'Oh, Freddy. This feels amazing. It has its own energy. How did you get it?'

'Well, many weeks ago I met Erika and Sven in Dominica. Erika gave me the Talisman and, truly, I believe it has somehow brought about huge changes in my life. I wrote to the Russian girl, Svetlana, and I shall meet her when we visit Europe. Lily and I are planning a trip together. But will you be the one to take it now, Eva?'

'How exciting! I'd love to be involved. What a wonderful story.' Eva was totally caught up in the thrill of the moment. In fact, they both were so engrossed in their exchange, they didn't notice that Lily and Adam had stopped talking and were sitting quietly, listening to the story as it unfolded.

Lily produced a camera. 'Let me take a photo of you with the Talisman, Eva. I've been here before, when Freddy needed a photo to send Lana.'

'Just a minute, I've had an idea.' Freddy called out to Roger. 'Hey, man, would you mind taking a photo of us all?'

Roger ambled over, springing on his toes, rolling his shoulders up and down in cool Rastafarian style. With a big grin, he took the camera from Lily. 'Sure, folks. No worries.'

Freddy continued to talk, but now to the whole group. 'Lana loves to hear what is going on with her Talisman and tells me she has created a large portfolio of photos and emails from those who have guarded it. It has travelled from Russia to London, then to the Canaries, and across the Atlantic. Now it is here with us.'

Freddy spread his hand out, expressively. 'Truly, my life has changed. First I met Lily, then I had this precious object in my care, and that led me to Lana.'

'Freddy, thank you so much.' Eva was overcome with emotion. After a few seconds she continued. 'I feel privileged you have entrusted it to me.'

'Who better?' Freddy smiled warmly. 'Enjoy it, Eva!'

Chapter 23

Harriet met her father's domestic LIAT flight from St Vincent and brought him back to the boat.

'Where's your mother? I would have thought she'd be back by now.'

'She's with Sven and Erika. In fact, she has moved onto their boat.'

'*Ménage a trois*, eh? We'll see about that.'

Harriet deflected him by suggesting he have a drink with her. Later they could go on shore to join the reunion evening now that everyone was back at Hog. For herself, she could hardly wait to get her hands on Paul and wanted to plan how they could slope off into the woods, just the two of them. She couldn't get enough of him, and it was a joy to listen to his idealistic views of life, his fresh approach to everything, his humanity—but above all, she had to admit, his undiluted adoration of her!

It was to be a huge feast. Roger wanted to do a pig roast as he had just invested in the equipment and was keen to try it out. His idea was that offering a pig roast would be appropriate for Hog Island! The cruisers supplied the meat and fuel. Sven, having been a guest at many pig roasts in the US, was able to guide him, which he did with enormous tact. All the accompanying salads, potatoes, cheeses, and desserts were brought on shore, plus a quantity of beer and wine. Henry prepared his famously wicked rum punch, and Roger was invited to a tasting, prior to the party. He was also invited to join them for the evening.

'A Hog Island reunion without you just wouldn't be right,' Eva told him.

Harriet had been collected by Adam, Eva and Paul, leaving James to dinghy to shore when he was ready. He arrived late and clearly had been drinking. The group welcomed him warmly, and Prue went up to him for a perfunctory kiss on the cheek. She looked healthy and had the glow of a woman who knows she has value. Her light tan was complemented by a peach-coloured sarong that suited her complexion.

'You look well, Prue—well enough to come back on *Sorcerer?*'

'I'm not coming back, James,' Prue said quietly.

James absorbed her words, while a red fury started to suffuse his neck and face. 'Not coming back, Prue? What on earth do you mean?'

His raised voice was ugly, and everyone looked round to see the source of such aggression. In an instant, Erika went to stand by Prue, and Harriet moved to her other side. Prue had paled and shrunk a little. Sensing her fear, born of habit, Erika took her hand.

Observing this, James stood and stared, his mouth open. Then the vitriol started. 'So that's how it is. You prefer a woman. You dirty little lesbo. You like being fucked by a woman.' His voice slurred. 'I was right. I always thought you were frigid.'

The whole group stood aghast, in absolute horror. It was like a stage set. James with his back to the sea; Prue flanked by Erika and Harriet facing him, and the whole cruising community from the island in a semi-circle behind them. The only sound was the sizzling of the pig.

'No, not exactly,' said Prue bravely, standing her ground. 'I just don't want to be with you any more.'

'She has moved in with us. We are looking after Prue now.' Erika faced James, seemingly unfazed by his fury.

'Yeah, yeah,' he sneered. 'So this is my repayment. I look after you and support you all these years, and you leave me for—a woman!'

Sven made to move forward but Eva caught his arm, saying quietly, 'No, Sven, that will inflame him more, and he's out of control already.'

'I think you had your money's worth, James,' Prue answered. 'I've been invited to take up a teaching post where I can be a real Miss Blossom, without the degradation.'

'With your lesbian doxy, I suppose? How dare you humiliate me.' James' hand grabbed her arm viciously, painfully, and with all his force he struck Prue's face. She crumpled.

Erika reacted like a tigress protecting her young. 'You disgusting, perverted bully. You've abused Prue since forever,' she yelled at him. 'You evil, repulsive fat-carrier, parading your tart while your wife suffered in hospital.' In a flash she hit him—a smoothly controlled upper cut to the jaw—powered by perfectly toned muscles and a hatred so pure that it worked!

James fell, blood pouring from his face. He lay there, unattended.

Erika dropped to her friend and took her bruised head onto her lap. A teeshirt soaked in salt water was handed to her, and this she placed gently on Prue's face. She had passed out, fortunately, unaware of the rest of the drama. Harriet and the others, who had never met Trixie, were shocked at the revelation as well as the violence. Paul put his arms round Harriet and sat her on the ground, holding her shaking body tightly.

Henry and Adam grabbed James by the arms and dragged him to the water's edge where Roger was already revving the engine on his big tender. They hauled James' deadweight into the boat, assisted by Warner who had joined them. The boat then roared off towards *Sorcerer* where the four men dumped him, unceremoniously, into the cockpit.

'That should cool him off a bit. His dinghy is on shore and that's where it will stay,' Adam commented.

'It may even develop a terminal leak,' added Henry. Then he shook his head. 'Repulsive fat-carrier indeed! And wow, what a punch! Quite a woman that Erika!'

They motored back to shore and carefully carried Prue to the Island Packet, this time in Roger's boat.

Sven's only comment was one of admiration as he helped support Prue to her cabin. He looked at his wife. 'Erika, you are awesome, just awesome!'

Erika blushed and simply nodded. She cared for Prue, giving her homœopathic arnica and putting her to bed, carefully anointing her swollen face with the pulp from her potted aloe vera, then gently holding her through the night.

Well before daybreak the next morning, Paul rowed Harriet to *Sorcerer* in his parents' dinghy. Quietly they boarded, removed Harriet's few belongings, and slipped away. Following events of the previous evening, Adam and Eva had offered Harriet a berth on their boat. Of course, they knew the berth itself would not be used much. They approved their son's first passion and recognised Harriet as an interesting and sophisticated woman. They agreed he couldn't do better for his initiation in the fine art of love—though Adam insisted to Eva it was more a baptism of fire!

Shortly after dawn James and *Sorcerer* disappeared, the inexplicably damaged dinghy, half submerged, was still attached to its kedge anchor in the shallows!

A week later, Prue's bruises and shock were fading. The small community returned to normal, though the previous feelings of peace and wellbeing had been shattered.

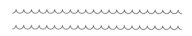

Everyone felt uplifted when Freddy Muller came on the VHF, calling all cruising vessels at Hog Island. He invited everyone to bring a picnic on shore next evening as he had persuaded George to give a talk on cruising Cuba, from a yachting perspective. The idea was well-received and all of them were glad to have a new focus.

Henry brought one of his super-lounger chairs for Prue, and she sat in the centre of the group who, now fed and watered, were waiting for George to start. The present time was peaceful and full of friendship, and Prue's future was exciting and meaningful.

It was a balmy evening and not too hot. The chiggers, that embedded their poison in most of the tender Caucasian flesh, were the only downside. So subtle were they in their attendance that their visit would not be noticed immediately. But they would be remembered over the next two weeks, in the form of tiny, unbearably itchy, red spots.

The semicircle this time was relaxed and expectant. Most of them anticipated visiting Cuba so to have the subject brought to them by such a knowledgeable man was a huge bonus. Fellow sailors thought highly of George and his gentle manner of story-telling. True stories about his adventures were not only informative but entertaining. Several cruisers from the nearby anchorages at Hartman Bay and Woburn had heard the VHF message and motored round to join the Hog Island group. They were made welcome and settled down to listen to George, who was now taking his place in front of them.

'Hey there, fellow cruisers! Sadly, you will have to rely on my powers of description to stimulate your imagination—no handouts or overhead projector to define the talk.' He paused, and without hurry looked at each person in the circle, in the manner of all good orators. 'This will be an informal talk, more of an outline of a country than a sail plan, and I shall invite you to ask questions at specific moments.

Cuba is a must on any sailing itinerary. It's a magnificent country, with a huge variety of things to see and do. There are the ancient and historic buildings of Havana and the rolling red earth slopes of the tobacco-growing fields. The beaches are not heavily populated, and the dive centres are world famous with fabulous coral reefs to explore. Less attractive, but important historically, are the huge old Russian guns still trained on Washington DC, while all makes of American cars from the fifties ferry tourists round the capital. It is actually illegal to run private vehicles as taxis, but this infringement is largely ignored. On the whole, I found the police very human. Maybe this is because they all have family members indulging in banned activities. Who knows?

The people of Cuba are very poor. Making a living by using private cars as taxis is only one such activity. Accommodation and meals in private homes are also offered to travellers. Packs of forbidden lobsters and cigars are bartered on the QT in exchange for the highly sought-after US dollar. You need to understand that most of these services or goods are available to the visitor in government establishments at three times the price and half the value. One of the things we noticed about the practical effect of communism is that employees don't seem to have pride in what they do. We often noticed a lazy attitude to service in government hotels or restaurants. Now, if you want to talk to them, and your Spanish is good enough, the attitude would be entirely different. They love conversation!

The commodities not available to the average Cuban are things we take for granted—dairy products, potatoes, soap and toilet rolls. In addition, only the top hotels have toilet seats so there is a definite market opening there.' George smiled. The audience, catching his play on words, laughed.

'Bog-seat billionaire! Doesn't have a good ring to it,' Henry called out.

The group erupted!

'Does have repeat possibilities though,' offered Sven.

'Sounds like a deep-seated problem!' Adam raised his voice over the hilarity.

'Seat of Power,' Daz sang out, in a voice full of laughter.

'Is that the power behind the throne?' ventured Paul.

'Okay, okay. Stop!' George held up his hand as the jokes and laughter threatened to take over. 'Yes, we've all needed a good laugh but shall we get back to Cuba?'

At this admonition, Paul, Harriet, Frances, and Daz, all sitting on rugs on the ground, with one voice yelled, 'Ooooooo!'

George, realising he'd been a bit pompous, grinned. 'Sorry, guys!' Then he tried to pull together the threads of his talk.

'Let's talk more about the people of Cuba. Other things that are difficult for us are their treatment of animals. Thin workhorses, drawing big carts with seats, sometimes drop dead in the shafts. It is actually illegal to shoot a sick or old horse, and they are overworked and underfed with no veterinary care or proper rest. Their owners can't afford foot care and decent tack for the animals, causing many to live in pain. Freddy asked one man why he used a metal chain noseband across the animal's face when leather would not cut and cause bleeding. The Cuban replied that a leather band would break eventually, and need repair or replacing—the metal one would last *siempre*, forever. Sadly, we couldn't fault his logic!

Cock fighting is legal and some religious practices use chickens and goats in a very cruel manner, though I won't expand on that here. Dogs seek food scraps round the restaurants and some have pups to feed. The level of their mange is appalling, raw and bleeding bodies, with the skin literally hanging off in strips. Their distress is just awful to see, and there is no control on stray dogs and cats breeding. When we asked a local man if there was a refuge for strays, the idea was greeted with amazement. Perhaps by now some misguided rich crank has invested in such a place, but truly the level of human poverty that we saw, makes the idea of an animal refuge, rather than a human one, seem downright immoral.

In the market in Havana, we saw a woman in a wheelchair, legs extended and supported on a platform. Both legs were covered in open ulcers—they must have been horrifically painful. She couldn't afford the medication to treat the ulcers, if indeed it was available. We also met a taxi driver, an ex-aeronautical engineer from the days of Russian employment. He suffered badly with emphysema, and asked if we could send him the necessary antibiotics. If not, he would continue to suffer until he died at a relatively young age. He was fifty at the time. The other downside of the socio-economic situation was that highly qualified people, like the engineer I just mentioned, earned so little that they supplemented their income by doing menial jobs like waiting tables or serving at bars. And many women use prostitution for extra cash. In fact, as male tourists, the prostitutes were a pestering nuisance. A strange dichotomy of emotions for us, as we found the level of prostitution not only unattractive, but also sad. I'm not taking a moral stand here. Prostitution will always exist, but to have to survive that way is awful. So many folk there simply offer what the tourists will pay for, whatever that may be!

We met a young couple, brother and sister, who started a car spray-painting business. Working as hard as they did, they should have made a fortune but free enterprise is not allowed. Every can of paint had to be accounted for and each job had a government-imposed price. Highly skilled doctors were paid forty US dollars per month, dentists thirty US dollars per month. Less skilled workers were paid in pesos. I say *were* because that was a year or so ago and maybe the situation has improved. Such, my friends, is the reality of communism!

We were told by locals that they longed to open up trade opportunities with America but Castro, who has been a wonderful patriot and leader in his day, was not up for that. Hopefully, things will change. The US administration is just as bad. Cruisers checking in at Key West told us that Cuba is simply not on the map at the U.S. Customs Service! And although Americans are not permitted to visit Cuba, in reality there were many more US yachts visiting there than any other nationality. Of course, in so doing, their insurance is negated and therefore their risk considerable.' George paused, and drank some of the beer Roger brought over to him. 'Any questions so far?'

No one responded, except to say how much they were enjoying his talk.

'We loved Cuba, Uncle Freddy and I.' George grinned at Freddy. 'One amazing thing about the people is their innate musicality. Informal groups gather in sheds and garages, playing instruments and singing—and where there is music, people dance. They dance in the street, bars, *cafés*, and supermarkets! We saw tiny children and very old folk, dancing in public where and when they felt moved to do so. Families dance together in the evenings, and there are dancing contests between schools. We saw huge groups of children practising movement, and yes, they are taught how to move. Their teachers would be working with them, and locals would line the street, watching and swinging in time, traffic at a standstill. What wonderful priorities! The arts in general are subsidised, and artisans of all types work tax-free, so of course they are in abundance. Many of them are truly excellent, and some even tour abroad.

We found great friendliness and hospitality, in spite of the poverty. When you visit, be sure to spend time at Viñales, the tobacco-growing region, Trinidad, the old colonial town, and of course, Havana with its many wonderful historic places and buildings. Another must is Isla de la Juventud, which you can sail to. The main town there is Nueve Gerona where the Presidio Modela, a national prison built in the 1920s, is well worth a visit. In the mid 1950s Fidel and Raoul Castro were imprisoned in the hospital wing of Presidio Modela. Interestingly, as a qualified lawyer himself, Fidel prepared his own defence during his incarceration. He failed, and was convicted to fifteen years in prison. During the early months of his sentence, he wrote *La historia me absolverá*. The manuscript was smuggled out by his supporters, and I have a copy on the boat, in translation of course.

If you hire a car, you will discover it's difficult to find your way around, unless maybe you use your handheld GPS. Actually I've only just thought of that solution. The custom is to pick up local hitchhikers who will show you the way. However, a knowledge of Spanish is necessary as it's only in the tourist centres that Cubans speak English. And be warned, those resorts manage to achieve the usual sort of characterless similarity to other resorts anywhere in the world. But of course, that was just our perception. On a sailboat, you have a great advantage. That is to see the real Cuba.'

George stopped talking and looked around. 'I've catalogued photos in folders on board, if anything here has stimulated your interest. Okay, folks, any questions?'

Following tremendous applause and cheers, he turned his attention to his beer, and the evening continued in the easy manner it started with George as leader of a discussion group rather than a lecturer. It had been a successful event, much needed to replace the memory of the previous gathering on shore and the cruisers eventually returned to their boats, feeling buoyant and uplifted.

Chapter 24

T aking a young man in hand proved to be a good idea, a more than rewarding experience, as it happened. Once the fumbling had been overcome and his confidence and staying power grew, he became a gifted pupil-thirsty for knowledge and greedy for research . . . and so naturally intuitive. Their trysting place was on the other side of Hog Island, away from the anchorage, a deserted beach fringed with palm trees. After many meetings, it was here that it happened!

Coitus perfectus, that's what it was! Harriet lay on her back under the shade of a palm tree, hot sun sometimes slicing down between its huge leaves, teasing her body with stabs of fire. The heat pierced her memory, and her body felt light and alive. She remembered every last detail of that coupling and told herself that if she never had another, it would be the ultimate.

Had it started deep within or was it without? A light sort of rumbling became a gentle staccato. Gradually my body became aware of something different. My toes started to twitch as every nerve ending responded to the meaning of awareness. A dreamlike state took over my brain, co-joined with a lethargy creeping up my legs. My breasts had a life of their own, the nipples huge and erect, quivering and expectant as my arms and hands joined in the search. My fingers found his tiny nipples—fingers feeling as if they had been supercharged. They sought, found, scratched, moulded flesh. And then the pulsing urgency began.

It must have started in the cosmos. Then my pulsating, overtaken body joined in. He rocked me sweetly, happily drowning in the juices of my passion, his wonder and maleness filling me up, answering my need. I felt engorged—at one—a great floating, rocking, squeezing cunni-locked-cock. Yes, floating, rocking, as my hips raised me up towards heaven. He must have sensed this was unusual, special, as he tuned into me. His own pleasure seemed to be in mine. This was the time for the Big One. My big O. Just mine! He rocked me more, and harder, deeper and harder, yet at the same time almost softly, so delicate yet insistent was his plunging into me. Then my waves of pleasure took over. Yes, deep, touching everything. Sexy! Sexy! Sexy! But somehow, spiritual too. Is this karma? Tantra? Why am I floating on waves of splendour. Is this reality? Is that me screaming and shouting or am I chattering or crying? Or is it all silent within me? I have no idea! It was the ultimate huge internal hurricane, its eye pierced with sweetness and knowledge of eventual and hopeless surrender. The hurricane became violent, its noise changed into a sort of shouting, howling that joined my passion—a very male noise as he impregnated the world. What superlatives are there to tell how my orgasmic transition screamed out its destiny in helpless submission, until eventually, just eventually, I subsided and we subsided into a sort of nirvanic torpor . . .

Chapter 25

I t was just two days later that Roger came to open up the bar. *En route*, he motored over to *Green Flash*, hailing Adam and Eva by knocking on the hull.

Adam appeared quickly, and greeting Roger, invited him on board for a beer.

'No, man, thanks, but I got things t'do. Jes wanted to let you know that folks here is discussin' a storm. Looks like it's blowin' up real bad and may head our way!' He raised his hand and roared off.

Adam relayed the news to everyone at the anchorage, and they decided to review the weather reports every hour. Twenty-four hours later, it became clear that a Tropical Depression 9 had strengthened to tropical storm status and was named Ivan. After two more days, Ivan was categorised a hurricane, and the National Weather Service noted that the very rapid strengthening was unprecedented at such low latitudes in the Atlantic basin.

'Where are Daz and Henry?' Adam enquired of Eva. 'Do you know?'

'Not exactly. But I do know they are at Caribbean dance workshops and staying in some hotel on shore.

Surely they will be hearing hurricane alerts on the radio or TV. Everyone must be talking about it.'

He tried again, unsuccessfully, to reach them by satellite phone. By now there was a sense of urgency as they had decided to get to a safe building on land. Over the next few hours, all the cruisers at Hog anchored their boats as securely as possible, packed precious items just in case, and headed for the mainland with an awful feeling of trepidation. They were, after all, leaving their homes.

On the evening of September 6th, the group that had become a close-knit community, gathered in the dining room of the Renaissance Hotel in St Georges.

It was now clear that Hurricane Ivan, labelled strong category 3, nearly category 4, would almost certainly hit Grenada the next day.

At last Adam made contact with Henry. 'For God's sake, man, where are you?'

'Just collecting some documents from the boat. Where are you all?'

'Dining room of the Renaissance in St Georges. But get here asap. Be safe, Henry. At this stage, nothing else is important. Just get here, will you?'

'Thanks, Adam. Don't worry, we're on our way. We'll be there soon.'

In the hotel, everyone stayed on the lowest level where the reinforcements were strongest. Some three hundred people gathered together with what little items of survival they had carried in. They tried to sleep or rest as best they could, forming little groups for mutual support, all of them nervous and scared of the unknown.

George and Frances sat close, holding a shaking Dog between them—all bravado gone as he felt the atmospheric pressure change and sensed the terror of the humans around him.

Local people came in for shelter. In the tradition of people who'd been there before, they told ever more terrifying stories of the trail of destruction left by hurricanes, thereby increasing the drama of the horror being enacted outside.

At 6am on 7th September, hotel staff sealed all the outside doors by pulling the huge iron bars into place.

The small group of cruisers were better equipped than most to deal with the emergency. They were used to being challenged by sudden weather changes, and although this was way out of the norm, they had packed their squashy bags well. Water was a top priority, and they all had brought large empty collapsible containers with them, which they filled before taking refuge in the dining room.

Eva and Lily both had the foresight to book suites in the hotel as soon as they heard the storm warning. They invited their friends to make use of the rooms and when it was confirmed that they would need to sleep downstairs, they stripped the rooms of bedding and towels, to be shared by them all. They sat huddled together, each getting comfort from the others, while the storm screamed its fury outside.

At this moment, Eva suddenly knew a calmness, a sense of peaceful resolution. She felt as if her hand was guided to touch the Talisman and, as her fingers traced its familiar contours, realised she must share it. She drew it out of her belt-bag, and gently placed it on the floor in the centre of their circle.

The windows were boarded up but it lay there, glowing in the dim light. Eyes were drawn to it immediately.

Prue gasped. 'The Talisman!'

Eva nodded. 'Yes. Here we have a unique friend.'

Freddy touched it in greeting and explained. 'Some of you don't know about the Talisman's journey to the Caribbean. It all started with Daz, who was given it by a Russian man in St Katharine's Dock just prior to the departure of *Wild Foxes* and *Green Flash*. Lana, it's creator, attached an explanatory label. You can read that yourselves. Recently, she wrote me the story of its progress up to Grenada, because those who were given the Talisman had sent her photos and emails. They told of personal achievements in the face of some challenge or problem, always linking this to the Talisman with no understanding, just the certainty of knowing it was so. Daz told Lana of the comfort and strength found in order to support Henry's dream of sailing, and that was achieved in spite of great initial fear and misgiving.'

Freddy picked up the Talisman and gave it to Lily. She kept it in her hands for a short time, and then George touched it for the first time. In turn they held it and read the label, each experiencing different emotions.

Paul was moved. 'I hope it protects Daz and Henry, wherever they are.'

'No! That can't happen.' Prue spoke with firm conviction.

They all looked at her questioningly, startled at the strength of her voice.

'Daz gave me the Talisman in Graciosa, greatly extolling its powers and the courage gained from being its temporary host. But it was strapped round my waist in my body-belt at the time of my accident, and it certainly didn't protect me!'

'What happened, Prue?' Eva encouraged her to continue.

'I felt the sensation of the Talisman on many occasions. I can't describe it more clearly than that. I was in hospital, in a lot of pain and sleepless for many nights, getting depressed and frightened too by thoughts of the future. I suddenly remembered the Talisman! I found it had survived the accident intact and that night, as I held it, slept deeply for the first time. I felt my healing had begun on all levels. In truth it's simple. Somehow it guided me. It helped me fulfil the need I'd disregarded for years. But it couldn't, of itself, shape destiny. Believe me, I thought about this very question a number of times during the weeks I was lying in that hospital bed, and later too.' Prue fell silent, but there was more to come. 'Ultimately, I believe it gave me the strength to confront James, and maybe it also brought me to my friends, Erika and Sven.' Prue now sat between them with the resolve of a new woman, smiling, in spite of the howling wind and the awful *bangs* and *crashes* outside. 'I gave the Talisman to Treasure, my Bajan friend, who worked in the hospital. She gave it to someone in Monserrat, but I never knew who it was.'

Erika spoke up. 'That was me! Having the Talisman entrusted to me was an experience I can't put into words. Sven?'

Sven took her hand and continued her story. 'Erika used to be pursued by demons. She made life rigid and judged others harshly. There was no softness in her.'

His wife nodded as tears trickled down her cheeks. Prue squeezed her arm and handed her a tissue. Erika smiled through her tears at this practical gesture.

'I have learned to love,' she said simply.

They were all silent with their thoughts.

Erika held the Talisman as if in a trance. 'We'll survive this hurricane, but many won't. We have our memories, our faith in each other and the future. Will you all close your eyes?'

As if it was the most normal thing in the world, they obeyed her quiet, persuasive voice.

'Can we offer our thoughts and love to Daz and Henry. Let us send strength and peace to them both.'

They were silent in their projections. The vitality of their missing friends was in their hearts as they sent their messages and prayers.

Erika continued. 'I believe the Talisman has revisited Daz and Henry in this hour.' She handed the Talisman to Freddy.

Taking it from her, he told his own story. 'On the first occasion I encountered the Talisman, Erika gave it to me in Dominica. You cannot imagine the pain I felt on seeing this beautiful thing. It was as if my daughter was with me again. She, Marie, used to paint tiny, exquisite birds on porcelain shapes she had created. She was killed in a car accident at the age of twenty-two, the same age Lana is now.' Freddy paused for a few moments, collecting his thoughts. 'Life is not easy for a strong-minded paraplegic determined to be independent, especially in Russia. It is in my mind to offer her my sponsorship. Perhaps I can make life better and enable her to fulfil her talent. Lily will be beside me. We have discussed the idea. I think of the gifts I have received through the Talisman—the gift of getting to know Lana and being ready to embrace a relationship with Lily. It has given me the chance to really live again . . . indescribable! Did Lana project such power into her Talisman so that people like us could take something from it? By the strength of the feelings we generated and the love we put back into it, somehow it's re-vitalised, re-energised. What do you think?'

'Like a sort of personalised reverse psychometry,' Eva offered.

'What is psychometry?' George was always fascinated by these new and unscientific ideas.

'It's a type of New Age hocus-pocus.' Frances seemed less impressed!

'Actually, my sweet daughter, it's not hocus-pocus. Imagine a healer, who is so open in awareness, that simply by holding an object belonging to someone else, mind-pictures of that person's fears and hurts—painful memories too—can be received. By this means, someone who suffers can be helped. I see no reason why this cannot be used in a reverse way. After all, Frances, it's only an extension of healing, just another kind of healing from the one you practise. Maybe you are right, Freddy.'

'And that is why I gave the Talisman to you, Eva. You! A woman of great wisdom and spiritual wealth. A woman who has already earned the Talisman.'

'My God. Full circle!' breathed Adam.

The group stayed as they were, close physically, but now even closer in their unity of minds—while the storm raped the land and raged itself into extinction.

Chapter 26

The reality of life outside was appalling. The wind ravaged the trees, and although the catamaran was in a protected area, a designated hurricane hole, this was nothing against the possibility of a direct hit. The sky was greyish black and menacing, the sea bucked against this sudden onslaught of wind. Local wildlife that could get away had done so long ago. So too had the friends they made in London, and the others they had met at Hog Island.

Henry and Daz had been on the mainland for three days, looking at real estate and then for fun attending a series of dance workshops that were being run by a visiting celebrity.

This had given Daz the idea that a new guest spot at the club could feature Tin Pan. 'Me, playing a single drum while singing, dressed in a colourful Caribbean number, with bare feet and much hip swinging. Might even try a little wucking-up. That should get the punters going!'

'Not unless I'm the one doing the wucking-up,' Henry retorted. He recalled the incredible dancing they had seen here in the Caribbean, where men and woman fitted, spooned into each other, front to back.

It was pure—no, actually totally unpure—vertical simulated sex.

Hips bucked and gyrated and the happiness generated by these sexually liberated people was fun, especially with Daz, who had grinned up at him, saying, 'Our favourite position!'

He remembered getting a hard on, and it wouldn't go away. Such was the effect of Daz ...

The situation in which they now found themselves was Henry's fault entirely. He had insisted on getting back to the boat to collect some documents and personal papers, but when they tried to return to the mainland, the outboard failed. It was too windy now to find the spare engine in a deck locker, much less fit it on the dinghy. And then the weather went mad. There was nothing they could do so they went to bed with a bottle of Bollinger.

Thank God the fridge is still working, thought Henry. In passing, he flipped the switch on the music system and Freddy Mercury's voice filled the boat with *Too Much Love Will Kill You*. For a while, the Champagne and music absorbed them as they lounged on the bunk, simply enjoying the pleasure of the other's company.

Huge anchors, four in all, secured the boat which now was awaiting its fate.

Probably safer here than on the nearby shore of Hog, Henry tried to console himself. 'Let's crack open another bottle,' he suggested.

There were always a few bottles of Champagne in the small locker fridge he had designed to be fitted by their bunk.

Henry's arms encircled Daz, whose head was on his shoulder. 'My darling boy,' breathed Henry into the top of Daz's head. 'When we come through this we must find a place for ourselves, perhaps on the river at Henley, and get a couple of those little dogs you like so much. What are they? Yes, Westies.'

'Henley for Henry,' quipped Daz, dismissing the seriousness of their situation. Then as quickly, he countered, 'and if we don't make it, we'll be together always.'

The childlike simplicity of the way Daz expressed himself, and his capacity for loving Henry, never ceased to be a wonder to the older man, who now just gathered him even closer into his arms. Suddenly, all sound stopped! It was eerie! It was nothing!

Henry, as always tuned to the elements, became aware of the calm. 'Oh my God, it's the eye,' he said softly.

Daz stirred. 'What's the . . . ah, the wind seems to have dropped.'

We don't stand a chance, Henry thought. *What to do? Can't tell Daz. Must tell Daz* . . . 'Darling Daz, you are the most precious thing that ever happened to me,' he started and then he stopped. *What can I say? I've fucked up the life, probably ended the life of one beautiful person.* Henry agonised. *I love the boy so much, he is so full of life and talent . . . and love.*

Briefly, the man who had been Henry's other long-term partner, came to mind. An ambitious photographer and leader of the gay rights movement, Ralph had used and manipulated everyone who stood in his way, anyone who did not allow him to control the situation. Last heard of in Florida, he was having a clandestine affair with a married industrialist and apparently caught in such a sticky web of deceit that he was helpless. How different life was with Daz!

He decided he would use the much-debated e-perb system that gave immediate satellite contact with Goonhillie in the UK. No one could help them, but at least someone would know where they were. Getting out of the bunk, he went to the chart table and pulled the red tag. Then he had another idea. Maybe his satellite phone would work. Daz was sleeping again. Thank God for the amount of sleep young people need! He quickly made contact with Carlos who was shocked and upset at their situation. Writing down the exact position of the catamaran he promised to contact the authorities and arrange for a helicopter to be sent to airlift them out.

Henry hesitated, then said, 'If anything goes wrong, if I don't get back, you should know that Foxes will be your baby. It's all in my Will.'

'No, Henry. Just get your bent ass back here asap, do you hear me?'

Henry could hear the choking in Carlos' voice.

'Okay, keep your shirt on. It's just in case.'

The line went dead. What to do now? Henry went out on deck. He walked along the hulls, down one side and back along the other, pausing to admire the chic lines of his beautiful boat, briefly stroking a stanchion and guardrail in passing, and then checking again that everything was tightly secured and all the anchors were holding well.

A faint noise, like a *scream*, was starting from somewhere far away. Henry now moved fast across the cockpit. Going inside the boat he secured the double doors, and quickly checked round the galley and main saloon areas. Nothing lay around, everything was stowed or tied down. He moved back to the bunk and took out the lee cloths, securing them to the outer side, and then pulled down and tied the mid bunk lee cloth he had designed for use in rough weather. The strength of the equipment gave him confidence, and leaving just one opening, he roused Daz. 'Go for a pee now, my sweet. It's going to be a bit rough soon.'

Daz clambered out and was back in just a few minutes. Henry followed his own advice, then joined Daz in bed and tied the remaining outside rope to the strong hook. He then took another rope and lashed them together, round their waists.

By this time, although it had been less than five minutes, there was a distinct chilling, prolonged howling outside, and the boat rolled. The wind squalled, then flung itself with renewed fury at the tiny island, its inhabitants and its visitors. The boat started rolling badly, and Henry knew it was down to the anchors holding, or it would be only a matter of time before they flipped over.

They clung onto each other as *Wild Foxes* pitched, and took up a frenetic dance. It was terrifying, and there was no need for any explanation. Their situation was clear and Daz, although sometimes foolish, was no fool. With an ear-splitting sound—like many rifles going off a simultaneously—a tree cracked, was lifted up and flung against the boat! Then another! An almighty noise like an explosion ripped through the catamaran.

'What's that?' whispered Daz.

'My God, it's the mast coming down.'

Henry's voice revealed his horror. With a great bang, as the wind screamed round the boat, the huge 66ft mast crashed down. Not having come clear of the starboard hull, it weighed down heavily and, as the angry sea hurled itself at *Wild Foxes*, the portside anchors gave up their struggle and pulled out of the sea bed.

Slowly, almost majestically, the port hull raised up, describing a huge arc as it slowly rolled over. The gaping hole where the mast had been embedded now became an open channel for the sea to pour in.

With great calm, and enormous love, Daz wrapped his arms ever more tightly round Henry. 'Let's just stay where we are, together, my love.'

Throughout the long, slow roll of the boat, Henry and Daz were as one, locked in each other's arms, legs wrapped round, and faces pressed together.

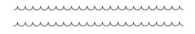

Hurricane Ivan roared and screamed. The huge catamaran was picked up as if it was made of matchsticks and hurled onto Hog Island, then picked up again and tossed lightly into the sea on the other side of the island.

But Henry and Daz were already at peace, the love within them living on.

When the wreck was found, far from being a macabre scene, it was spine-tingling with a powerful feeling of forever. The two bodies were still entwined, their facial expressions unexpectedly soft and peaceful. The bunk within the cabin walls was intact, remaining round them like a protective shell.

One of the rescuers clumsily pulled out a handkerchief to wipe tears from his eyes. 'A true love-nest,' he gasped.

Epilogue

An identical announcement was printed in all national newspapers on Friday 17th December 2004.

Yesterday, the ancient church of All Hallows by the Tower, London held a moving memorial service for Henry Springer and Daz Lee, who died together when Hurricane Ivan hit the West Indies island of Grenada, on 7th September 2004.

Henry, aged 55, owner of the famous club, Foxes, will be remembered for his generosity in supporting the training of young disabled athletes, two of whom gained a gold medal in the Paralympics. He also paid for entertainers each Christmas to perform in council-run homes throughout London.

Daz Lee, aged 24, was the constant companion and partner of Henry. According to his friends, his sparkle and vivacity and his great talent as a singer, was only exceeded by his enormous capacity to love.

The club, Foxes, is bequeathed to Carlos Franco. The new owner said the club would continue to run in the tradition in which it was founded.

Eva Pitman presented a moving eulogy and Lily Trampton sang a Caribbean hymn. Paul Pitman performed his own composition on the organ, simply entitled, *Requiem*. On the church porch just after the Blessing, the stirring sound of *The Last Post*, played on the trumpet, echoed through the building.

Among the large congregation were the cruising friends who escaped the devastating hit made by one of the worst hurricanes in history:

Eva and Adam Pitman
Freddy and George Muller
Frances and Paul Pitman
Lily Trampton
Prue and Harriet Bucket
Erika and Sven Pedersen
Margreet and Warner Frank
Svetlana Bossi
and the Talisman rested quietly in the pocket of its creator ...

> *We are all visitors to this time, this place*
> *We are just passing through.*
> *Our purpose here is to observe,*
> *to learn, to grow, to love.*
> *And then we return home.*

> *—Aboriginal Philosophy*